Digg Dogg

and the

Depression Playlist

by Lucas Pops

When you wake up still tasting Tequila,

feeling shame, fear, and regret in equal

measures, it's good to have a friend who,

without judgement, gives you a shoulder

to cry on and maybe a simple good thing

like some eggs and sympathy.

-Anthony Bourdain

CHAPTER ONE

CLARK

After…

The faded letters on the marquee dangled in such a crooked fashion you'd have thought a child had arranged them. Ironically, that would have fit the production. It felt like any minute one of the many giant "G's" could just fall from the sky and crush the protesters marching outside the theater.

A girl can dream…

Final performances are today. We just have to get through this last matinee, then we can be done with Kansas City. Only a few more cities after that and then, well, we'll see what comes next. Since it's the middle of the day, we only have a few demonstrators out right now, the hardcore devotees. Their hilarious homemade signs reading, "Neuter Diggsy!" and "Digg Dogg needs to be <u>Put Down</u>!" and, of course, the ever popular and viral, "#kancelthekidshow".

Honestly, the small gathering at least adds a bit of commotion to the front of the theater, even if it is unenthusiastic. Because inside the lobby, it's a fucking ghost town. The PA system is blasting *Learning How to Smile* by Everclear, so appropriate. The local ticket taking ushers can't even be bothered to stand upright as they slouch over their boxes. I grab the theater manager, some mouth breathing, daddy's-friend-got-me-the-job type of winner, by the arm and yank him near the front doors.

"Can you at least try to get your employees to stand the fuck up straight and attempt to look professional?"

Mouth-breather nods and bumbles off towards his lackeys. I'm certain he'll try to be the good guy and tell them about the bitch from the pervert's show wants them to stop leaning for the nonexistent customers. I know this because he wouldn't be the first insecure man to call me a cunt for being assertive. I want nothing more than to pull this fucking hair tie out and release this migraine

of a ponytail. I usually just keep my black strands tucked underneath

a tour baseball cap, but I forgot it in the hotel room this morning and

am forced to shove it all in the back of my skull to keep it out of my

eyes while I work like the boss I am. The lanyard around my neck

keeps clacking against my clipboard. Another thing I wish I could

lose is this fucking lanyard. But then I'd miss out on all the

Suburban dads staring at my tits, pretending they're reading the

badge while they ask me where the restrooms are for their piss pant

kids.

I head over to the merch stand, still covered wall-to-wall

with *Digg Dogg and Friends* stuffed animals and t-shirts. This time

last year, this display would be barren. Now, it's overflowing with

leftover crap. I check the sales. I don't know why. I guess out of

habit. I already know they're going to be abysmally low.

I continue my path over to the box office to check in with

Autumn. She's the old lady that runs the ticketing booth. I've gotten

to know the attendants in every city we've toured over the years. I prefer the booth dwellers that shoot straight with me. And Autumn is no exception.

"How's it looking so far?" I ask.

The old bird swivels around in her chair still focusing on the phone in her hands. Even upside down, I can tell she's reading one of her old romance novels that she recently upgraded into an eBook. I kind of preferred when she would lug one of those old books around and read it in front of everyone, half naked dudes on the cover, Autumn didn't care who knew. Now, she just looks like she could be tweeting.

"Not looking like a sellout today, Clark." She says in her dry tone and matching ambivalence as her face remains glued to her screen.

"I'm shocked" The sarcasm oozing out of my mouth so thick it could be… I don't know… I'm too tired for good analogies.

"How bad?" I ask.

Autumn has already turned back to the front window and dismissed me for interrupting her reading. "Pretty sure there's more employees in the building than guests."

"How about tonight?"

"Just as bad. There's still time though. We could get a few more tickets sold."

"Sure."

My path of ennui continues as I make my way back to the dressing rooms. I cut across the stage as the crew resets everything for the upcoming performance. There's usually a buzz in the air right before show time, but not as of late. Now, everyone just goes about their job in silence, like we're going through the motions. I inspect the giant childlike cutout house, making sure the bold colors aren't fading too much. The door has been physically and symbolically bolted shut ever since Mr. Bob was written out of the production. I had suggested that we remove the house all together, but since we couldn't come up with an acceptable replacement, it stayed, hovering over the show like Bob's shadow. The house meets my standard of approval and I pass by Diggsy's Doghouse to the right of it. It's still in good condition too, and so I make my way

backstage.

I pop my head into the first dressing room and yell to the

actors that they've got five minutes to positions. Vinny is standing

by a chair wearing the top half of his stuffed frog costume as he

thrust his pelvic into the backside of Ryan, who is bent over the

chair wearing the top half, minus the head, of his giant stuffed cat

costume. You'd think seeing these two Adonis's going at it would

shock me and it did, the first few times, but by now I can literally

pick these boys' penis's out of a lineup. And I mean literally thanks

to their matching Black Heart tattoos above their crotches. A tattoo

that I also happen to have.

It's just another thing that this show has ruined for me. I

mean, imagining these two gorgeous creatures pounding away at

each other used to be the highlight of my sad sex dreams for a time.

With Vinny having the type of sculpted muscles you'd have thought

a gay mad scientist had cooked up in a lab they were so perfect. And

Ryan with his casual charm, a *Prince*-like aloofness that just

radiated chemical sexuality, his slender frame and features just gave further credence to my belief he was a bastard child of the Formerly Known one. There's a famous quote about how it's better to never open your mouth and be thought a fool than to speak and confirm it. Or something like that. Ryan has the opposite in the fact that he never says a word and yet comes off as the coolest person in the room. Pairing him up with Vinny is just plain unfair. These two have no right to not only be beautiful bodies and faces, but beautiful souls as well. Plus, they bring out my filthy mouth whenever I'm around them.

"Soon as I finish stretching Kitty Kat here," Vinny huffs out to me between thrusts.

"Tickle the balls, Ryan. Five minutes to positions"

I turn to leave them to conclude their business, hoping none of said business ends up on their costumes.

Which reminds me.

"And get your frog legs on, Vinny!" I yell back to them as I make my way to the next dressing room. But before I can reach it, I'm cut off by Zoey in her mouse costume with the head under her arm. I don't let her slow me down though, and we do a walk and talk.

"Clark! A quick word?"

"Five minutes to positions, Zoey."

"It'll only take a second. It's a logistical question. Your department, yes?"

She forces my hand and I have no choice but to stop and listen to her try in vain to change my mind on an already settled matter. The top of Zoey's skull barely reaches my chin, so I am towering over her. She's got the kind of cute little girl face that creepy older men love to explain basic stuff to just to hear her giggle an ignorant response.

"Make it quick," I blurt at her.

"I know it's obviously too late for Kansas City, seeing as this is the second to last show, and I know you said Chicago was a no go—"

I let out the biggest, most exhausting of sighs. I had the slightest bit of hope she wasn't asking me this yet again.

"And Detroit, you said, was out of the question, but since it will be the end of the tour, could we possibly consider I get my own dressing room for New York?"

This bitch.

"Zoey, if I could get you your own room, I would, but I can't."

"But I'm principle cast now. I shouldn't be getting into character with Background."

"What's wrong with Background?"

"Nothing! Sorry, I was Background before Sunshine left. I just think I deserve my own dressing room."

I let this anxious and annoying little ball of blonde spin her wheels as she continues to apologize for disrespecting her fellow performers while still trying to elevate her own status. I honestly could get her a dressing room of her own, if it wasn't for the fact that she keeps pissing me off with her persistence.

"The theaters we've booked only have three private dressing rooms in them. You've got the least seniority, so you're out."

"Can I at least get dressed in Vinny's room? He gets ready in Ryan's anyway."

"You'll have to take that up with Vinny."

I leave her standing deflated and devastated as I continue my path. We both know that even if she had the balls to ask Vinny, he would just mockingly tell her no in a way that is equal parts humiliating and emotionally crippling. As much as I love Vinny to death and just talked him up to the moon, he can still be the cattiest of bitches.

Ever the gay cliché.

I think I have freed myself of my boil, but she stays affixed to my ass by catching back up to me as I arrive at my star's dressing room.

"Can you talk to him for me? They listen to you."

"I'll see what I can do." As in, the three of us are going to laugh our asses off when we talk about this.

"Can I speak with Mr. Harrison about it?"

I try to hold back the giggle that was sneaking out of my throat at the idea of "Mr. Harrison" giving any type of shit about the show right now.

But I am a professional.

And in my most professional of voices, not in any way sarcastic or fake, I calmly explain to Zoey, "Our lead is an artist. An artist that requires peace and tranquility before he is to give a grand performance that will brighten the lives of the children and their parents, who paid to see him. He is only to be disturbed by someone such as myself, who has built up a trust with him over the years—nay, decades, and is able to not derail his inner Digg Dogg."

"Oh, I am so sorry! I'll leave you to it!"

Zoey puts her mouse head on and scurries off. I take in a deep breath before opening the door to his dressing room, expecting the worst, hoping for the best, ending up with the usual.

As soon as I open the door, I'm hit with a wall of marijuana

smoke that had to of filled the entire room before I ventilated it.

Mixed in with the hallucinogenic cloud escaping is a pollution of

noise he likes to refer to as his "Depression Playlist". It's a playlist

he likes to blast from his Bluetooth speaker that mostly consists of

deep cuts from artists that committed suicide or songs from the

second act of different musicals.

Right now, it's playing something that doesn't fit into any

of those categories. I think it's *Coming Undone* by KoRn, but it's

hard to be certain as the contact high that's already hit me has me a

bit confused.

Inside, I find him. Passed out on the floor in his giant

stuffed dog costume surrounded by empty bottles of ginger beer and

a few half-drunk liquor bottles. It's all the same brand of rye

whiskey and ginger beer with some Angostura bitters mixed in just

to switch up the floor's pattern. On the mirrored counter, I can see

he must have attempted to garnish his cocktails with lemon wedges

that he tried to cut with a butter knife in what I'm guessing was

pretty comically unsuccessful judging by the mess.

The suit he's wearing, an anthropomorphic Boston terrier, had warmed the hearts of a generation of children. A generation that has now grown up to realize the whole show they used to love turned out to be a lie. The head of the costume is still hanging by the door where he left it after last night's performance. It's the only thing in his dressing room that has any kind of order to it. The rest of the room is a mess of disarray and despair. I hover over sleeping beauty as he slowly wakes from his slumber, aided by a few swift but firm nudges from my foot. The scruffy, unkempt beard covering his face still has the dried vomit on it that I hope was just from last night and not, as I suspect, from several days ago.

I attempt to lift the man in his urine-soaked costume by scooping my arms under his shoulders while he stirs awake. In the struggle my earpiece and microphone are knocked off my head and dangles around my neck. We knock over the bowl of peanut M&M's that are still delivered to the dressing room as a part of Bob's artist rider. The ironic fact that those very candies bouncing and scattering down onto the floor were more than likely a result of child labor thanks to the terrible chocolate trade our world turns a blind eye to is not lost on me.

As I get him situated on the nearby couch, I get a chance to readjust my headset as well as my mindset, just before the first gurgled words burp their way out of his mouth.

"Five minutes to positions, Boss?"

This is the star of my show. This is the man that I have attached my career and life to for the past decade. A man I care deeply for. And up until recently, that wasn't a bad thing. When he wasn't what he is now, this bodily fluid covered mess.

Back when he was Murphy Harrison.

Back when he was Digg Dogg…

CHAPTER TWO

MURPHY

After...

The funny thing about alcohol is it's basically a poison.

You put a poison in your body and enjoy the effect it has. I wouldn't

say I enjoy the effects, more like their necessary medications.

Because now, life outside my whiskey loaded world is not a life I

currently want to occupy. At least when I'm fucked up, I only have

to care about what the poison is doing to me and how I have to focus

on basic functions, like keeping all my liquids inside of myself. And

even though I fail at said tasks more often than not, at least it's

better than what awaits me when I sober up.

Once again, Clark is doing all she can to Humpty-Dumpty my ass back together again. She's been doing this almost my entire career, but now I've made it even more difficult for her.

Well, me and Bob.

He kind of got this whole downward spiral kicked off.

"God, this costume smells like piss!" she says as she covers her nose.

"That would probably be from the piss I took in it earlier, but I don't want to jump to any conclusions... I couldn't get out of the suit in time."

Clark instinctually grabs a trash bucket by the vanity mirror and hands it to me. I'm confused at first, until I realize this woman knows me better than I know myself and I immediately, uncontrollably, vomit into the receptacle.

"I'll get the suit cleaned after tonight's performance so it'll be fresh for Chicago. Looks like we're cutting the audience participation segments tonight. The kids might get drunk off your fumes."

She sits down on the chair next to me as I pull my head out of the bucket. I wipe the residual puke on my sleeve as Clark unzips her fanny pack. She hands me a stick of gum before taking the trash can from me.

"You make sure there's no hecklers?"

"I did my best to screen for eggs and fruit, but I can't promise any yelling. Security knows the drill if any protesters get inside."

I fumble with the gum wrapper, my costume paws making life difficult. Clark waits a moment, enjoying my struggle before setting down my puke bucket and helping me out. As I pop the stick in my mouth, Clark grabs a water bottle out of my mini fridge and chucks it to me before walking out with my throw up container in her hand. I truly love that woman. She has been my keeper for too many years, and I don't deserve her efforts.

I stare off at the one bulb on the vanity that has burnt out. Feeling my hangover and letting the pain zone me out. Using my teeth to screw off the cap, I chug the little bottle of water before willing myself to my feet. And believe me, that took a lot of willpower. The simple act of finding a reason for waking up is something I struggle with daily now. I drag my dead corpse of a body over to the doorway and grab that stupid fucking dog head off the hook and exit towards the stage.

The shine of the stage light glows all around me. It's the perfect mood lighting for when you've got the remnants of an entire bottle of whiskey seeping out of your skin. Nothing like bright, searing spotlights to remind you that your head is trying its damndest to split in two.

I feel like I've become the *Loneliest Whale in the World.* That mammal that scientists have been following because it lets out this one-of-a-kind frequency that no other whales can hear. So, this blue whale just keeps floating around the ocean, belting out it's high-pitched call at 52hz, hoping for a connection that we know won't be heard.

The music cues up, that fucking theme song that haunts my nightmares. I swear when me and Bob were coming up with the show's theme, all I asked was that it not be something like this. This upbeat earworm of nothingness. I wanted something iconic and hopeful. Like *Mr. Rogers* or *Sesame Street*.

Hell, I'd even be okay with *The Muppets* or the theme from *Reading Rainbow*. Even though it turns out one of the iconic songs from *The Muppet Show* was taken from a porn film. I guess that explains why Jim Henson originally wanted to call the pilot "Sex & Violence". I would have liked to hear that theme song.

Instead, I'm stuck with this unholy abomination of a high-pitched methed out child's fever dream. It's accompanied by a small, scattered smattering of clapping coming from the audience. If I looked out into the crowd, it would probably feel like a De Chirico painting, all barren and surreal.

At least it's not as terrible as all that shit *Moonbug* and *Pinkfong* are putting out now. All the focus we put into making quality children's programming and it all got undone by flashing colors accompanied by butchered nursery rhymes and shitty animation that got inspired by our lazy musical efforts.

We felt at the time we were living in the shadow of Raffi and needed something repetitive and catchy. Little did we know it would haunt us for the entirety of our careers.

As I take my position behind the dog door, I wait for my cue to enter. My hangover apparently starts to get worse because the crowd noise seems to be getting louder. I blame it on the alcohol at first, but then it starts to get deafeningly loud, and I know it's not that. All the colors around me starts to drain away. My mangy suit is back to its pristine freshly made state. I look over to my right where there should be nothing there. He's gone and I should be staring at black curtains, but instead I'm back in a memory.

Back in a good time…

Back before…

I look to my right and there he is.

It can't be real. I'm pretty sure it's not.

Bob is waiting at his position.

CHAPTER THREE

MURPHY

Before…

I've heard people talk about out of body experiences, so from what they've described, this isn't it, but it's the closest thing I could reference for what is happening. When I said the color drained away, I mean that literally. Everything around me is just varying shades of grey. It's almost like a memory, but the memory has changed.

It's not how I remembered it, and yet… it is.

Mr. Bob gives me a wink and a thumbs up as the theme music starts to reach its climax. Bob's a tall man, at least a head taller than me, and he's always been skinny, not lanky, but slim. His height ended up working out for us because with the Digg Dogg costume on the two of us would end up meeting eye to stuffed eye. Even though I could never really see that well in the suit.

Bob has a warm face. The kind of warmth that makes you feel comfortable in his presence. The kind of warmth that reminds you of a safe feeling.

A feeling that everything will be okay.

I look down at my suit and it no longer has the shabby appearance of a lifetime of hard times thrust upon it. It looks like it still has hope and promise in front of it. I can't even feel my headache right now. The clapping has reached a fever pitch as the announcer in the theater booms out over the speaker system.

"And now! Here he is, kids! Digg Dogg!"

Bursting through the doghouse door in full Digg Dogg attire, shattering the flimsy corkboard door, I plow my way onto the stage.

The crowd erupts in child-filled applause.

The music abruptly cuts out.

Digg Dogg (yes, I sometimes refer to my character in the third person when I'm playing him, fuck off) yells out to the crowd, "Uh oh! Mr. Bob isn't going to be happy about this, is he, kids?" I use a dopey fucking voice as Digg Dogg that is nowhere near any kind of octave I would ever use myself.

The children in the audience yell back their answer to me as Mr. Bob steps out from behind the house door to an equally loud crowd reaction. He's got his grey pants held up with violet vest and a matching tie. Standard "Mr. Bob" outfit that would become both mocked and iconic. After posing in the doorway and letting the cheers die down, Mr. Bob walks over and inspects the doghouse's broken opening.

"Digg Dogg! Did you break your door again?"

Digg Dogg replies with a sheepish side to side head shake. It's actually kind of a challenge to display remorse under all that felt fabric.

"Diggsy?"

This time it's in a sterner voice as I nod Digg Dogg's head

in admittance.

"Well, thank you for being honest."

Mr. Bob outstretches his arms to embrace Digg Dogg in a

great big hug as the crowd awes in delight. I cover the microphone

that's by the side of Bob's mouth being held in place by wrapping

around his ear and whisper, "Dibs on the rack in row three."

Bob swivels his head to see the large chested woman in the

third row of seats with her child at her side watching the show. He

just shakes his head with a grin as we release our hug. That's

always been the thing between me and Bob. I was the crass asshole,

and he would be the sweet bystander putting up with me.

"Now let's clean this mess up," Bob tries to continue with

the show. "Hey! Maybe our friends can help us clean? Whadya

say?"

He turns and stands upstage to address the crowd, "Would

you guys want to meet the gang?" The audience screams in

response. "Well, then, let's call them out here!" Mr. Bob shimmies over to the side of the stage as an up-tempo backing track kicks in and the stage lights turn colors rapidly as if it's goal was to set off a seizure.

"First, we've gotta get our favorite feline out here!"

The audience cheers her name as Digg Dogg calls her out onto the stage.

"Baby Pants Kitty Kelly! Oh, Baby Pants Kitty Kelly!"

Ryan comes out wearing the giant stuffed cat costume to a raucous applause. The costume is of an angelic kitten with the top of the hair done in a pink bow and wearing a frilly diaper. It's funny how we always introduce Kitty Kelly first when she was really just a token female character. We originally came up with the design with no real thought to her motivations. We just needed to add a woman. Then, as we started to develop the show, and it grew in popularity, the character started to become a feminist icon, even though she's in a diaper and a tutu and is played by an effeminate gay man.

Bob continues to tease the next cast member as Digg Dogg yells his name to cue Vinny.

"F-F-F-Fab Frogg Freddie!"

Vinny hops out onto the stage in his giant, stuffed frog costume as the crowd cheers him on. The costume is a green, spotted frog with a set of sunglasses and a snazzy vest. Our attempts to be cool when we started the show was with a hip-hop frog created by middle-class white dudes, is now loved due to the resurgence of terrible nineties nostalgia fashion. We're fully aware that we continued the tradition of white people stealing from Black culture, and there have been plenty articles written about him, but the defenders will always say it's just a kid's show and not to take it too seriously. At least we had Vinny stop using a stereotypical Black voice for the frog once he took over the role. The same racists trolls using the "kid's show" defense, suddenly switched gears and vilified us when we changed up the "legacy of the character".

Bob screams out, "And finally—"

"Chester Cheddar!" I have Digg Dogg cut off Mr. Bob to yell out the final friend.

A white mouse wearing a monocle with a fancy vest and jacket on the top half, the bottom being just the mouse legs, scurries

30

out. I don't know why cartoon animals are always portrayed pants-less, but that's just how people seem to want them to be. I think it's Zoey inside the costume. This could very well be back when my ex-wife, Sunshine, used to don the rat. We've rotated so many people in and out of those suits over the years, Only myself and Bob remaining from the beginning. The gang joins together for a group hug as the backing track fades out. We all release our embrace as Mr. Bob and the Dogg take center stage.

"Well, Diggsy, looks like the gang's all here."

I'm starring into Bob's face as everything else fades away just as the backing track had done a few second ago. The throng of children, the cast and crew, the lights, the stage, all of it has faded into nothingness. It's like that easy trope TV and film use to show two characters falling in love, everything gets coated in darkness except the main cast members.

Except it's not me and Bob falling in love, it's just a coated world of darkness. All I can focus on is Bob's next words that seem to repeat in my head.

"What are we going to do next? What are we going to do next? What are we going to do next?"

The light that had faded away has returned, along with my suit's weathered appearance. The grey has also subsided, bringing color back into my life. That all sounds delightful, like when Dorothy landed in Oz, but it's really just a jarring snap back to reality. I'm frozen in place, all alone at center stage with the rest of the cast in the background, waiting for me to continue. The small, scattered audience is barely into the show, several of the children are watching other, more exciting programs on their parent's phones.

The theater announcer repeats over the speakers, "What are we gonna do next?"

I jolt Digg Dogg out of his trance and have him nod emphatically before the rest of my body language returns to this performance.

"We're gonna need a clean-up song!" I belt out.

The few children paying attention in the crowd are the only ones cheering as another backing track kicks in. The rest of the cast joins Digg Dogg at center stage as they work through a choreographed routine, singing and "cleaning" up the stage.

My body betrays me as I let my eyes wander over to the door of the house, wanting to believe Mr. Bob could still walk through it like nothing happened.

But knowing he won't walk through that door ever again… I still can't deal with that.

CHAPTER FOUR

CLARK

After…

The sound of the "crowd" has faded from the theater and all that fills the auditorium is the cold echoes of a mixture of children's laughter and their crying. The final performance tonight went off without incident. I didn't think Murphy was going to make it through the afternoon performance, let alone the night one. But the bastard pulled his shit together for the kids. He may be a pathetic excuse for a human at the moment, but the man cares about his little fans.

I do my final rounds of the building, making sure that there's no psychos waiting to make a statement by vandalizing the show. Not that I could do anything if I came across someone. It's more of a therapeutic walk than anything else. I check in with merch to get their final numbers and it's just as depressing as I figured it would be.

After that, I get my Autumn fix in. Box office numbers are just as disappointing for the night show as they were for the matinee. At this rate, the tour is operating at a loss. I'm not sure how much longer we're going to be able to maintain this pace. I half expect to have the plug pulled any minute now.

I make my way backstage again, to see to it that the crew is staying on task during load out. I want to yell and make sure everyone's careful with the staging and equipment and to keep them moving so we stay on schedule. But it's kind of difficult to be a hardass when you're not sure you'll be able to pay them.

Hell, I don't even know if my paycheck's gonna clear next month, with all the vendors and sponsors that yanked funding. At least Chicago is paid for.

Time to check in with my star.

He's sitting in a chair in front of the vanity mirror in his dressing room as I enter. He's still got the bottom half of his Digg Dogg costume on, and his top half is covered in a white teary-cloth robe. In his hand is an empty champagne glass. In his eyes is a vacant look as he stares off at nothing. On his "Depression Playlist" blasting from the speaker is the *I'll Cover You* reprise from the musical Rent. I walk over and grab the opened champagne bottle from the ice bucket it was chilling in and fill his glass before taking a swig myself. He looks back at me over his shoulder as I plop down on the chair behind him.

"No toast?" he asks.

My mouth his still half full of champagne, partially dripping out down my chin, as I apologize and hold up the bottle to toast him.

"To closing out Kansas City with a bang."

I cheers to him as I take another rip from the bottle before asking if he's ready for our next town.

"Packed up my hotel room right after today's matinee," he replies.

"Really?" I ask.

"No. I'll deal with that shit in the morning."

Murphy gets up from his chair in front of the mirror and makes his way over to me. In the same motion, he downs the entire contents of his champagne flute as he drops into place on the couch next to me. He holds out his glass and I refill it, knowing I should probably slow him down, knowing that I couldn't if I tried.

"You make sure my room is prepared for me?" he asks.

"Your usual welcome basket has been set up at the hotel and not the theater dressing room, as requested."

Murphy's cell phone starts to buzz. He struggles to get it from his pocket underneath his costume before finally pulling it out. He stares at it quizzically for a moment before turning it to show me.

The ID on the cell reads, "UNKOWN CALLER".

"Ex-wife's lawyer again?" I ask.

"Probably just more tabloid scum trying to get a Bob quote from me."

"You ever think about giving someone an interview?"

He ignores me as he lifts his phone up and shoots it towards the trash can across the room like it was a basketball, smiling even when he misses the shot. I don't think he realized that was the same trash can he had vomited into earlier in the day and that it hadn't been cleaned out yet. You'd think the smell emanating from it would give it away, but the whole dressing room is a cacophony of smells that it's hard to really nail down any one specific disgusting odor. Although, frankly, I'm starting to get used to the constant stench of my star's accommodations.

"This thing is going to blow over," I tell him. "Some other scandal will come out about some Hollywood starlet's nudes leaking, and we'll be back to selling overpriced stuffed dogs to the children crying to their parents for monetized love."

Murphy leans back and takes another big gulp of his champagne, emptying the glass again. I stare at him for a moment, trying to read his thoughts as he keeps his head back, looking up at the ceiling as if he is willing himself to fly straight through it.

I feel like he's handling Bob's arrest the same way he had handled losing Rey, so I bring up this feeling to him. He tries to dismiss it, not by reassuring me that he's matured since his last mental breakdown, but by avoiding the conversation all together and trying to sweep it aside.

"I'm just saying, we almost lost you once. Can we try to keep it somewhat together this go round?"

"I make no guarantees," Murphy replies.

"Can you at least try different coping mechanisms this time?"

"But my usual mechanisms work so well." The sarcasm rolls right off his booze covered tongue as he takes the bottle from me. He tosses the glass sideways over his shoulder without a care as it bounces off the wall and crashes onto the floor next to the couch. Taking a rip straight from the bottle as if nothing happened, as if that broken glass wasn't coming out of the tour's budget. As if we're not going to be paying overtime to the theater cleaning crew for this dressing room.

He's such a fucking asshole.

"How is it you weren't the one that was canceled?" I ask.

"I know. We all thought I'd be the one to fuck up this gravy train." He replies.

I make one last final plea for him to get his shit together. I mean, I know he's not going to get it together anytime soon. I just need him to keep from completely losing it. At the very least, I tell him he needs to talk to me if things ever get too dark, if he ever gets too far gone. I tell him to keep looking forward because that's what I'm doing. I'm focusing on events and tasks on the horizon. Having things to focus on down the line makes the present not so depressing. I take the bottle back from him and we toast to Chicago, the upcoming town, before I take one last drink and walk out with the bottle, leaving him reaching for air as he tries to retrieve it.

"Now get some sleep. The last thing you want on a long drive is to be hungover," I say to him over my shoulder.

I down the last of the champagne, which was just the suds and backwash at the bottom at this point, as I exit the dressing room, leaving Murphy alone with his thoughts. A dangerous place for him to be, but that's where we're at in life now.

Trapped in our own dangerous thoughts.

CHAPTER FIVE

CLARK

Before...

You ever heard of a Fire-Priority List?

It's a thing people will set up, either physically written down or some just keep it in their heads. It's a list of things you would prioritize securing safely in the event you woke up to your house being on fire. Most people's first priority, outside of their own safety, is loved ones. Children, spouses, pets, those are always first and foremost on the list.

I do not have any children, a spouse, or even a pet.

Next, is the valuables: phones, laptops, jewelry, the things not so easily replaced. I mean, I have a phone and laptop, but I'm not that attached to them, plus my jewelry doesn't have much value, sentimental or monetary. Maybe documents come next for you: birth certificates, marriage certificates, house deeds. Once again, none of those things come into play for me if my rented apartment goes up in flames.

No, for me, aside from getting my ass out of the house, the only thing I would grab, my prized possession, is a framed photo of Mr. Hooper from Sesame Street, *as drawn by Big Bird. It's signed by Caroll Spinney, the actor inside the suit, and it's the only thing in the world I care to not get burned. Although ever since HBO bought out the workshop the Street has become gentrified like every other urban neighborhood.*

It's actually a reflective life lesson.

I stare at my favorite photo as my, not boyfriend, more of a fuck buddy, who's currently filming episodes of his show on the other side of the world, breaks it off with me over the phone. Murphy is over in Europe shooting footage for a Digg Dogg special and has apparently fallen in love with his co-star, Sunshine.

"Ever since that night at Bob's, I couldn't get her out of my mind." He pleads with me to see his reasoning. *"I wasn't planning on doing anything, but we ended up spending the night together, and I'm sorry, Boss, but I'm in love."*

"Her pussy is that good?" I bark back at him.

"It's not just the sex. We had a genuine connection. I have to see where this goes."

He has to see where this goes?

He used that same phrase with me, but it had a different context. With me, "see where this goes" was nonchalant, noncommittal. He didn't want to get tied down to anyone, since he was a megastar, but still wanted to sleep with me when it was convenient for him. With her, "see where this goes" is a prophecy, a destiny. He wants to take all the relationship steps with her and hope she will go with him on that journey.

"So, you're just calling to take care of your loose ends, right? You want to stop whatever it was we were and go back to a professional relationship? Or are you also firing me?"

"You really think I could ever fire you? You practically run my life when we're on tour. I'm totally fucking lost out here without you!"

"You were able to find your way to Sunshine's pussy with no problem." A cheap shot, I know, but his first response was to compliment my work ethic and not me as a lover, so fuck him.

That's pretty much the last coherent word I get out of him. He pretty much shuts down after that comment and we end up silently hanging up shortly after. I don't know exactly how to feel. On one hand, I knew there was no future with him from the start. His status would always have him in another world than me that we could not coexist. But still, it's never a good feeling when someone chooses someone else over you.

Shortly after I received an email from him, thinking it was some kind of NDA from his lawyers I would have to sign so as to not disclose our relationship, I was surprised to find it was actually from his mind:

"I don't want to lose you as a manager, but more importantly, I don't want to lose you as a friend. If you can no longer work around me, I understand, but I don't want you out of my life. We both know we don't belong together. You say it's because of my celebrity, but it's not that and you know it. We are great friends. There is no one outside of Bob that I care more for in this world. I don't want to say I regret us having sex, because I got to know you on an even deeper level because of it, but I would take it back in a heartbeat if it meant we could no longer be in each other's lives. I genuinely did not expect to have these feelings for Sunshine, but they are here, and I can't ignore them. You know she's a great woman because she is your friend too. And deep down, I feel like you know me and her are a better couple together.

Can we please just be okay?"

Signed,

Shithead

I did forgive him.

I went back to work on the next tour with them and, honestly, they did make a great couple. I was always friendly with Sunshine before, but once she started dating Murphy, we became even closer. I finally had another woman to hang out with after years of being stuck with Bob and Murphy.

She got me into jogging.

We would run together while on tour, feeling safer going for runs in strange cities if we were partnered. It was an easy way to keep in shape and gave us time to talk. It became such a part of our routine that I continued it long after she left the tour, even though the safety aspect has dropped now that I run by myself. Dipping and weaving down busy sidewalks as pervy men would stare at us flying by in our ass-tight yoga pants, we would just laugh and bitch about the two assholes making our lives hell.

Murphy was still cheating on Sunshine while on tour.

Even though they were a couple, they had separate rooms booked and would sometimes sleep in their own suites. It mostly depended on if Murphy was going out with Bob that night. Sunshine would stay in and didn't want to be woken up by him drunkenly stumbling back at late hours. She knew that he would bring other women back to his hotel room, thanks to the panties and/or condoms left behind clueing her in.

Hell, it got to the point that we both had to routinely take turns kicking random groupies out of his bed in the mornings so he could wake up and get ready for his performance.

All the while, it never bothered Sunshine.

I'm sure on some level it did, but she never let it be known. When I asked her about it, she said, "It's not the women sleeping with him you have to worry about. It's the women trying to take your life you have to look out for."

She knew with his status; Murphy couldn't help himself with the women throwing themselves at him. But, for her, all she cared about was that he came home to her after the spotlights turned off...

For Sunshine, the physical didn't matter. All she cared about was that she wasn't getting replaced.

Like I did.

Shit. That's what happened to me…

It was only a few years after our breakup that they got engaged.

He proposed on stage, in the fucking Digg Dogg suit, after the curtain came down for our last show in New York that ended that current run. They ended up doing a destination wedding on the cliffs of Negril, Jamaica. Bob was, of course, the best man. And I shit you not, I was Sunshine's fucking Maid of Honor. I actually walked Murphy down the fucking aisle since his mother was too ill to travel and his father had been out of his life since forever ago. It almost felt right for me to be almost giving him away that day.

A déjà vu of our breakup call, only this time in person, I gave my blessing for these two to be together, leaving me alone.

My wedding gift to them?

The only thing on my Fire-Priority List.

Goodbye, Mr. Hooper.

CHAPTER SIX

MURPHY

After…

I'm alone in my hotel room.

It's the last night I'll be in this room, so I say fuck it and go all out. I've been trying to figure out the best way to recreate that Kansas City memory but haven't been able to get close to touching that moment. I can't tell if it's because I'm in the wrong state, but then again, I don't remember if it was the Kansas or the Missouri side last time. I guess I'll start by broodingly staring out the floor-to-ceiling window of my room.

It's like I'm Batman.

I watch the city from behind the glass as the Power and Light District is awash with the night lives of happy people.

Seriously?

I'm such an asshole.

I'm envious of theoretical people.

Hell, I'm sure there's people down there who would give up a left nut just to stay a night in this swanky ass hotel room. And then they'd give up their right one for this complimentary robe they gave me. It's like wearing a non-sticky marshmallow around my shoulders it's so soft. Now that I've freed myself from the sweltering heat of the Dogg pants, I can finally let my testicles breath underneath this robe. It's also handy in wiping the condensation off my cold glass so the fucker doesn't slip out of my hands. I give it a drag across my hip to dry it before bringing it up to my lips.

My phone is in my other hand as I scan over a list of barbeque restaurants that deliver to my area. I scroll through them until I finally find the one I'm looking for. Of course, they don't have online ordering as an option.

They're gonna make me call them.

God, I hope she doesn't still work there.

What am I worried about? Even if she did, and she was the one who picked up, she wouldn't recognize my voice over the phone.

At least I don't think she would.

Fuck, I should just find another restaurant, but this is my last chance in this town, so I might as well do it right, just to make sure.

I dial.

It's a dude that picks up.

Perfect.

I order a pulled pork sandwich because that's what I got that night. It comes with a side.

What was it I got last time?

I get coleslaw.

I don't think that matters that much.

Before they get me my total, I ask about the biggest tub of BBQ sauce they could give me.

It's not big enough so I get two.

After I hang up, I finish off my drink before heading to the bathroom. This is supposed to be a nice hotel, but they don't have glass door showers. They have clear plastic curtains like every other basic bitch hotel. I guess we had to downgrade since the show has been playing to empty auditoriums. It actually works out perfectly for me. I yank the curtain down off the rod and bring it out to the commons area of the room. I've moved the chairs and the couch since they have to be pushed up against the walls in order to lay the curtain out completely flat. It looks like I'm about to perform some black-market organ harvesting in the middle of my hotel room with how the furniture and plastic sheets are arranged.

I've become a Batman villain.

Even though I'm not planning on drawing any blood tonight, things are still going to get messy.

I'd better take off my necklace.

I place it lovingly on a side table. The little metal circle that dangles from the rope clinks on the glass surface. The little lowercase "r" in the pendant's center is losing some of the black paint, but the indent of the letter is still visible. As I rub the metal lettering, my mind starts to go back to her.

Nope!

Not today.

I've already locked that shit down deep so I can deal with it another time. I've got enough crap to work through right now.

Did I already finish this new drink? I'm gonna go grab a fresh one from the fridge.

It's called a Horsefeather, Rye Whiskey with Bitters and ginger beer. It's what Bob and I would always drink whenever we traveled to Missouri.

Or was it Kansas?

I don't know why we decided to drink local offerings. Our first tour, we found a bar near the hotel and that's what they served, so we kept ordering them every time we came to town.

Damn, that one went down quick. Better get another one to have with my food.

Fuck, this delivery's taking forever.

I'll switch to just rye whiskey until it arrives, so I don't drink all my ginger beer.

I should have gotten the bigger bottle.

Is there a size bigger than the handled ones?

Oh well, at least the food has finally arrived.

I set the two big ass tubs of sauce in the center of the plastic curtain on the floor and eat my sandwich in the chair.

It's kind of tough to eat without anything to set my plate on, but I make it work, kicking my feet up over the arms of the chair and let them dangle as I use my shins to hold the plate.

After I finish my food, I go to throw it away and completely miss the trash can. That's gonna suck for the maid to clean up. Especially since it's probably going to crust over being on the floor all night.

Couple more shots of rye and then—

I open up another ginger beer.

Only a couple left.

Luckily, there's a knock at the door.

She's finally arrived.

I would have had her come sooner, but this was the earliest she could schedule me in for. I open the door, happy to find she's not a complete gargoyle.

Her ad didn't show her face, so I was kind of shooting in the dark.

Not ideal, but she checked the boxes I cared about.

She's wearing a short, tight dress. I think it's some kind of

red, but it could just be the lighting or my inebriation.

I invite her in as I sit back down on the couch with

my drink.

She's taking in the room and, of course,

she's worried by what she sees.

I reassure her that I'm not going

to murder her, that it's just to keep the

room clean.

She doesn't believe me.

Why would

she?

And she informs me that she's got a friend waiting

downstairs and in case she doesn't show back up

in an hour, he'll be coming up.

She also says

something about "Water Play"

being extra.

I think she's talking about me

pissing on her.

Or her pissing on me.

I tell her it has nothing to do with urine or poopy

things.

I tell her not to worry about it as I pull out a wad of cash

from my robe pocket and toss it over to her.

She unfolds it and starts to count it as I take

another swig of my drink.

It's empty again.

I grab another bottle to make

another round as she makes a phone call,

I'm guessing to her friend downstairs and

tells them everything seems to be on the

up and up so far.

I'm kind of relieved

that she doesn't recognize me.

After she hangs up, she puts the money and her phone back in a small purse she has dangling around her shoulder.

I sit back down on the couch and play some music from my phone.

I go with *69* by Teyana Taylor to set the mood.

This fucking Horsefeather is already almost half gone.

She sets her purse down by the edge of the plastic, keeping it in her sights, as she casually removes her small dress, followed by her bra and underwear.

It's so matter of fact, like she's just undressing in front of a mirror and not a complete stranger.

I'm worried she's going to be one of those hookers who are basically just an expensive assisted jerk off.

Her body is curvy as she's

probably in her early thirties, but still

tight, nothing disgustingly out of shape.

Perky breasts that surprised me by being pierced

with little rings. A few indistinct tattoos across various

spots on her skin that I don't care to focus on since my

vision's a little blurry anyways..

She sets her clothes on top of her purse

before she walks over to me on the couch. She

asks me if I want to begin with a massage on the

tarp, and I tell her to start by sucking my dick.

She obliges by squatting down

on the floor in front of me, bringing her

hands to my lap. She pushes apart my

robe and buries her face in my crotch.

No condom as she

wraps her lips around my cock.

I knew tonight

was going to be dirty,

but I didn't expect this.

Whatever.

I go with it.

Her hair is a big ball of curls, just like the waitresses' was.

That's really the only reason why I picked this

girl. The hair matched.

I let my mind wander back to that night

as I roll my head back in pleasure.

At least I'm hoping it's

pleasure. In truth, I don't really feel

anything anymore.

Her head starts bobbing up and

down now. And I'm enjoying it. Thank

the Gods.

I was worried I wasn't going to be able to

get hard. Because, you know…

Whiskey Dick and memories.

She's really moving now, her curled mane bouncing slightly off step with the rest of her head. I can tell she's trying to get me to finish from just a blowjob. If she can get me to cum quick, her night's over and its less work for her.

So, I stop her before she accomplishes her mission.

I stand her up as I rise from my seat.

I guide her over to the tarp.

My erection, still peeking out of my robe, pokes her in the stomach while I lead her over to the plastic with my drink in my free hand.

I can still see her saliva shining on the shaft of my penis and it apparently left a little wet mark on her stomach where I had bumped her.

Like a cute little sloppy kiss.

I pick up one of the tubs of barbeque sauce and hand it over to her.

She just gives me a quizzical look as I drop my robe revealing the tattooed artwork that covers my body, adding another layer of questions I can see grinding away in her skull.

Although her shock at my ink isn't as bad as others I have seen.

Some people have gotten so used to seeing me as a children's entertainer that they couldn't imagine any sort of "edge" to me.

I got the idea to start getting the work done when I heard a story about how Mr. Rogers always wore long sleeves because he wanted to hide his tattoos that he had gotten when he was a sniper in Vietnam.

Pretty sure that story was made up though.

Still…

I tell her I want her to stand over me and pour the
tub of sauce all over herself.

I want it to cover her body and the excess to drip down onto me as I
lay underneath her.

She says okay with a bit of trepidation as
I take my place on the floor.

She steps over me, putting each
foot on either side of my stomach.

She asks if this is, like,
really good sauce or something
and I tell her not particularly.

She shrugs as
she pours the sauce
onto her chest, letting it
dribble down to my
waiting flesh.

I stare up and admire her perfectly

trimmed pubic hair from under her as she takes off

the Styrofoam lid.

I never knew it before now, but I get why guys want

women to stand over them and get pissed on.

Not that I want that to happen to me.

Not that there's anything wrong with that.

No kink shaming here.

But staring up at a vagina is one of the

most beautiful sights one can see in this life.

That sounded creepier than it was meant to.

What I was going for was that having a naked woman stand

over you, getting to really see her in all her womanly glory, is really

quite a thing to behold.

If only I could get her and the room to stop spinning.

She rubs the sticky vinegar sauce all over

her chest, lathering herself with the remaining

contents of the container as I try to take another

sip from my drink.

A task that proves rather

difficult while laying down, no matter

how hard I crane my neck.

She's attempting to

make her little lather party as

sexy as possible, asking me if I

like that between fake moans.

I sigh.

Not because of her performance, she is

convincing, but because, even though I'm still hard, I'm

not where I need to be.

I'm not in the memory like I want to be.

I hand her the other tub, thinking more would do the trick.

She empties the second sauce container; this time it spills down her

back making her shiver with sudden goose bumps.

As much as she tries to avoid getting it above her

shoulders, she instinctively rubs her neck and splashes some of the

barbeque on her chin.

I also notice some of it has gotten into her hair and

I kind of enjoy thinking about how pissed she's going to be

when she has to wash it out later.

I know, I'm an asshole.

The liquid on her body has started to dry

and get even stickier than before.

Her enthusiasm is starting to wane.

She asks if she should keep going or if there's

something I want to do next.

I can't help but let out another sigh, not

directed at her, but at myself.

I tell her I don't know. Tell her

to sit on it. -My dick, that is.

She asks if she did it

wrong.

She must have thought that sigh was for her.

I don't even know what it was she was supposed to be doing right, let alone how she could have done it wrong.

I tell her not to worry about it.

She lowers herself on top of me, resting on my thighs.

I watch as she struggles to wipe her hands off on the curtain before reaching for her purse, using just her fingertips, trying and failing to not get any sauce on her bag.

The woman pulls a condom out of her clutch and tears it open.

After placing the red rubber on my tip, she rolls it down until she reaches the base before sliding herself on top of me.

It feels nice to be inside her.

I let myself enjoy that moment.

That feeling when you first enter a woman's warmth, it's euphoric.

She starts by gyrating on top of me before

proceeding to work herself into a full bounce.

I start to drift into it.

She drops down and presses her chest to mine, covering my

face in her curls, while bouncing her ass up and down on my cock.

I try to push her hair out of my face so I can reach

for another sip of my drink.

Our bodies are practically stuck together

thanks to the brown condiment we're covered in.

She pulls away and arches her

back, launching her head to the sky as her

enthusiasm is something to be

commended.

I almost for a second

think she's not faking it.

Her feet are now flat on the ground as she
repositions herself to use her knees to fully spring up and
down on my member.

Her body's slapping against mine with an
accompanying clap as she puts her full force into
pounding me.

She's actually going to make me cum,
and I am thankful for this momentary reprieve
from my world.

My sticky lady can tell that I am
nearing climax and tells me not to cum
inside her, to let her know when I'm
going to finish.

Which I almost laugh out loud
at her precautionary measure considering
my bare cock was down her throat just a
few minutes ago.

But I oblige.

After a few more thrusts from her pelvis, I tell her I'm about to shoot.

She falls back off me, her ass landing slapped onto the floor back between my legs, as she instinctively grabs my cock and jerks it up and down to keep me on-course to orgasm.

What she didn't expect was for the sauce to become so dry and sticky that the condom would come right off with her, still stuck, attached to her pussy.

Her tugging still did its job and my load flies into the air, startling her enough to let out a yelp.

Her legs slip out from under her, and she collapses onto the ground as we lay there, catching our breaths.

With the air coming back to me, so does the rest of the world and my problems.

The color of the room seems to drain away again.

Tears start to well up in my eyes as I say

fuck it and quit with the struggle of trying to drink

my whiskey without spilling.

I just let it rip upward as liquor

pours out of the sides of my lips.

A single tear and a sip

of whiskey drip down my chin

as I lay with a hooker covered in

barbeque sauce and cum…

…I've become my grandmother.

CHAPTER SEVEN

MURPHY

Before...

Laughter erupts from our tiny booth.

It's both startling and fills the quiet hotel bar, bringing all the attention to the two men sitting in said booth. Friends continue to laugh and obnoxiously make the entire room about them. Bob orders another round of Horsefeathers, drinks that we always get whenever we're in Kansas.

Or is it Missouri?

"You did not go home with that waitress?" Bob chuckles as he asks his probing question of me.

"She came back to my hotel room to change out of her work clothes. And what was wrong with the waitress? She was hot," I reply.

"You met her while she was working, she must have wreaked of barbecue sauce."

The bartender that is taking care of the whole restaurant drops off another round of drinks to the booth. It's late at night now and only the employees can be found mingling around the hotel's bar.

"I mean, yeah, but what's wrong with that? It was good barbecue."

The two of us cannot contain our laughter as we burst out again, receiving snide, sideways glances from the annoyed employees who just want to go home.

Bob takes a chug from his fresh glass to choke back his giggles before saying, "Dude, you are grimy as hell!"

"What was I supposed to do? You left me to run off with that soccer mom."

Bob shrugs. "She drove all the way from St. Louis. I had to show that suburban housewife a little appreciation."

"Oh, appreciation?" I make a thrusting motion with my hips, completely realizing how crass this gesture was, removing all the kindness that usually shines through Bob's face as he hangs his head to hide his boyish giggles.

"Didn't she have her kids with her? I knew I saw them at the Meet 'n Greet." I ask.

"She left them in her room with old episodes of the show on their iPad." Bob's response receives a judgmental glance from me. He quickly defends himself. "You don't get to judge me with your brisket smelling ass."

I shrug him off as I go to take another drink but stop as it's about to reach my lips. Mostly because of a puzzling thought I have to express. "Are you saying my ass smells like brisket because I had sex with the waitress, and it rubbed off on me or that I enjoyed smelling her ass which is similar to brisket?"

"Her ass smelled like brisket?" Bob asks, confused.

"More like pulled pork."

He can't hold back his fluids as he spits out the ginger beer and whiskey being pushed out by uncontrolled laughter. "What does that even mean?" He struggles to ask as he fights through his fit of hilarity.

I can't help but match his manic elation as I smell my own clothes. "I guess I could have showered before meeting back up with you."

Bob returns the same judgmental glance I had just given him before the two of us burst back into our riotous wheezing.

The color slowly begins to return to my face.

I look around and start to realize I'm back in this hotel room.

Not the bar.

I'm still in the center of the room, practically cemented to the floor with sauce and semen and slightly too sobered up to be okay with my situation in this room. The hooker props herself up on her elbows, sucking in air, and asks if I'm good. I give her a half-hearted thumbs up as she gets up and walks over to the bathroom to clean herself off.

I watch her from the bathroom doorway.

She turns on the shower and lets the water-reduced barbeque sauce slosh all over the floor, thanks to the lack of shower curtain stopping the splashdown. When she finishes rinsing her body off, she takes a small hand towel and starts to pat herself down, focusing on getting the crusted brown crap out of her nipple rings.

She takes her whole self in while checking out her figure in the mirror before stopping dead. She brings her face in close to her reflection, eyeing in disbelief what she is seeing.

"You got sauce in my fucking hair!"

CHAPTER EIGHT

MURPHY

After…

I fucking love Chicago.

There's something about this city. It's like New York without all the New Yorkers. If only Chicago loved me back. There's a fresh set of protesters outside the theater. We just got into town, so the first few shows are always a minefield of party crashers trying to derail the performances. If it's anything like the other cities, they'll start to lose momentum as the days roll by and we can get on with life.

I think I'm in the clear tonight. Usually if a protester tries anything, they do it during the opening number. They'd never wait until the closer, especially with all the kids we invite up on stage. It wouldn't make sense to cause a scene for the final song, all it would do is end the show early and by then, we wouldn't have to issue refunds, we'd get to keep the box office.

No, it doesn't look like anything's going down tonight.

The background dancers are teaching the little bedwetters on stage how to shuffle like chickens. Feathers keep flying off the dancers' bird costumes because apparently, we don't have the money in the budget to fix those raggedy old suits. It's time to put this whole crew out of their misery and end this shit-show.

"Let's give it up to the Plücker's, everyone!" I point to the frolicking chickens, trying to remember which ones I've "plucked" before by looking at their lean dancer's legs. The audience gives a half-hearted applause as the birds give a little shake of acknowledgement. I look over to find the Frogg and the Kat out of positions. Fucking Vinny and Ryan. They always end up next to each other for the finale, even when I told them to flank me.

Whatever. It's not like it matters anymore. The only person still giving it their all is the rat.

What's the new girl's name again?

Something childlike.

Lily? Sure. I'll go with that.

"And, of course, we have to thank our helpers!" I point to the children as a louder cheer comes through, mostly from the parents of the kids. Stagehands guide the snot-leakers down off the stage and back to their folks.

Time to go home.

"And from all the gang, I want to say a big thank you for coming and playing with us today! And as always and forever—" I pause to let the crowd echo with me, "Love Loudly!" That was probably the loudest the audience had gotten all night, and it still was subpar. The curtain comes down, and that's one more nail in this show's coffin.

We're almost sealed up and ready to be buried.

I make my way back towards my dressing room and towards my happiness poison. I haven't decided how I'm going to fuck myself up to start my night. It could be beer, rum, whiskey, vodka, coke, pills, weed. It's nice to still have some mystery left in

my life. All I know for sure is I'm going to end my night sippin'

tequila and fucking a whore. But first, I have to get out of Digg

Dogg.

The head is the easy part.

The strap slips off my chin and I turn off the little air

conditioning fan inside before I hang the helmet on a hook by the

door. It's everything else that's a pain in my furry ass. I pull at the

arms first, but they never seem to give. I drop onto the couch and

attempt the legs, but the round, plush stomach always gets in the

way. I say fuck it and claw at the back zipper to the extent that I

could practically tear the suit to pieces if I had any kind of sharp

point on my fluffy paws. It never used to be this hard to get this

fucking dog off me. Maybe it's these new cheap cleaners that they

take the suit to or that I've gotten chunky since becoming a recluse.

I've gotten so frustrated at this point that I've just given up

and sit there pissed off for a moment before failing at another

attempt to free myself. That's when the rat pokes her head into my

dressing room. She pops off the head to her costume to show that angelic face that I just want to stick my dick right into. Not because

she's particularly attractive or anything. I mean, she is, but it's

mostly I just want to shut her up and ruin that sweet, innocent face

with my dirty cock.

God, what the fuck is wrong with my mind sometimes?

"Hey, Mr. Harrison, is this a good time?" she asks as she

enters the rest of the way into my room. I tell her, sure, why not,

before failing to remember her name. Which is very evident to her

thanks to my awkward trail off. Being the sweetheart that she is,

she tells me her name again.

It's…

I've already fucking forgotten it.

She just plows right on, not caring that I've worked with

her for several months now and haven't bothered to learn anything

about her, let alone what to call her other than *rat*.

"I was just wondering if I could get some insight into the

thought process you had when creating the Chester Cheddar

character?"

My thought process?

What the fuck is this bitch talking about?

I'd answer her, but she just keeps talking. I would tell her to shut up and get out of my room, but she's taking her costume off as she rambles on. She's doing it so nonchalantly, as if she's just changing in front of one of her girlfriends. I'm reminded of the hooker from Kansas City. I know she's just trying to distract me from her annoying personality by getting naked, and I'm okay with it because it's working.

As her top half comes off, I see her pink bra barely holding back her perky chest. Yet another thing I'd be okay with sticking my dick into.

If only she'd stop talking so much.

"Like, what was it about my character that made him a vital part of the gang? What was the inspiration behind him?"

The inspiration?

We needed a bunch of animals to sell as stuffed toys and a fucking mouse seemed the logical choice from a zoological standpoint. I'm starting to think this chick is trying to trap me as she drops her bottom half and is now showing me her matching pink thong. Who the fuck performs a children's show in a fucking thong? She's inching towards me now, and I get the feeling this isn't just a simple striptease anymore.

Does she think she can cash in like Bob's victims by going after me? I'm about to blow up on her when Clark comes in and saves the day.

"Zoey, are you trying to make this into a shared dressing room?" Clark is unfazed by finding a half-naked girl in my room. This is not the first time this has happened. This is the first time it's happened because the girl just wanted her own place to change, though.

"What? No! I'm-I'm just so comfortable with our star that I-I felt I could… Um—" The girl continues to stumble over her words as she picks up her costume and slinks towards the wall.

"Or did you think with everything swirling around Bob and the show that you could add to it by trying to force a harassment case on Mr. Harrison? Get back to your changing station with the rest of background."

The blonde blurts out several more pathetic apologies as she tries to scurry away. She ends up dropping a few pieces of her suit and when then she reaches down to pick them up, I'm given a firsthand look at her "Highway to the Danger Zone" while she's escaping out the dressing room door.

"Did she wear a thong during the performance? For a fucking kid's show?" Clark asks as she closes the door on what's-her-name's backside.

"I mean, it does get hot in these costumes. Maybe I'll start rocking one," I reply.

"I assumed you already did." Clark plops herself down on the chair next to the couch. It's funny how even though I'm in a completely different city, they always seem to set up my dressing room to be the exact same as the other ones.

"Do you think she was trying to seduce me or is she really that oblivious?" I ask.

"I think she's like many women who find you are a completely non-sexual creature."

"Then explain how we used to have a shitload of groupies?"

"I still can't explain that," she replies.

It really is a mystery. In the beginning, it seemed like it was the money and fame that would attract women to us, but as we got older, it seemed to be a father figure thing that was taking over their attraction.

Of course, all of that is gone now.

"Vinny and Ryan just invited me out for drinks, you wanna join us?" she asks.

"I don't know. I kind of had plans, but I don't really have a time frame on them. I guess I could go for one drink. Where are they thinking of going?"

"Does it matter? There's alcohol."

"Good point."

She gets up and walks towards the door to exit, knowing I'm staring at her ass in those yoga pants that are somehow work appropriate. I don't know how that works, that skintight clothing is okay in a professional setting. I'm just happy she's comfortable making her butt a beautiful treat for my eyes while still doing her job.

She doesn't even turn her head as she calls back to see if I need help with my suit. She knows my answer is going to be nope, so she doesn't even break her stride as she leaves me to continue my frustrating struggle.

I pull at my leg, this time higher up for leverage, but I ended up tripping myself with the momentum, knocking me over to the ground. I can already feel the checkered red scar forming on the side of my face from the rug burn I've just received.

I've got my ass up in the air with my hands around my knees like I'm presenting my puckered hole to get fucked while sporting a swollen, tender face from being burned by carpet.

I've become my grandfather…

CHAPTER NINE

CLARK

After…

He's just standing there like a dumbass. I bet he thinks he's being all brooding and dark, but really, he's just looking like a mopey bitch. That's too mean. I don't know why I lash out at him. It's not Murphy's fault we're here.

It's Bob's.

Still, I should have looked up this bar's address before letting Vinny whisk us over here. I should have known we'd end up on this street, his street. He's just staring at the sign on the streetlight, the little brown honorary placard underneath the big green proper named board. The big green sign reads, "FRANKLIN

AVE." The little one underneath it is bagged up by a black cloth. I know what's under that cloth. He knows what's under there.

His legacy.

I grab him by the shoulder to pull him away, trying to reassure him that it's only temporary, but his feet remain cemented to the concrete sidewalk. I have to get him out of the area before he starts to breakdown and cry in front of this stoplight like a deranged homeless man his appearance giving credence to that assertion.

As I finally convince him to walk away with the promise of alcohol, we're suddenly accosted by several flashing lights blinding us as they repeatedly blast our eyes.

"Hey, Digg Dogg! Digg Dogg! Do you think Mr. Bob did it? Do you think he's guilty?" A random paparazzi snaps pictures at a rapid rate, trying to capture Murphy's face in some grotesque expression so they can sell his depression to whatever magazine is paying the most for pain.

"Diggsy! Diggsy! Did you know about what Bob was doing? Did you cover for him all these years?" Another paparazzi vulture screams out at him as he continues to try to disorient us with his constant strobe of photo flashes.

I push Murphy towards the bar, turning our backs to the photographers as they continue to harass him. They don't dare go inside after us, though. These parasites remain out on the sidewalk in public spaces where they can accost anyone they feel like.

I turn around to give them the standard legal fuck you. "Mr. Harrison has made his stance on his partner's alleged indiscretions clear, and any further questions can be referred to the *Feels Like Fiction* production offices." I turn and go enter the bar, not saying what I really want to say to them, aside from a few lewd gestures and accompanying curse words. I get Murphy inside before he can hear the last one bark at him, "Do you have anything to say to Bob's victims?"

His victims?

I'm sorry, but I can't speak to them because I am one of them. Not directly, but I am one of the people whose lives were destroyed by that man. I'm one of the people left in the wake of his selfish destruction, left to pick up his mess.

They want Murphy to speak to them?

He's even more of a victim than I am. He loved that man. He was his creative partner. They had been associated as one entity since their careers began and have not strayed from each other for over two and a half decades. And now it's all been ripped away and that man, Murphy Harrison, is never going to be able to recover from this hurt and betrayal.

But that won't stop Murphy from trying to drink his way to recovery. As if alcohol will help him find his clarity. He's already got himself a shot of whiskey and a beer in front of him when I join them at the table. Vinny and Ryan must have ordered us drinks when they got here, because they've already got an elegant brown tequila in my hand as I sit down. We've got ourselves a booth at the back of the bar as I try to apologize to Murph for letting the tabloids find us. He just waves me off with a somber response, calling me "Boss" at the end of it before downing his shot.

His nickname for me. Boss.

It's ironic because I have to order him around like his boss and make sure he's staying on task, but in actuality, he is the one cutting my paychecks. If I were really his boss, and he was pulling this self-destructive bullshit, I'd fire his ass in a heartbeat. Yet I am the one answering to his breakdown.

"What happened?" Zoey asks. Popping up out of nowhere like an annoying little meerkat. I can't believe Vinny let her tag along. She must have strapped herself to the roof of their Uber. Murphy explains what happened as Zoey listens intently, fascinated by everything the man says.

Vinny could care less, though. He's facing away from us, and his eyes are scanning the bar for anything he finds ascetically pleasing. The place is a small, dimly lit speakeasy style lounge. Everything in the place is covered in either dark leathers or rich stained woods. There's a three-piece jazz band in the corner setting the atmosphere with low mellow tunes. Right in front of the musicians, there's a guy dancing that seems to have drawn Vinny's attention.

He leans his head over to speak to Ryan.

"You think that guy is family?" He nods to a muscular guy in a t-shirt so tight calling it painted on would seem like too thick of a layer. Vinny continues, this time allowing us into his conversation. "It's always tough with the muscle heads. Everything is already so tight on them it's hard to tell if that outfit was a queer choice or a necessity."

"You mean it's difficult to tell if he's gay or not?" Zoey says in a tone just asking to be mocked.

"Yes, Zoey. I mean if they're gay or not." Vinny's snark cuts through her so sharply I smile, imagining it drew blood.

A normal human being would have just taken the jab and then lay out on the mat, but Zoey seems to be genetically programmed to poke the bear as she replies, "Aren't you and Ryan a thing?"

"Me and Ryan are more than a thing, Blondie, more than any 'thing' you could ever hope for. That doesn't mean we're stuck with each other like a couple of monogamists. If we want to bring in a bulge in a tight t-shirt, that's our business. We are secure enough to have a level of trust you can't even begin to think you will ever have the maturity for."

Zoey practically knocks her drink over, trying to fumble out an apology. I swear whatever it is she's drinking, it's barely even a step up from a Shirley Temple. I honestly don't know why I dislike Zoey so much. Maybe it's her over eagerness at being a bit player in this walking death show. Or maybe it's that seeing her put her foot in her mouth brings me too much joy and I feel I have to hate her to justify it. Either way, she gives me plenty of ammunition in both departments.

"Calm down. No one's offended here." Vinny lets her off the hook as he gets up from the table, taking Ryan by the hand, as they walk over to the muscular dude. His opening pick up line can be heard over the bar's low, ambient music as he yells out, "Hey, you with the nipples. I bet you got a six-pack on your butthole! I wanna see it!"

I swear, that man knows how to speak to people's hearts.

I chuckle to myself as I take another sip of my tequila. Vinny always knows to get me the good stuff, and he did not disappoint with this selection. I'll have to ask him what brand he ordered me. I'm trying to avoid listening to Zoey's schoolgirl like questioning of an obviously bored Murphy. Until I am pulled back to reality by the sound of my name, followed by a question mark.

Zoey is asking me if I've been enjoying Chicago so far.

How the hell am I supposed to answer that? I've only experienced the hotel and the theater and now this bar.

So, yeah, it's been great so far.

Zoey is perplexed by the notion that I haven't been able to get out and explore this city at all yet. I'm too exhausted mentally and physically to try to explain my world to this little girl. Luckily, Murphy responded for me, "Clark runs the entire tour. She doesn't get the luxury that us actors get to be able to just show up, perform for the unimpressed, and then fuck off. She has to make sure everything is running smoothly and on schedule."

Which reminds me, I really should go see my sister, who lives a train ride away outside Chicago. At the very least, I need to see my niece. But I'm too busy focusing on work that I'm worried taking a break will lead to me breaking down. This little night out is already feeling like it'll be too much for me.

"Yup, my life is this train-wreck of a show." I agree with Murph, hoping that'll put an end to this vapid conversation, but she just had to push it.

"This 'train-wreck' influenced a generation of children," Zoey snaps back at me with a bit of a bite to it. I almost respect that the little puppy finally learned to bark.

Almost.

"Whether that was a positive influence has yet to be determined," Murphy adds before downing another shot of whiskey. Where he got another drink from, I don't know. I never saw a waitress or a bartender refill him.

It was like alcoholic magic.

"I think it was positive." Zoey continues, "I mean, yeah, the Mr. Bob stuff is disconcerting and makes it tougher to watch old episodes, but that still doesn't erase the history and how that art made people feel."

"Hmm, yeah, I kind of think it does." I have to shut down her attempts at sincerity before she asks us all for a group hug. "And it's just a kid's show."

"It's not just a kid's show. It's how some people connected with their fathers, how some people learned empathy, it's how some shape their identity. And to be told that this part of themselves is now wrong… I guess most just can't live with that reality."

I can't argue with her there.

I once read when confronted with information that challenges core beliefs, we'll explain it away. When the person or thing we admire or love contains an unalterable flaw, the only possible change is ours, and the change is painful.

The music suddenly drops out and a little microphone feedback brings everyone to attention near the blacked-out front windows.

An overweight, but not giving a fuck, judging by the crop top and booty shorts, beautiful bear of a man holds the mic up and declares that it's now time to start karaoke and for people to sign up with him. I take that as my cue to slip out with an old Irish goodbye, but the whole table turns to look at me.

The sound coming from the speakers is my name.

Along with Murphy, we are being called up to perform. It still takes me a second to process. I could imagine someone recognizing Murphy and signing him up without his consent, but who here knows me? Then it hits me.

Those bitches!

I can see Vinny and Ryan across the dance floor laughing to each other as the peer pressure of the crowd reluctantly pulls Murphy and myself to the front. I don't even know what song those assholes chose for us as I pick up the second microphone.

The backing track kicks on and the little TV in front of us finally lets me in on the secret. I thought for sure they were trying to really embarrass us and would go with something like *Barbie Girl* or *Don't Stop Believing* or some other equally horrendous option. But the song we'll be singing is *Bad Memory* by Emily King and

Lukas Nelson. An actual beautiful melody with notes that suit our levels.

"I don't know this fucking song." Murphy leans over and whispers in my ear.

"Just follow my lead. The notes and lyrics are all on the TV."

"I know how karaoke works. I just don't want to embarrass myself by screwing up the song."

"If you knew how it worked, then you'd know the point of karaoke is to embarrass yourself" I wave him off and take my place in front of the monitor.

The first verse is just for me. As I follow the little yellow lines on the screen to keep me on beat, I look over to see Murphy's gaze has drifted out the window. He's still thinking about his street, or about what those parasites outside said to him. His verse is coming up, so I give him a little nudge back to reality.

As Murphy sings, I start to see a slow spark begin to simmer behind his hazel eyes. For the first time in a long time, he almost seems happy.

We hit the chorus and harmonize in a way that actually connects us. I didn't feel it at first, but it was undeniable when we hit the final note that we had found a beautiful rhythm.

Vinny and Ryan have already returned to our booth as we come back from our performance, and they strategically chose spots out of reach for me to strangle them.

"Fuck you for that." I spat at them as I take my seat.

"Good song choice though, guys. At least you didn't completely fuck us," Murphy adds as he sits down across from me.

"I'm sorry, but it was the only way to get the karaoke queen off of us. He was so clingy after he saw us strike out with the Tighty Whitey."

"Muscle Daddy didn't go for that butthole line?" I layer enough sarcasm onto that sentence that it's practically reached Vinny's levels of facetious.

"He. Did. Not." Vinny taps the table to emphasize each word and then changes the subject, "So the problem is that we're going after guys that want to talk."

"Yeah, that was the problem." I couldn't help myself. I had to slip that little snark in there. The sweetheart that he is, he ignores it and keeps going.

"Let's finish one more round and then go to a very loud club so we can find someone to just look at and grind against. You guys in?"

I am not down for a second location. I was barely up for going to this bar and going out to a club where I have to stand and pretend to dance sounds exhausting. I'm already on my feet for over ten hours a day, why would I subject my feet to even more torture? Vinny tries to convince me with light begging, but I resist.

They attempt to get Murphy on board with their raucous plans by appealing to his drug and alcohol affinity, yet somehow, that doesn't work. He coyly tells them he has plans. When they press him for more information he simply repeats, "Just plans." Then he gets up to say goodnight to us and head back to the hotel.

Zoey offers to accompany them, but suddenly Vinny and Ryan are too tired to go someplace else too.

Funny how that works.

And just out of the corner of my eye I can see Murphy talking to the karaoke host before he slips out the back door as the MC then announces, "And now to perform *Through the Storm* by Aretha Franklin and Elton John—Vinny and Zoey!"

CHAPTER TEN

CLARK

Before...

You can feel the electricity.

There's something about thousands of people gathered to experience a singular event that emits this wave of anticipation that you can't help but be moved. That anticipation gets rowdier when a good majority of the crowd is underage and not fully in control of their emotions and bodily functions. Security is about to have no choice but to let the screaming hoard into the coliseum and find their place amongst the sea of fans.

This is by far the biggest endeavor the Digg Dogg Show has ever attempted. An arena tour made up of venues that can hold in the tens of thousands. There's a road team in the hundreds for each performance as they have to essentially put on a rock concert in every town they go to. I've had to break us into A Company, B Company, and C Company in order to facilitate all the moving parts. And they have to deliver because every single ticket in every single city is sold out.

Furbies.

Teddy Ruxpin

Beanie Babies.

Tickle-Me Elmo.

Cabbage Patch Kids.

None of these came close to Digg-Dogg-Mania. These plush stuffed dogs that barely cost three cents to make were selling for thousands out of a desperation of demand at Christmas time. And the draw for anything else related to the show was even greater.

He was a world-wide phenomenon.

It's about thirty minutes to show time and the audience has finally been granted access to their seats. While they all file in, I survey the crowd for potential candidates to receive backstage passes. On a normal tour, I would be frantically running around taking care of final preparations. But with such a large crew, I've been able to delegate all of my normal headaches out to lower-level producers and can just concentrate on the bigger picture, finding hot pieces of ass for my stars.

You'd think that as the senior tour director I would be above such things, yet Murphy decided this was my primary duty. I mean, who the fuck goes to a children's concert looking to hook up with the stuffed dog? Plenty of damaged women apparently, because my job doesn't seem to be about finding a rare specimen, more it involves picking out the shiniest.

This is what my life has become.

I spot a few ladies with appealing assets and approach them with laminated lanyards for after the show. The women are so grateful for the opportunity to meet "such amazing men" that it causes my skull to develop a headache from trying not to roll my eyes after each sentence spewed out by these gold-diggers.

The show went off like an awakening. Playing in a stadium is all about giant gestures and spectacle that reaches everyone across the vast space. So, they put on the grandest, loudest experience possible to the point that all the kids in the first ten rows have to wear noise canceling headphones.

I'm making my way backstage now, flashing my credentials every few feet since nobody knows anyone on this tour. It's such a large cast that they have several trailers set up to house them all. Under my arm is a long, narrow cardboard box that has the front flap half torn open from security inspecting it. I pass by a small grouping of little children sitting on the ground in a tiny circle, all of them focused on the portable DVD player in front of them. I've almost made it to Bob and Murphy's trailer when I'm stopped by one of the new guys, Vinny something or other.

"Clark. A word."

"What can I do for you, new meat?" I reply to the living-at-the-gym piece of eye candy.

"I was led to believe that I was brought on to play Fab Frogg Freddie, a principal cast member."

"You were—you are. What's your question?"

"If I am part of the principal cast, why am I getting dressed with background?"

I just let out a sigh.

I shouldn't be dealing with performer drama. He should have brought up his grievances to one of my underlings. They would have dealt with this situation with a softer touch, but I am way too important to have to deal with shit like this being put on my plate.

"Listen, Donny, was it?" I ask, purposefully condescendingly.

"It's Vinny."

"What the fuck kind of grown man calls himself Vinny?"

"I—"

"Don't care," I cut him off. "Listen, you're only here because the Original Freddie got too old to squat up and down for two hours every night. I don't give a shit where you drop your jockstrap before and after each show. As long as you keep those brick crushing thighs in hopping shape, you can consider yourself

employed. But if you come to me again with asinine complaints, I will call up some bar in West Hollywood and find myself a replacement muscle daddy to slap on that green suit. Understood?"

The pretty boy stares at me for a moment, dumbfounded, before his face opens up with a wide smile. "I like you."

"Damn right you do," I reply before trotting up the metal steps that connect to the nondescript white trailer housing Murphy and Bob. These assholes each have an individual trailer and this joint one for them to party in. I open the door and I'm immediately hit with a thumping bass rhythm and a curtain of THC laced smoke.

Inside the dimly lit trailer, I find an image you would think is reserved for the after party at rock concerts, not for a children's program. The low light and foggy atmosphere, coupled with the inappropriate music, something by Lil' Wayne about a Wifebeater, *sets the vibe as several women drape themselves over Bob and Murphy. They're all laid up on a set of couches, laughing as they down shot after shot. No one in the group acknowledges my presence as I stand in front of them trying to keep a professional demeanor. So, I just drop the box I had been carrying all over the goddam stadium at Bob's feet as it makes a metallic thud.*

"I'm not your fucking mailman, Bob. Stop ordering your shit in my name for me to deliver to you." I bark at him making sure I come off especially shrill to really drive home the sitcom wife aspect of my relationship with these douchebags.

"Sorry, Clarky, I'm a little too famous to use my own name. If people see 'Mr. Bob' on a package, they'll likely steal it and sell it to the tabloids."

I'm pretty sure this is all bullshit, but it did have some air of truth to it. The two of them had lost a lot of their private lives to their new icon status. They were no longer just stars of a show for kids anymore.

They had become cultural staples.

Bob picks up his box and pulls out a few small round metal pieces and a long steel rod. He starts connecting all of the items together until it becomes one set. Everyone is looking at this contraption with several questions inside their heads, but only I have the balls to ask what we were all thinking, "What the fuck is that thing?"

"It's a branding iron," he answers, as if that's only the explanation needed.

"Why do you need a branding iron?" Murphy asks before grabbing the rod from Bob to inspect it.

"I'm thinking of buying a ranch up in Jackson Hole."

"So, you bought a custom brand before you bought the ranch?" I ask.

"Actually, this is just a prototype. Not gonna buy the ranch if I can't get the logo right."

Murphy presses an end to one of the women's thighs, faking the sound of sizzling flesh, to joke with her.

I couldn't have known what I had been an accomplice to or how I had inadvertently caused the suffering of others with the simple act of delivering a package to its rightful owner. I couldn't have known how those badges I would hand out at shows would seal the fates of so many. All I thought I was doing was my job.

I hadn't known I was working for the devil.

CHAPTER ELEVEN

MURPHY

After…

The stitching is starting to give way.

It is literally coming apart at the seams. I've had this blazer for longer than I can remember. He bought it for me as a gift after the show got picked up. I used to only bust it out on special occasions. Now it's a fraying reminder of better days. It's kind of funny that I went out to a nice bar in sweatpants and a hoodie, yet when I get back to my hotel room, I change into a formal black suit and tie. At least these accommodations are better than Kansas City. It's a little more fitting that I'd be wearing a nice outfit in these kinds of rooms.

My snifter glass is empty again. I have to will myself up off of this leather chair in order to make my way back to the bedroom, just to rummage around in the welcome basket to find the bottle for my refill. The basket is on the dresser. I should probably move it, so I don't accidentally mess up the beautiful display in front of it.

Written out in delicate little white lines made of pure, uncut cocaine reads, "Welcome Digg Dogg". It's that level of detail that makes me love Clark and her beyond satisfactory job performance. I sift through the little airplane bottles of liquor until I find a winner. The large bag of popcorn from some local shop just seems to be getting in the way so I take it out and throw it in the garbage. I don't know why she insists on putting items from the host city in my welcome gift bag. All I really require is the alcohol, coke, and my special request for Chicago: Cigars. I pull a hand rolled premium out of the humidor and make my way back to my chair, after a courtesy snort before leaving the room, of course.

Back in a comfortable spot, I crack open the little glass container and pour it into my snifter. It smells like an Extra Añejo. I mean, obviously, that's what the label on the bottle I had Clark get for me says, but what I meant was that the aroma from the glass just screams crafted quality. It's got a beautifully smooth caramel note that matches its coloring. I poured it into a snifter glass so I can smell the rich agave as I sip and drift away into a Jalisco dream. This is the same tequila I always drink when I'm in Chicago. Whether I'm at the bar with the cast or alone here in my hotel room, I don't care about the cost of the bottle. I use my butane to light the cigar and suck in the first glorious puff when the knocking at the door calls my attention.

I announce that the door is open, since I propped it ajar with the swinging latch for the lock. Coming through the entranceway is a stunning brunette wearing a long coat that goes down to her bare knees that guide my eyes further down to her bright, sleek black high-heeled shoes.

"Hello there. I take it I'm here to see you?" she says it more like a statement than a question.

She flips the latch and closes the door before slipping off her coat, revealing the lingerie she's wearing underneath. I requested when I called her that she has something sexy to wear, but I didn't think she would travel while being so scantily clad. She's in her mid-twenties, old enough to not be a naive new adult, but not too old to have been beaten down by the world yet. The lingerie she chose is a little black number that amazingly matches her red bottomed designer shoes. The corset style is tight, snug to her slender body. The pattern dances with the illusion that it's see through in the right places, while barely covering others. Her panties, also matching black, ride up and hug the top of her hips before diving underneath her in a small, sleek V.

I pull a wad of cash from my pocket. By far the most I've paid a girl all tour, but if she's even half as good as she looks, it'll have been worth it. She sits down sideways onto my lap, kicking her feet up, before taking the money and carefully counting it while I cue up a song on the Bluetooth speaker. I went with *Flowers* by Troi Irons because the singer's voice has a sultry sexiness to it.

"They let you smoke in here?" she asks.

"Ask forgiveness. Not permission," I reply.

I offer her my cigar as she takes a puff while it's still being held in my hand, her bare butt cheek getting cupped in my open palm. She sets the money down on the side table next to us as she lets out the smoke. I can tell she wants to try my drink. I would normally tell anyone who attempted to syphon my booze to go to hell, but this woman could ask for my mother's pinky on a platter, and I'd hack that fucker off for her.

She leans back against the armrest as I pour it directly into her mouth. I bury my face in her chest as she takes the snifter from my hand, allowing me to use said hand to reach over and slide those black panties down to her feet, careful not to burn her with the cigar.

"Hmm," she moans. "So. Do you want me to call you Digg Dogg or Diggsy?"

I pull my head away from her chest. Something I thought would require an entire football team to remove me from, but apparently finding out a hooker used to be a child, a child that used to watch your television show, and is still a big fan, is enough to pry me away from a pair of perfect perky breasts.

I ask if she's still okay with our arrangement, even with the whole Mr. Bob stuff.

She assures me that I am not the one on trial, that he's the fucking asshole, and that Bob was the one who ruined her childhood.

That's all I needed to hear to regain my erection.

She must have been able to feel me bumping against her backside, because she reaches over and flips the handle on the side of the chair, reclining it and me backwards. She lifts her right leg, with her underwear dangling from the ankle, and slowly swings it past my head while lifting her other leg and resting them on my shoulders. I hold up the cigar so she can take another drag. The hooker uses her spare hand to undo my pants. She pulls my cock out and starts moving her hand up and down, while sipping on my drink with her other hand.

She lets a long, tequila infused line of saliva drool down her mouth and onto the tip of my dick, using it to ease her stroking. She continues to work my cock with a cascading succession of high projectile spitting to add lubrication, accompanied by intermittent moans and affirmations. I lean my head back in pleasure as I inhale more bliss from my cigar.

She asks me if I'm ready for a condom, so I produce one from the side table's drawer. I hand the golden square to her and she uses the spit covered hand to take it from me. After using her mouth to tear it open, she rolls the condom down the length of my dick, using one hand without spilling a drop from her glass.

This woman has skills.

She grabs the handles of the chair, using her legs to propel herself forward, and slides herself on top of me as I enter her. Even through the rubber, I feel her warmth wrapping around my shaft. She leans forward and tips the snifter to my lips to let me finish my drink before tossing the empty glass over her shoulder. She spins her legs around while still keeping me inside of her until both feet are planted on the floor as the recliner thrusts me back up.

I'm looking at the back of her head for only a second before my eyes instinctively guide their way down the curves of her back and all the way to her glorious, perfectly peach shaped ass.

I know I should come up with a less clichéd analogy than a peach for the shape of a woman's ass, but this backside is asking for me to take a bite out of it like the ripe fruit, it's all I can think of.

She's immediately placing her hands on my knees for leverage as she leans forward and starts to bounce up and down on my lap. I'm letting out sounds I've never made before, but it doesn't matter because they're drowned out by the sound of her cheeks smacking against my thighs while she rides me. I watch as my dick disappears and then reappears from inside her. I can see streaks of her wetness have started to accumulate on the white rubber. She's actually enjoying herself.

At least her body is.

She's building up such speed that I swear I am about to blow already. She must be able to tell because she suddenly stops, telling me to hold on a second and not to cum yet. She leans back against my chest waiting to make sure I didn't unexpectedly finish before giving her hips a little wiggle and pulling her corset off to let her breasts out of their cups. She brings my hands up to play with her perky, erect nipples while her fingers slide down between her legs to play with herself a moment. I can feel her pussy squeezing around my cock as it pulsates from her digit play.

She wants to take this to the bedroom before continuing.

I'm guided by the hand into the bedroom after dropping out of my pants and underwear along the way. I'm straight *Winnie the Pooh*-ing it as we enter the bedroom area of the hotel suite, having no bottoms on and just my top half of the jacket and shirt. When she notices the coke on the dresser, I agree to let her partake as she grabs the tiny glass tube next to the basket. She uses it to inhale an entire letter into her nose before moving over to crawl onto the bed with her backside pushed out towards me, like she's a cat presenting herself. I take off my blazer, shirt, and tie and follow her onto the soft mattress.

I kiss her on her right cheek and give it a light bite as she starts to giggle.

I ask her if it tickles.

To which she replies, "No, it's just—Doggie style from Digg Dogg? I'm thinking about how I'll tell my friends. It's just too funny."

My smile fades as I thrust into her, sending her off balance before she snaps back. I continue to thrust, hard.

I grab at her hips and go supernova.

There's no slow build or sensual movement anymore. She's just a cock sleeve for me right now. Her warmth and wetness have gone, but only for a moment. Her insides are now burning, and the condom is so slick I can see the residuals on my shaft again as it peaks in and out.

I tell her I'm going to cum on her asshole.

I don't know why I want to do that. It's not something that gets me off, but it's something that needs to happen, because it happened back then.

She's huffs out her approval, not that I needed it, telling me it'll cost extra.

I pull out of her and yank off the rubber that slides right off with ease. She grabs hold of her cheeks and spreads herself for me as I use my hand to pump out a gushing stream right onto her puckering backside. She releases her grasp and lays down flat on her stomach, kicking her legs into the air.

I get up and proceed to take the lowercase "g" of coke straight up my nose.

"Can you get me a towel, or can I roll over onto the bedspread?" she asks.

After the initial pain in my sinuses subsides, I turn back to her and say, "I have you for the full night, right? Don't clean up. We're going again."

I stick my cock right in her face.

I know she doesn't want it in her mouth because it probably still tastes and smells like condom, along with the residual semen still on the tip. But with the amount I'm paying her, she happily takes me all in. I'm still hard from cumming just a little bit ago but ramming my dick down the back of her throat keeps me at attention. Plus, the little blue pill I took beforehand is helping me along.

I normally don't need medical assistance, but since I knew I had this girl for the night, and I would be going multiple rounds, I popped one to ensure I would be ready. At my age, multiple rounds are a thing of the past without a little aid. It takes some pre-planning nowadays, but maybe I'll have a reinvigorated night that doesn't require it.

I continue to thrust into that little mouth of hers like it was her ass earlier. I grab the hair on the top of her head and make it bounce at high speeds. I can hear her gagging in rhythm like music to my ears while feeling her spit wad up and drip down my balls.

I never understood where the phenomena of Throat-Fucking came from.

It's such a visceral, carnal position. Oral sex is already such a one-sided sex act, that now the person giving is being literally fucked in the face as hard as can be for the receiver's pleasure.

I can't recall anything in the naughty sections of my history books ever talking about a dick getting repeatedly rammed in order to fully degrade a partner. It's like their face has been turned into a Fleshlight.

Even older pornography, and by older I'm not talking 1970's full bush era, I mean burgeoning internet age, when things just started to get dirty, didn't have the rough oral that seems to be standard fare now a days.

Just something I ponder as her mascara starts to run down the sides of her face now that her eyes have started to water from lack of oxygen. That red lipstick she had on is now smeared across my cock as I keep fucking her mouth harder and faster. I finally slam her face against my pelvic, forcing her to deepthroat me all the way down to the base and holding her head there while she struggles for breath. She gives me the courtesy tap out on the side of my hip and I release her head.

She snaps back, taking a big breath in with a shit-eating grin behind it.

"Hmm. Come on, choke me with that dick, Daddy Dogg."

The color completely drains out of my world as the words

that come from her mouth send me back into a memory.

And with that…

I'm reminded of my daughter.

CHAPTER TWELVE

MURPHY

Before…

"Say hello to Daddy Dogg!"

That was the best greeting I could think of to welcome Bob and Clark into my opulent, dick-measuring beachside home while holding a bundled-up newborn in my arms, giving them both a big, one-armed side hug as they walk through the door. The grand entranceway is a sea of white contemporary architecture, a typical Hollywood douchebag homestead. It's the kind of home Midwesterners imagine a successful musician resides in. Its living room is devoid of an entertainment unit, instead opting for floor to skyline ceiling windows looking out over the Pacific Ocean beachfront. I told the realtor to give me a house that location managers for television shows about drug kingpins would use on the regular.

"Oh, my god, let me look at that baby!" Clark squeals as she reaches out to take the bundle from my hands and gaze at her in awe. She recently cut her hair to give herself bangs and with the horn-rim reading glasses she's got on; she looks like an Asian Zooey Deschanel. Bob has grown out his beard since we're on hiatus between episodes. He congratulates me on becoming a new father, but I'm deflecting the praise I don't feel I've earned yet.

"I can't help but comment on the fact that I did nothing to bring this miracle into the world. I was only really there for the fun part in creating her," I reply.

Clark tries to assuage my insecurities manifested in sarcastic jokes by reminding me that I'm practically a dad to millions of children on TV.

"I'm a pet to a bunch of kids," I state before pointing to Bob and saying, "He's the father figure."

"Shut up, Murphy. You created perfection here," Clark says without taking her focus off the little one.

Even though I usually try to cast off any type of compliment thrown my way, I'll take in the flattery when it comes to my new daughter. Clark just keeps gushing over her and calling her breathtaking, to which I accept as fact, because I know deep down in my heart that it's true. This little girl is the most beautiful creature I could have ever thought to grace my life. The moment I saw my own face fixed with the childlike features of a cherub angel reflecting back at me, I suddenly knew I had a bigger purpose, that of a father.

I cried in that moment.

I cry a lot more now. Things that wouldn't have affected me before now touch at my soul. It's like a raw nerve has been removed from my body and exposed for the world to see.

"Yes, she is gorgeous. Speaking of gorgeous, where's the wifey? Sleeping?" Bob asks as he makes his way over to the open kitchen.. He opens up one of the sleek white cabinet doors and looks around inside. My friend's movement in the kitchen is effortless

because he feels more at home in my house than his own. As he

continues to scan the shelves, he calls out to the two of us in the

living room, "I'd imagine she must be exhausted, what with her

doing all the work while you're off making your stupid children's

show. No champagne glasses?"

"They're still at the New York apartment. And, hey, I'm a

modern dad. I take care of my fair share of diapers and get up for

the midnight feedings."

Bob pulls out a set of crystal Irish-cut whiskey glasses and

sets them down on the white marble countertop before her grabs a

bottle of Prosecco from the wine fridge. He chides me about not

believing in my contributions to the baby's daily care as he pops the

cork on the bubbly and then pours it into the whiskey glasses. Before

we can toast, Bob gets one last shot in by asking, "And that nanny

you hired, she's just here to lounge around and look pretty?"

"She helps out around the house." I try to hide my guilty

look behind the glass as my sheepish smile betrays me. The other

two just giggle at this exposure. "You were just hyping me up as someone who's going to be a great dad. Now you're knocking me

for hiring a nanny?"

"Admitting you have help doesn't make you any less of a

dad." Clark doesn't even look me in the face as she delivers her

response. Her focus is and always has been staring deeply into the

eyes of that baby girl.

"Thank you. But can we still leave the nanny out of this?

She's not even here right now," I say in my defense.

"Is she single? Is she hot? Answer the second question

first." Bob spits out his quip as I retort with an insincere, "I hate

you." But Bob laughs it off and reaches out for his turn to ogle over

the child.

Clark hesitates to give her up, stating, "Don't drop her."

As she reluctantly hands over the burrito of blankets that's wrapped

around their source of affection.

"I can't drop her at all? Am I allowed to drop her a little

bit? Like, what's my range for the fall?" Bob's joke falls flat as our

need to protect the precious little one is no laughing matter to the two of us. Bob is actually being a good friend by keeping it light and joking. I'm still a wreak over this birth.

There was... complications.

As Bob takes my baby into the crooks of his arms, she immediately starts to fuss and lets out a whimpering cry that threatens to elevate into full-blown screams.

Fearing this could wake up Sunshine, Bob bounces the baby in an attempt to calm her as he adds a sway before breaking into a soft, whispered lullaby, "Shh... Shh... Sunny days, sweeping the clouds away... On my way to where the air is sweet... Can you tell me how to get..."

The precocious ray of sunshine in Bob's arms starts to settle herself, soothed back to sleep by the sweet song.

"Why wouldn't you sing the Digg Dogg theme?" Clark asks as this gang share a drink and continue to fawn over the newborn.

"Because Sesame Street *is a classic," I say, smiling. "And ours is dog shit."*

CHAPTER THIRTEEN

CLARK

After…

This goddamn song again.

The show has had some really heartfelt, significant songs over the years. And yet, it's this fucking diaper song that sticks around. To the point that we have to close to intermission with it every time.

Every. Damn. Time.

It's one of those earworm tunes that gets stuck inside your brain and won't leave you alone until you physically remove it with a tack hammer. It doesn't help that children usually insist on having it played on repeat day and night. It's a simple melody with a repetitive chorus that sees the whole gang asking Baby Pants Kitty Kelly to give up said baby pants, her diapers, with the rational that she's too big for them.

Why this one song caught on more than the other quality ones they put out, I'll never understand. It's just like how most modern pop music over the last two decades came from the same guys. Almost every pop song has been produced and written by these two Swedish dudes whose translations come out as gibberish, yet the beat and melodies make them 'classics'. No one cares that this song is annoying, they just like to dance to it. My current remedy is to put my Airpod in my free ear and listen to better songs. Currently, it's the appropriate *Waiting for the End* by Linkin Park playing.

The whole cast is on stage finishing up this fart of a song. As they hit the crescendo, a set of confetti canons go off, sending streamers into the audience. A little bit of flash and flair to keep the snot-nosed ticket holders from leaving during the break. As the curtain comes down, I am forced to leave the comfort of the soundboard to deal with my divas backstage.

I'm first intercepted by Zoey bitching about her dressing room situation again. I've started to come around to her personality, not finding it as grating as before. I began by looking inward at myself and why I felt animosity towards her in the first place. It was almost some kind of misogynistic predilection to disregard her and see her as less than because she didn't fit into my ideals of what an acceptable woman should be. I was compelled by societal influences and pressures to see her as an enemy to myself simply because I felt threatened by her youth and beauty, when in fact, I should be embracing her as a part of my tribe.

Still, that bitch isn't getting her own dressing room anytime soon.

After I shut her down, I am accosted by Vinny and Ryan, who seem to take umbrage with the fact that they had to take a reduction in per diem for the Detroit leg of the tour. I assure them it will be reimbursed and added to their pay rate, once we get our cut of the ticket sales from Chicago and bring us back out of the red, but they still feel the need to hate me for the rest of the day. Finally, I make my way to the dressing room of my star. His new handler for the next segment, some perky young thing, is waiting outside his

door to be introduced by me. She has to take over today because the

usual handler called in sick this morning. I enter without even

knocking to find an unsurprising sight. Murph has taken the caps off

of five airplane liquor bottles and has proceeded to down all of them

in one big gulping handful.

After he finishes dissipating his alcoholic shakes with his

little medicinal friends, I bring in the wrangler. She's wearing a

security lanyard similar to mine. Her brown hair is in a ponytail,

tucked under a baseball cap sporting the tour's logo on the front.

Similar to the one I'm usually wearing. She's distractingly pretty for

a stagehand. My first thought is to be suspicious of her, but then I

remember I dealt with the same things when I was coming up. Back

when I was distractingly pretty, as opposed to the distractingly tired

that I am now.

I let Murphy know that this beauty will be walking him

through the crowd in a bit. It's like I'm feeding her to the wolves as

he immediately gets up to drool over her. I can practically sense his

erection pushing against his dog suit as he shakes her hand. I leave them alone, I know, so dumb. But they do have to go over procedures, and I have to get back to the soundboard to double check the post-intermission levels. The procedures they go over are how they're going to execute the next segment.

Basically, Digg Dogg opens the second act by walking from the back of the theater through the crowd. It's a great way for all the kids to see him up close and for him to get personal interactions with his little fans. The issue with that though is that you have a millionaire primadonna in an obstructed view costume trapesing through a sea of small, grabby, unpredictable monsters hopped up on sugar and sleep deprivation, as the matinee and night shows usually interfere with nap and bedtimes, respectively. So, we always employ a handler from the local theaters to escort Digg Dogg through the crowd and to act as a gatekeeper from the hordes of screaming acolytes. Although, as of late, the hoards have more or less been small groupings. But we still need to dispatch someone to make sure he doesn't trip over a small child and topple to the ground. Thus, the need for them to go over coded commands for how they'll proceed and what route to take before going out into the wilds of the stands. Hand signals for if he's okay, or needs attention,

or, in an emergency, needs her to get him the fuck out of there.

I make my way back to my position as the tech is dimming

the house lights to start the show back up. The spotlight is

positioned to follow Digg Dogg as he makes his grand entrance

from the back left corner of the crowd. He really is good with the

kids. The few audience members we have for tonight's performance

start to gather around him as he tries to hug and high five everyone

that still paid to come out to see him, despite everything surrounding

the show. I notice the handler is getting caught up in the task at hand

and has started to continue towards the stage without Murphy

behind her. She's getting further and further away from her ward as

he is caught up with his admirers.

Normally this isn't that big of an issue. He gets too into

interacting with his fans all the time and will sometimes stray. But

she is noticeably at too great a distance from him now, and, of

course, that's when it happens.

Some angry, sweaty adult man swats at the back of

Murphy's costumed head, screaming obscenities at him. I can't hear all of what he's yelling from where I'm at, plus the backing track is blasting through the auditorium, but I know it has something to do with Bob and his scandal. I immediately yell for security on my headset, and they're on top of the sweaty guy in seconds. They've been trained and debriefed on dealing with protesters out front and taking care of any infiltrators. So, the big beefy guards spring into action the moment I call on them. This isn't the first time that anyone's taken their outrage and directed it at the show, trying to disrupt it. But this is the first time someone physically attacked Murphy though, and it starts a bit of a melee.

Murph pushes back at his attacker as security tries to break them up. The shoving match spills into other theatergoers, who feel the need to protect themselves and their offspring caught up in the fracas. This results in an all-out mosh pit of small children, suburban parents, and a furry dog caught in the middle.

I want to go out there and help him, but a tiny little thing like myself would just get trampled. So, I focus my abilities on corralling whatever children and their families are on the outskirts of the tussle towards the exits away from the commotion. I duck down just as a stuffed Digg Dogg comes flying by and almost hits me in the face. I look over to see Murphy's costumed dog head rolling down the aisle, followed by the rest of him being carried by security towards the backstage area. I dart over and grab the head before trailing after the group.

The security team sets Murphy down on his feet before they shoot him through an exit door. But as he's about to disappear, he comes face to face with a small child standing off to the side. The two lock eyes and I can see the magic being shattered in this kid's world. He is looking into the angry, sad, defeated eyes of the man behind his hero. It's like he just saw a drunken, puke covered Santa Claus get taken away by the police in handcuffs and the cops rip off the beard to reveal your dad in the costume before sticking him in the squad car.

Weird. That was a very specific example.

I'm pretty sure that's a memory I might have repressed.

This show does wonders for my psyche.

CHAPTER FOURTEEN

CLARK

Before...

Murphy had never told his friends and family of the trauma that occurred when his daughter was born. I only knew because as one of the people running his life at the time, I was privy to things above friends and family. Rey had come into this world with a degenerative blood disease that forced her into the NICU the first few weeks she was alive. The happy couple just told people they were taking some extra days at the hospital before coming home. Mostly because they didn't want to risk anything getting out to tabloids while they were particularly emotionally fragile. Murphy would watch her tiny little body, covered in tubes and wires, through plexiglass enclosures, while being completely helpless to do anything but stand by and cry. His daughter had recovered and came home without any incident, so Sunshine and Murphy decided to still keep the illness to themselves.

They focused on welcoming their happy, newly healthy baby.

And she was the happiest baby. I mean, yes, most babies are smiling and happy, but speaking as someone who's worked around children most of her career, I can say this baby was always happy and smiling. Like, big smiles all the time, just pure joy. She would accidentally throw her plate of mushy food all on the floor, and you wouldn't even get mad at her because of the giant smile on her face. You would never know the illness that had been hidden away when she was born.

But it didn't stay hidden.

It came back.

The family became regular visitors at the hospital with nothing but pain and tears to show. She would get better, well...

better enough to go back home. They would gain a semblance of hope that life could be normal, but it was always fleeting. And they would be right back in an emergency room soon enough. His daughter's body was giving out and there was nothing the doctors could do for her...

CHAPTER FIFTEEN

CLARK

After…

This is it. The final straw.

I can't keep doing this anymore. I can't keep picking this man up off the floor and holding his world together. I'll have to have my resume updated. The work on this show has to be glossed over a little now, but I'm sure I could get on as a stagehand somewhere else. Twenty years as a tour manager, you'd think I'd have my pick of new jobs.

I'm going to start looking tonight.

I'm done.

Back in my star's dressing room, I canceled the rest of the night's performance, you know, due to the all-out riot that broke out just a few minutes ago. He's pacing and is visibly rattled. Not anything new, but this time it's justified. Security was able to pick him up out of the crowd and get him safely backstage without serious injury to anyone. The children in the audience will likely need therapy about seeing their idol get assaulted in front of their impressionable young eyes. Digg Dogg's handler, who was supposed to be by his side to protect him from any kind of incident such as this, is standing in the doorway in frightened guilt.

"I am so sorry, Mr. Harrison! I was distracted by you hitting on me earlier and I wasn't paying attention—"

"Get her the fuck out of my sight, Clark!" Murphy screams at her, cutting off her pathetic apology. I know he's serious when he calls me by my name. I close the door on the girl, who cranes her neck around the gap, looking to me for reassurance. I try my best to give her a nurturing glance, to let her know she's going to be okay, but I know nothing I can muster will ease her worry. Honestly, what was she supposed to do? Even if she had been closer to him, there was nothing that little hundred-pound girl could have done but get knocked out of the way.

"We're cutting the walkthroughs! I am not leaving the stage ever again!" Murphy barks at me.

I plead my case against that move. Digg Dogg coming through the audience and getting up close with the children is the favorite part of the show for the kids. But he doesn't care. His personal safety is more important to him, which I understand, so we agree to cut the walkthrough segment for the rest of the tour.

The whole time we argue, he is struggling to take his costume off. Like some dopey cartoon character, unable to get off a pair of too tight pants, he comically thrusts his arms out of the fur. I've made my way over to the couch and sit, watching him spin his wheels. I still have the Digg Dogg head in my hands as I rest it on my lap, so I pat at the fabric like it's a real pet.

"I can't do this anymore," he laments. "I thought since the TV show was put on hiatus, hiding out on the road was the best way to avoid all of this, but it's not working."

He grabs the small trash can by the vanity, places it in front of himself on the floor, a deliberate movement, then kicks it up into the air, sending the can and debris flying everywhere.

"Well, that's what happens when you do that," I state in a very matter of fact tone, unfazed by his latest outburst.

"I'm the one—I'm the one paying for Bob's shit!"

"We all are affected by this—" I try to continue, but he cuts me off.

"No! I'm the face of this show! I'm the one in the fucking costume! This fucking costume!" Murphy gets frustrated as he yanks at the suit again. He yanks it so hard to the point that he falls straight to the floor while he was attempting to drop back into the chair but completely missed it.

He lays there, dejected.

"You done?" I ask him as he reluctantly nods. I should leave him down there. This asshole thinking he's the only one who was hurt by Bob's betrayal. Like he's the only one who had their entire life turned upside down. I should leave him to wallow in his own self-destructive tantrum…

But I don't.

I bend to his level and help him get out of the costume.

"This won't happen again. Security was on it and you're never leaving the stage. Let's move on and finish out Chicago." I say to him as he squirts out of his fuzzy cocoon. His whole body is a sweaty mess, but at least this time he had the decency to wear underwear, something he's not always so courteous about.

He pulls himself up to the makeup chair in front of the mirror as he notices his cell going off with a phone call coming in.

The ID reads, "UNKOWN CALLER" again, like the other time.

"What the fuck is this now?" Murphy exhaustedly exclaims.

"Tabloids again?"

"No, this is the burner only a few people have this number." Murphy states as he rejects the call yet again, but this time he pulls up the digit number from the caller log. He clicks at his phone after I tell him to search the number, trying to get to the source of his nuisance. It takes longer to load than either of us would like thanks to the terrible cell reception and shitty Wi-Fi that comes with this theater's thick, acoustically built walls. When he finally gets his answer, he reads it out loud to me, "Carlton County Correctional Facility."

"Isn't that where…?"

"Yup."

"His bail was denied again?"

"Yup."

"You think he's calling to get you to write a character letter to the judge?"

"Yup."

He confirms what we both already knew. What we always had feared would happen. The inevitable confrontation. Murphy finally having to face his demon and listen to his side of the story.

Bob was calling.

CHAPTER SIXTEEN

MURPHY

Before...

Looking back on the original Digg Dogg costume, with its visible stitching and cheap matted fur, I still can't believe that horror show of a suit was ever allowed in front of children, let alone didn't get us sued for inducing nightmares. I drop the unrefined version of the Digg Dogg costume onto a bed as the sounds of children running and playing outside these four walls I currently occupy, sends nervous chills up my spine. This suit looks like it was handmade by a man who has never excelled at crafts and was tasked with creating a life-sized, professional dog suit.

An apt assessment. I am said man.

Bob stands nearby in front of a mirror, straightening his bowtie. His "Mr. Bob" ensemble already looking like the eventual finished, polished product that it would come to be known by. The stark difference between the quality of the two outfits is not lost on me. I stare at my friend who looks like a professional, who you would allow, welcomed into your home. And then I look at my mess of a situation on the bed, that looks like a mascot for a homeless shelter. Just another sign on high from the gods that we should not be in this house, at this function. So, my nervousness brings me to do my best attempt to bail.

"This is degrading, Bob. We didn't create Digg Dogg to wind up doing kids' birthday parties."

"We're not doing kids' birthday parties. We're doing one kid's party. One kid whose mom is the producer on the Happy Kidz Show, who can get us booked on a prime slot, that could lead to our own show, thus preventing us from doing kids' birthday parties."

"Still, I feel like I'm whoring out," I reply as I arrange my outfit on the bed, trying to make it look any less horrible than it is. The bed is an unnecessary California King. It doesn't even take up *the entirety of the room, which still has the space for us to have practiced our dance number just a few hours earlier. When the party host directed us inside my first thought was, we had to have been brought to the master bedroom, when in fact this was just another guest space in this opulent mansion. It almost feels like a power move having us come to see her wealth and extravagance so she can drop her dick onto the table and show us who the real man in this relationship is. Letting us know that we are the little struggling artists, and she is the almighty executive in charge, holding our fate/balls in the palm of her hand.*

"Think of it as an audition. She needs to see how kids react to it before putting us on TV."

Bob's reassuring words do nothing for my anxiety. If anything, the pressure has made me feel worse, making me hold my stomach as a deep growl comes from within my midsection.

"Whatever end that needs to come out of to make you feel better, do it now. I need you on board and on game, quick." Bob points to the adjacent bathroom as I head straight in that direction, closing the door behind me.

Inside the bathroom, I turn on the sink faucet and splash some water on my face. I've seen it done in TV and movies all the time, but it does nothing to calm my nerves. I drop my pants and sit down on the toilet in an attempt to relieve myself. It's a small, half bath kind of space with the toilet directly next to the door. I guess the guests need all that room for dance routines, but not an adequate space for shitting.

I breathe in and out, in and out, closing my eyes trying to calm down and reach a center, remembering what that yogi at that free session I went to tried to teach me. His name was Chad, and he tried to sell me coke after the class, but he still imparted some wisdom.

The door suddenly bursts open, startling the shit out of me, literally. As I cower in terror, a little boy pops his head inside and looks at me. The two of us stare at each other for a moment, face to face without a word exchanged, before the kid finally breaks the silence.

"Whatcha doing?" the boy asks.

I'm taken aback by his lack of decorum, but reply,

"Poopin'."

"Why?"

"Because I need to."

"You look sick."

The kid's got me there.

"I'm nervous," I tell him.

"What's nervous?"

"It's like scared."

The kid holds off on the questioning as he eyes this strange, unknown man on a toilet. And just like that, the boy leaves, closing the door behind him.

I sit in silence for a moment before I call out for Bob, wondering where the hell my partner had gone and how he missed the small child busting in on me while I was incapacitated. There is no answer from Bob, so I try making an attempt to regain my composure with a calming breath in and out again, eyes closed for maximum concentration.

But before I can fully Zen out on Master Chad's teachings, the door is knocked open again, and the boy reappears, this time he has a light blue balloon floating above him, being held in place by a string connected to the boy's small hand. The kid hands the balloon to the stranger in front of him.

"Here. Now you won't be nervous," the child says.

"How's this going to help me?" I ask.

"I filled it with my brave thoughts. Now you won't be scared."

The kid turns and walks away, leaving the door wide open behind him. I sit there holding the string with the blue balloon floating above my head while my pants dangle down around the base of the toilet bowl.

Bob pops his head into the restroom, wondering what's taking his partner so long. He stops, dumbfounded as he takes in the sight before him. I don't even look back at Bob with embarrassment.

No, I have gained a newfound confidence in my situation. The ridiculousness of the balloon and my poop, coupled with the sage advice of a wise beyond his years five, maybe six-year-old, has given me a kind of clarity I never would have discovered otherwise.

Bob continues to look at me for answers.

"I'm a little black rain cloud," I exclaim in a fucking pitch perfect impersonation of Jim Cummings voicing Winnie the Pooh. *Giving Bob even more questions in his head than before.*

I pull my sorry ass off of the toilet, yank my pants up while still holding the balloon and with the kind of cocksure attitude that would put General Patton to shame, I declare, "Let's do this shit!" before marching out to throw on that haggard looking Digg Dogg costume I made with my own two hands.

Bob just looks at me and then back into the bathroom before asking quizzically, "Did you win a prize in there or…?

CHAPTER SEVENTEEN

CLARK

After…

I find him sitting in his underwear.

Not the comical tighty-whities, but a classic, black with grey band boxer brief set up. It's an odd mix of sexy and pathetic. I left him alone to deal with the choice he was wrestling with, whether or not he was going to talk to Bob, while I went off to see to it that the rest of the show was reset for tomorrow. I honestly thought he had gone back to his hotel room it was so late. He's facing the mirror, but his gaze is somewhere else, somewhere far away.

Wherever his mind is at right now, I hope it's some place nice.

Digg Dogg's fuzzy empty head is on the vanity in front of him while he holds a glass of wine in his hand, as if he is toasting to his friendly pet. I try to take this all in and really absorb what I'm witnessing, but the giant stack of paperwork in my hands is starting to weigh my arms down. So, I throw the papers onto the chair and grab the glass of wine from his hands.

He's got his depression mix playing on the speaker again. It's a song I recognize but can't quite place this arrangement. I sneak a look at the display, since I don't want him to think I'm not fully absorbed in his misery. The song is *King of Wishful Thinking* but it's not the original version from the '80's. It's a more slowed down cover from this singer named Letta. Her soulful singing allows you to actually hear the hauntingly heartbreaking lyrics and I understand why he put it in this mix.

He doesn't even turn his head to acknowledge me when I tell him, "I honestly don't know how the fuck we can keep operating at a loss for much longer." I rub my eyes before taking a sip and asking, "What is this a blend?"

"It's Orin Swift." he answers. "You're changing light bulbs on the *Titanic*, Boss. You need to accept that we are going down, been going down."

"You're doing all you can to make us go down faster. What do you think is going to happen to the show if the other creator also ends up in jail for drugs or soliciting a prostitute, or both?"

He swivels his head around in his chair to finally face me. "Um, you're the one providing those drugs. And how do you know about the hookers?"

"I provide coke for you so you won't get busted buying it from someone we can't trust. But I can't help you if you get busted by an undercover cop you tried to pay to blow you."

"Hey, I usually always ask if they're a cop first." He taps his index finger against the side of his temple, as if he said something truly genius.

"That does nothing to protect you," I break the news to him.

"It doesn't?"

"What happened to all the groupies and single moms you used to pull?" I ask because back in the day, he was even more of a whore. You wouldn't think a children's television star would be such a filthy womanizer, but I remember he and Bob would end up with rock star levels of naked females in their hotel rooms after each show, sometimes during the shows, too.

You would have a weird mix of both panties and diapers getting wet while they were performing.

My god, that's disgusting.

Why did I think that?

Oh, yeah, those two used to say that all the time.

Boys are gross.

"I mean, I could get women back when I had money and was famous," Murphy laments. "Now that syndication has been pulled and merch has dried up, I don't have enough cash to make women forget. And I'm less famous now and more *in*famous. The ladies don't go for that. At least hookers don't judge and are cheaper than therapy."

"Is it though? I feel like with your shitty negotiation skills you overpay your call girls."

"That is probably true. But with therapy I don't get to have sex unless I end up with a terrible therapist."

"Fine. I'll forgive your drugs and hooker-ing," I submit.

"Hooker-ing?" he asks.

"I don't know. I'm tired."

"And it's not like I have any prospects here on tour. Background dancers ain't gonna fuck me because they know I can't advance their careers now that I'm essentially blackballed." He walks to the couch to join me, taking the wine from my hand before continuing, "I'm not desperate enough to let Zoey trap me."

"Don't *ever* let it come to that."

"Would you prefer I stay in my hotel room and order in an adult film?"

"Murphy, I swear to god, if this is just a backhanded way for you to get permission to watch one of my sister's scenes."

"What? I wasn't even thinking about your sister, the pornstar." He says like a dainty southern belle to drive home the sarcasm. Yes, my black sheep half-sister ran off to LA and sold her naked body to celluloid. She thinks I hate her because of that, because I'm apparently the good sister whose work enriches the lives of children, while her work promotes the process of making them. But I get it, I've been out there, and I've seen what the fame industry can do to a person. We've actually gotten back in touch lately. She contacted me about leaving and trying to live a "normal" life around the time that this whole scandal broke. It kind of leveled our social statuses to the point we could be sisters again.

"You've already watched it." My eyes narrow as I glare daggers at his stupid face.

"I may have seen a scene or two" he flashes a childish grin behind the wine glass.

"You're an asshole."

"Well, our ship sailed a long time ago. So, I felt it was okay to lift that ban and pretend it's you I'm watching getting railed" he says as he takes a sip of his wine.

"Our ship sailed?"

"Yes, we drifted apart like boats on the ocean."

He really doesn't get it.

He thinks he's being poetic and glib at the same time. So, as usual, I have to spell it out for him. I could start a fight, but don't have the mental capacity for it. I guess I'll just opt for comical jabs.

"Drift apart? More like I didn't appreciate the fact that I would sleep with you after you hadn't even showered since fucking some other girl the night before."

"Again, I apologize for that. I'll shower next time."

"Not the biggest issue there, but at the very least, I should be first draw," I say in a playfully biting tone. A tone that is very familiar between the two of us. It's kind of our default setting when we talk to each other.

"Absolutely, Boss. You are now and forever first dibs when it comes to blowing me." He matches my sarcasm by upping the ante.

"I feel so honored."

We share a weary laugh.

A laugh we both needed to let out.

Yes, even though I used to be one of those dirty whores that found themselves under Murphy Harrison, I still ask myself why I let him do bad things to me.

The truth?

For one, he was different back then. Aside from the fact that he was fitter and actually well-groomed. He also seemed to genuinely care about this show and the influence it had on its audience.

As we like to say: He wasn't devastated by the world yet.

We let our laughter slowly weaken and die out to low wheezes as the creeping silence between us sets in. We don't get to remain in the quiet for long though as the noise of people breaks through, coming from the stage area outside the dressing room.

"Oh, shit, the angry mob's finally come for us," Murphy says, raising the playful sarcasm level up again as we go to investigate the commotion. He throws on a pair of sweatpants as I toss him a sweater that had been draped over the back of the couch. Before we exit the dressing room to find what awaits us on stage, I catch a glimpse of one of his more hidden tattoos.

The little black heart above his cock peeking out from his Calvin Klein underwear waistband.

CHAPTER EIGHTEEN

CLARK

Before…

I have never been one for tattoos. Not that I had anything against them, but I never really saw the benefit in paying a lot of money for someone to hurt you and permanently scar your body. I don't mind them on people, sometimes it did enhance someone's features, but it never was anything that really stuck out to me as necessary or even needed.

So, it came as a quite the surprise to everyone, including myself, when I agreed to join the entire cast in invading a local shop and getting inked. I was still the responsible one and called ahead to inform the establishment that they were about to be overwhelmed with a bunch of artists coming in to overload them. Plus, I had to make sure we had enough security guards free to come secure the area.

I had chosen a small little place with only a few tattoo artists on staff for maximum discretion. It was tucked away in the Logan Square neighborhood on Chicago's West Side. The shop was your typical Bohemian artist sanctuary, covered in framed artwork from the employees, spray-painted walls, horror film nick-knacks in every conceivable corner. A blend of base thumping hardcore rap and screaming heavy metal blared out over the shop's speakers as myself and the rest of the principal cast of children's entertainers entered through the glass doorway.

We weren't greeted with a customer service smile from a happy desk clerk, or anyone for that matter.

Instead, a portly Hispanic man, covered in long hair, on his head and face, as well as a body of ink, grunted at us from a chair while reading Vonnegut. We all stood in the entranceway awkwardly for a moment before we were finally acknowledged by a petite black woman sporting a green FRO-hawk. Her ears were *filled with big black gauges to accompany her lip and nose piercings and, of course, she had sleeves of tattoos on both arms being exposed by the turquoise tank top she had on. Whatever bra she had on was not padded at all because I could see her nipple ring piercings etched through that tank and she knew we could all see them.*

She didn't care, and I loved that about her.

You ever meet someone, and you want them to become your new best friend? But you don't know how to go about it since adults can't just say, "Hey, let's be friends".

I checked us all in, trying to come off as cool as possible in front of my new bestie. It was going to be a fairly easy process as everyone was getting the same tattoo, a solid black heart.

Bob's idea.

He felt that we were all lost souls, dead inside, and that this show brought us all together and had given us a purpose, to guide the youth away from the things that made this group black-hearted in the first place. It was a beautiful sentiment, and everyone appreciated his effort at comradery even if it did kind of insult us in the process, but we also couldn't deny its truth. Murphy had added to it by deciding the placement of the tattoo should be right on the pelvic region. He didn't have a succinct reason for this decision. He just felt it would look cool if it was just above our cocks and vaginas, respectively.

My hopefully future maid of honor took Sunshine to the back first to be the inaugural inductee into our fucked up little club. She was giving her a flirty look that I had seen a million times by now. Everyone I love ends up choosing Sunshine over me. Granted, in this case it was just the fact that Sunshine was standing in the proximity to go first, but it still felt like she was getting picked.

Had I known what was in store for me, I would have gladly shoved Sunshine into the hardcore chick's arms. Because my turn was up next as another artist popped out from behind a curtained room to take my breath away. To say I was immediately taken aback by him was an understatement on par with saying Tarantino takes in the occasional movie. He had the prerequisite tattoo coverings that are to be expected of a person in his profession, that's not what got me. No, it was his piercing green eyes that seemed to shoot right through me like the bullets in the opening chapter of One Hundred Years of Solitude. *His perfect jawline and broodingly dark features made me want to desperately feel how tight his powerful arms could hold me down. My gaze swept slowly over every inch of this perfectly etched alt-Adonis.*

He called me again and I realize I'd been just staring at him, dumbfounded as my name came out of his beautiful plump lips. White guys aren't supposed to have lips like that. Fuck, it's like his face was sculpted to be sat on. I compose my horny ass before finding myself alone with that perfectly angular faced artist in a small private room with my pants down.

He had manicured facial hair that wasn't overly done. It was taken care of enough to show that he gave a damn about his appearance but didn't overdo it to the point of vanity that makes you look like a bitch. A little black ring wrapped around the front of his bottom lip, piercing it and making it look all the more enticing.

Goddamn, do they only hire the insanely cool kids here?

His perfectly messy long brown hair kept in a man-bun tempting me to run my hands through it and grab hold for a nice grip. I tried to restrain myself from thinking such dirty things, but it didn't help that once it was just the two of us in this tiny cubby, I had to drop my pants and push my panties down far enough for the gorgeous man to do his work on my downstairs.

Thank God I had worn a sensible, yet sexy black bikini-cut thong here and not my comfortable, no-one's-supposed-to-see-these period panties.

As he laid me on the table and I held my underwear down, just barely keeping from showing full vagina. The artist started by shaving the area he'd be working on. I hadn't known beforehand that he would be shaving me. Luckily, I kept it pretty well groomed down there so he didn't have too much to remove. He gently spread a foam lather onto the front of my crotch and then slowly and delicately used the blue disposable razor blade to clear any rogue bump that would get in the way of his ink.

After he had shaved my pubic hair, he placed a temporary stencil onto my pelvic to get my approval of the placement and design. I very much so approved, and he pulls out a small cap of black ink and picked up his gun.

The first jabs of the needle felt like my skin was getting slowly tugged and torn, which it kind of was. It hurt, but not as badly as I had thought it would. The slight pain was nothing compared to the torture that was going on just below, though. The artist was positioned directly between my thighs and would accidently brush against the outside of my clothed labia every so often. Each time it would happen, he would look up at me with an apologetic glance, but never say anything as I would just return an approving smile. The whole process took less than an hour and after putting some clear antiseptic onto the fresh tattoo, he places some cellophane and medical tape over it to keep it from getting infected.

As I stood in front of a long mirror admiring the artist's work, I caught him checking out my ass that was hanging out thanks to my lowered pants and thong combination. He tried to act like a gentleman and turn away, but I wasn't going to let him off the hook.

I went straight for the kill.

"What time are you done with work?" I was never normally this direct, but the unintentional teasing this man had just done to my pussy had me feeling extra bold. I also knew that we had bought out the shop for just our group, so as soon as we were done, he was done. I proposed that the two of us go get drinks after, but he came with a better idea and pulled out a bottle of spiced rum from under his sketch desk.

He pours the two of us a drink into some plastic cups as he instructed me to grab a can of coke from the mini fridge in the corner. I hop back onto the chair I had been sitting in for the last hour, pants still down to my thighs, as he scooted up next to me in his rolling stool.

"I'm actually being a bad tattooist right now," he says before taking his first Cuba Libre sip.

"How's that?" I reply before sipping my own plastic cup, no iced drink. So classy, but fuck it, he's pretty.

"You're not supposed to drink after getting work done, blood loss and all."

"It's just a little tattoo. I'll be fine." I say.

"You're the expert." he grins.

We were on our third round when I felt loosened up enough to talk about the elephant in the room, how turned on I was by his grazing of my vagina during the tattoo.

"I mean, I know you were trying to be professional and couldn't help it, but I was kinda okay with it!" I blurt out.

"Only kinda?" he replies with that boyish grin that flushes the fuck out of my cheeks.

The two of us giggle about it for a moment before our lips find each other.

I pull his shirt off immediately so I could see all the artwork on his chiseled frame. His nipples had little black bell bars piercing through them, and his whole chest was covered in tattoos. I unbutton his pants to continue my search of all his ink. He steps back to pull it out of his underwear and, of course, he has a tattoo covered cock to show me. He had the head of a snake tattooed just below his belly button, and the body slithered down until the tail wrapped around his uncut member several times.

And I mean several times.

I grab hold of that tail and pull him close before telling him he needs to inspect his work a little closer. I push his head between my legs as he slides my panties and pants off my ankles. His lip ring teases at the bottom of my clit as the rest of his mouth envelops it while his tongue gives it some light flicks. I close my eyes and put my knuckles, damn near my whole fist, in my mouth to keep from screaming out. The walls to this little booth didn't go to the ceiling, and the door was only a long black curtain. His expert mouth was living up to the fantasy I had imagined for the last hour and just before I bring his body up to mine, I look over at the closed curtain to see an eye looking back at me.

As I scream, the curtain quickly shuts as the intruder goes back to hiding.

I leap out of the tattoo chair, over the artist, trying to cover myself up as the tattooist comes to my rescue. The artist isn't fazed, though. He rises to his feet, his hands are at his sides in clenched fists as he flexes his chest and turns up his chin to march towards my intruder, dick still hanging out of his opened pants. He rips open the curtain to find a startled Bob giggling at his discovery.

The artist says in a calm and cool tone, "Get the fuck out of my studio."

Bob stops laughing as it awkwardly trails off, assessing the situation has gone from playful to serious. He backs out like a dog with its tail between its legs, ushering the other cast members, who had gathered to gawk, out of the way as they all leave us be, closing the curtain behind them.

I turn to the artist, his snake covered dick, that just intimidated a man into submission, is now pointed at me, "That was the hottest fucking thing ever!"

"Mr. Bob's a fucking creep. Always hated that guy. The dog is cool, though."

"I wouldn't say he's a creep. We're just very close. I'm sure he thought it was funny."

"I don't know. Something about him." He looks off like he's contemplating something deep and fuck me, is his brooding doing it for me. He's probably the first person I had met that didn't like Bob.

Everyone loved Bob.

Our little interruption hasn't killed my mood. I pull my shirt over my head and jump into the artist's arms, wrapping my legs around his waist. He lays me back onto the tattooing chair and how fucking lucky am I that I wore a front clasping bra? Lucky enough that I found someone who knows how to unfasten it with one hand while sliding himself inside me. Dude has got some serious girth to him, but I'm so fucking wet, there's barely any resistance for him to go deep instantly. He grabs my chest with his left hand and teases my nipple as he starts to thrust.

Forceful, impactful thrusts. Like it's a tease as he hits me with his dick, but pulls it back, leaving me wanting another hit until he starts to move with a beautiful motion.

I don't bite my fist now, though; I let my moans carry wherever the fuck they want to go as the artist continues to pound

*into me while my head starts to dangle over the side of the chair.
He's leaning back so we don't rub our crotches too much, seeing as
how I have an open wound on mine thanks to his artwork.*

Such a gentleman.

*I still want to feel him against me though, so I flip my left
leg around and prop myself up on my side so he can push against
me from behind. Another set of loud moans escape my mouth as the
artist is now deeper than ever before.*

*I don't care that the cast can hear me on the other side.
I've had to listen to and accidentally walk in on them fucking
groupies so many times, now it's their turn to hear me. I'm taking
what I want, and it makes me feel powerful.*

*"Slap my ass as you fuck me!" I demand. He responds with
a massive open hand smack on my left cheek. It sends a ripple
through my body upon impact.*

*"Yeah, you like that, don't you?" he says as he rears back
and hit's my other cheek.*

"Fuck you're so deep! Give it to me!"

"Take it! Take this fucking dick!"

His thrusts into my backside are at a rapid pace now. I'm holding onto the chair for dear life as his speed has gone into hyperdrive. And I swear to God, it's like the orgasm he powered out of me is erupting from my mouth as I let out the loudest pleasure scream.

"I'm about to cum! I'm about to cum! I'm cummming! I'm cumming!"

He yells he's going to shoot too as he pulls his dick from my insides. Out of pure instinct and lust, I jump over and plant my lips right onto his cock so I can taste his pleasure. He grabs the back of my head and pushes me as far down that snake as my little mouth can go. He lets out deep, heavy moans as he shoots down the back of my throat with what seems like a gallon of fluid. I nearly choke as more and more pumps out and his strong arms keep my head pressed against his pelvic, until he slowly resides and falls back into his little stool next to the chair, exhausted and satisfied.

"Holy shit!" is all he can muster, outside the occasional, "Fuck."

"First time you've done it in the chair, or is this like a regular service you provide?" I ask.

"I have never done it in the chair. I don't know what came over me. I had to have you right away," he replies through exhausted panting.

I think I took his business card on my way out so I could at least learn his name and possibly call him up again the next time we were in Chicago, but it somehow got lost during our travels. I checked in with the shop on our next tour, but he wasn't working there anymore. He was just lost in the wind.

I got plenty of shit from everyone once I had emerged from my little romp. It was non-stop prodding from Vinny and Ryan on our ride back to the hotel. Sunshine got the vivid details over a glass of wine back in her room. It was all anyone could talk about the rest of the tour, except for Bob.

Bob had been quiet and standoffish to me for the next several days. I kept expecting an apology or some kind of talk about it, but that never came. We just kept on with our business until eventually we went back to our normal routine.

*We swept it under the rug in hopes it would never get dealt
with.*

Maybe I should have dealt with it.

CHAPTER NINETEEN

MURPHY

After…

The only thing we can see is the stage's Ghost Light

shining out into an empty theatre. It's eerie glow lighting the way,

so we don't fall into the orchestra pit or off the end of the stage.

We make our way out of the dressing room and towards the

light. Only to find Vinny, Ryan, and Zoey mingling with a small

group of random people drunkenly staggering around by my sets. A

few of them are trying on random costume items, Freddie, and a few

of the Plücker's heads obscure faces. They're taking pictures with

the infamous Digg Dogg House, no doubt posting snide and ironic

updates. They're all dressed up as if they just left a club and it looks

182

like this is where they chose to continue the party. Ryan and Vinny lay out on the floor, propped up on their elbows while they hand a bottle of vodka back and forth to each other, intentionally skipping Zoey as they pass over her.

"Vinny, Ryan, what the fuck are you doing?" Clark yells at them as she points at one of the party-goers, "You'd better be putting that head back exactly where you found it this instant!"

The partier lifts the chicken costume head she was wearing up off her skull and slowly steps backwards to the wings, no doubt terrified to the point of fleeing after she returns the prop in her hand.

None of that phased Vinny, though.

"Oh, untangle your tits, Clark. I'll make sure everything goes back before we leave." His body language was the face of unflappability.

Zoey? Not so much.

"I am so sorry! We will get everything put back immediately!" She is already falling over her own feet to clean the stage and make up for the audacity of upsetting Clark.

"Zoey, stop. It's fine. A misplaced bone isn't going to be the worst thing to happen to this show," Vinny tries to calm her.

Clark pours gasoline on the fire when she replies, "It is when we can't perform part of the show because a bone is missing." I could almost see a faint glint of glee in Clark's eyes as she watches the panic overtake Zoey.

"Oh, God, no! I wouldn't want to do anything to jeopardize the show!"

"Um, I'm pretty sure we've been in jeopardy ever since the truth about Bob came to light." Vinny's usual snarky responses don't seem to get to Clark, but this one appears to have breached her armor.

"If you really think the show is in danger, then why don't you just quit the tour?"

Before he can respond, Zoey chimes in, "Can I get his dressing room?"

Which is met with a "No!" from everyone in unison.

"I'm here because I love the show. Okay, Clark… At least I used to, before, you know, but it will always hold a special place in my heart." I can't quite tell if he's being genuine or not, due to the fact that his standard operating procedure is catty. He points at Zoey as he continues, "You think that bouncing bobble-headed fan girl is the only kid that grew up on Digg Dogg?"

Vinny hands the bottle of vodka back to Ryan as he gets up from the floor to approach myself and Clark. "When I got booked for this tour years ago, it was like my inner child just realized his dream. I loved, *loved* Mr. Bob and Diggsy. I even learned the routine from their early appearances on *The Happy Kidz Show*."

"Sure, you did." Clark doesn't believe him.

"I did! If Murphy still remembers the choreography, I'll do Bob's part right here!"

He's put me on the spot. I'm pretty sure I can still do that first number, the iconic one that still gets used whenever news reports about Bob want to recall our humble beginnings, but some of the other dances have dropped out of my brain either due to the passage of time or the drugs and alcohol eroding my memory.

I rub the back of my neck and try to stall. "That was almost

twenty years ago, Vinny. I'm not sure I can do *all* the steps."

"I'm sure we won't judge you too harshly." He gestures for

us to take center stage. "Sir?"

I reluctantly make my way towards the ghost light, moving

it out of the way so I don't trip over it and make even more of a fool

of myself than I am about to. The original routine, I was holding a

stack of letters Digg Dogg had stolen from a mailman in my hands.

So instead of reaching out at nothing like an idiot, I decide to keep

my hands in my sweatpants' pockets. The group cheers us on to try

to encourage the ridiculousness of what we're attempting. Ryan

pulls out his phone and starts playing the song. I can't believe he

found it so quickly. There's no way he had that already cued up.

Then I realize it's not the original version. It's *Caution* by

The Killers. They had sampled our song for this track, and it led to a

bump in our ratings thanks to the nostalgia. Either way, it'll work

for this routine.

Vinny starts to dance. He seriously has it down like he's

practiced it every day. Like it was still part of the tour's set list. It's my time to join in, but I just stay planted off to his side, swaying to the beat. I should join him, but I can't bring myself to do it. That song was our breakout performance, mine and Bob's. It is no longer the shining high point of my life like it once was.

Now it's a reminder of where things ended up.

Since I don't jump in, Ryan decides he can't leave Vinny hanging and takes my place. The two are completely in sync as they dance next to each other, side by side. They execute the spins and steps so gracefully and with so much enthusiasm that I forget what the song used to mean to me for a second and see it for what it was meant to be: an act of joy aimed at entertaining children.

I can't help it anymore and I count myself in—

5, 6, 7, 8!

I jump in and dance alongside them, still keeping my hands in my pockets, though, because I don't want to fully commit to the absurdity. But as I always suspected, eventually, the rhythm is gonna get you. That's when something happens to me that hasn't happened in a long, long time…

I smile.

Not just a smirk or the pathetically fake mask of normality I would wear to make people think I was doing okay, that unreal smile I was used to using. No, this is a genuine smile. It's actual, dopamine inducing happiness that is radiating across my face. And just like that, the song ends, and I am back in my world of reality, smile fading back to its hiding place.

The three of us bring it in for a hug that would have been heartfelt if not for a crying Zoey trying to insert herself in between us and join the embrace.

The rest of the night was a bit of a blur, thanks in no part to finishing off the vodka with Clark's help. The un-fuzzy moments that I can recall involved more dancing, a little more freestyle this time, and the rest of the party people mixed amongst us. I dealt with the typical fan questions from the non-acquaintances, who at least were respectful enough to not ask about Bob.

They gave the stock statements to me. *"I grew up watching you." "I love Digg Dogg so much." "I have a Diggsy tattoo."* People think it's such a shocking thing for me to see, but just about every other fan has inked that stuffed puppet onto their body that it's lost any shock value. I honestly can't recall any of the generic conversations I had with these star fuckers. What sticks out though was, when the fun started to wind down and people started to drift off and away, I ended my night in a good place.

It was one of those times when you could feel the sun coming up. Even though we were indoors, your internal clock is telling you the rest of the world is about to spoil your fun. The normal people were waking up and about to take back their city from us night dwellers. Clark and I are sitting on the edge of the stage, dangling our feet off the side, and talked. We talked for the first time not about the show or Bob or us, but about anything and everything other than our problems. We talked like we had never gotten a chance to talk before. We talked like college students in their first "dorm-room-deep" conversations. Still, we had let the weight of our lives drift away and were allowed to just be in the moment.

It was what my soul needed.

A human connection.

A connection that wasn't stained.

After…

This goddamn song again. I know I've said before how much I really hated that diaper Kat song, but this one has to be a close second. It's like a repetitive, irreverent mess. All the lyrics keep saying is, "Love Hugs, Hugs of Love" again and again. We just have to close out a show with this toddler abortion of a melody. I just know they were high as shit when they prematurely yank this tune into existence. But the kids love to sing along to it and it's a way to send them home happy enough to hopefully want to buy some merchandise on the way out.

Maybe I'm just extra sensitive today because Murphy kept me out so late last night talking my ear off about nonsense until the sun came up. But I think the main reason why I have such a dislike for this number is because it forces me out of my safe little box in the back of the theater. To end the performance, we have a bunch of pre-selected little fans come up on stage and sing along with the cast. It's a great photo op for the parents and an amazing traumatic experience for the kids involved.

But in order for all of that to go down, I have to be near the front directing the participants to their positions without wetting themselves or wandering off the edge of the platform. Now that I've corralled them all next to their furry friends under the spotlights, I sit back and wait for the dance to end so I can pull them back to their parents and close the curtain on tonight's program.

Without fail, there is always at least one child crying when they get up there. The pressure and the lights are just too much, and they can't handle their emotions, so the tears start flowing as they get overwhelmed. And sure enough, I'm watching yet another little girl start to lose her shit next to Fab Frogg Freddie. This little girl in

192

a pink dress with that stuffed Boston Terrier's face on the front, is

holding her hands to her face and has now officially lost it. She is

crying and screaming out for her dad so loud, I could have heard it

from Evanston. Vinny's a professional, though, so he plays it off

and keeps going with his performance, not letting her throw his

steps.

That's when I notice Digg Dogg is out of sync. He's at

least a full count behind the rest of the cast. I can see he is looking

over at the crying girl, like his focus is being pulled over to her by

some unseen force. I have no idea why this is affecting him, though.

She isn't the first screaming toddler he's dealt with, and this one is a

safe distance away that he should be able to drown out her yells.

I've seen him get kicked and punched at by a group of preschoolers

while still keeping in rhythm with a backing track.

So why is this one's wailing getting to him?

Then he goes completely off script and steps out of

formation. Digg Dogg is now walking over to the crying child,

skipping his cue to take them to the bridge of the song, and kneels

down to comfort her. The rest of the cast are so lost now they're just swaying back and forth, adrift in their confusion on what to do next. The sound tech in the booth is yelling in my ear what he should do next, so I do the only thing I can think of and bark back to cut the music.

Without the instrumental chimes filling the theater, the conversation between the two is getting picked up on Digg Dogg's mic. He's trying to assess what is bothering her. She just continues to sob out the words, "I miss my Da-da!"

"Oh, I'm sorry, sweetie. Is he in the audience?" Murphy searches the stands, even though I know he can't see anything past the blinding stage lights. He's aware now that the focus has turned to them as he's trying to help find the little girl's father, but the only person that emerges from the crowd is the child's mother, who I help onto the stage to go collect her kid. I see the woman gather her sad baby, scooping her up in her arms, as she apologizes to Diggsy. She speaks so softly it can barely even be called a whisper. The microphone is only able to pick up the slightest mumble, but her words seem to hit him so hard we can practically see the devastation on Murphy's face through Digg Dogg's foam head.

Diggsy holds out his hand for the child as the mom sets her down. The little girl, she can't be more than four years old, accepts him as they hold hands. It's a moment that feels like eternity before Murphy finally speaks in his owns voice, not the fake one he uses when he is in character.

"Your mom told me your dad passed away a few weeks ago?"

The girl nods.

"I can't imagine how tough that is for you. It's making you really sad, huh?"

The girl nods again.

"I know you wanted to come see me to forget, right? You wanted me to try and make you happy again. To take away your sadness? Diggsy has his own sadness too that he wishes he could take away, but not even this big dog can do that. I'm sorry that I can't change your sadness, but I want you to do something for me, okay?"

Her crying starts to slow, and she regains the breath that had eluded her down to short stutters.

"I want you to remember the happiness, the happiness that your dad brought to you. Can you do that for me?"

She wipes away some of her tears and nods her head again, but this time with more enthusiasm.

"Okay, so every time this sadness comes back, I want you to remember the happiness. Remember all the times you had with him. Remember his smile, his laugh, the way he made you feel. Keep him in your heart. The sadness will always be there, it doesn't go away. But if you hold onto the happiness, along with the sadness, the love will be there too."

Whatever progress she had made in calming herself down has evaporated and the waterworks flow again, but this time, it is accompanied with a smile. The little girl, with all her deep hurt, is smiling right before she jumps into Digg Dogg's arms and embraces him in a big hug, barely able to wrap her tiny arms around his neck. The mom, tears of bittersweetness in her own eyes, mouths the words, "Thank you" as she slowly lowers her hands away from her face.

Digg Dogg returns the emotional hug back to the child before releasing her back to her mother. But as he hands the girl back, he whispers, "As always, Love Loudly."

He ends it with the ASL sign for "more". He had been doing that since he first started ending the shows with the "Love Loudly" catchphrase. It was his response for the crowds that chanted at him. He actually used to do say "I Love You More" in sign language but has now become so iconic that all he has to do is sign the last word and everyone knows what he's saying.

As I help the bereaved family down off the stage and whisk them out a back door. I know the other theater goers will try and stop them and hassle them, as well meaning with kind words and gestures as they may be, the best thing is for them to be left alone right now. Security takes them the rest of the way because I have to intercept my star back at his dressing room to get an explanation as to what just went down.

CHAPTER TWENTY-ONE

MURPHY

Before….

It was just a week before Rey's fourth birthday, and we were back in the hospital again.

A nurse pulled me aside. She was matronly looking, so I automatically let her words hold weight being the Momma's Boy that I am. She wore a set of pink scrubs and tie-dye Crocs on her feet. The shoes would be a detail that would always stick in my mind, so whimsical in such a dire moment. She told me I had to tell my daughter that it was okay for her to let go. She told me I had to give my child permission to die.

I didn't understand what she was trying to say.

What father would let his daughter die?

Anger filled my heart at first, but she explained further. She didn't say to stop treating her or any type of euthanasia. What she was suggesting was to ease my child's aching soul. My ray of light was hurting and had nothing but fear for what inevitably awaited her. I needed to comfort her and ease her fears. She said I needed to let her know that no matter what happened, she would be okay, and she would always be loved and remembered.

This new clarity she had given me didn't help my hurt, but it did give me focus. I knew I had to do whatever I could to help my suffering child, even if ending the suffering meant more heartache.

Machines beeped and hummed.

I wasn't exactly sure what they did, but they made noises just the same. It's another detail of the memory that sticks with me, the sounds of the machines filling the quiet room. It's eerily silent. Like the Rothko Room. A place of equal self-reflection.

I stood in the doorway to that room that had been the sight of so much stress, pain, and uncertainty. We would sometimes end up being set up in the same room 114 during different trips to the hospital. I watched the mother of my child, my Sunshine, leave to go get coffee for the two of us and some food Rey would attempt to keep down, though we both knew she wouldn't.

I didn't discuss this with my wife.

In my heart, I was sure she would feel the same as me, but I didn't want to put this weight on her shoulders.

No, I would handle this myself.

So, while sitting in an uncomfortable hospital chair, holding my little girl in my arms while she was curled up in a little ball while crying from exhaustion. Getting her in my arms was a struggle because of all the tubes and wires we had to untangle, just to move her over to my lap.

As her father, I calmed her and told her that it would be alright, that she didn't have to hold on anymore.

I told her to let her struggles wash away and let what was to come, come. I told her she was loved more than she would ever know. I told her there was nothing in mine or her mommy's life that mattered more than her and that all we wanted was for her to find peace.

I said to that little not yet four-year-old, who got the most unfair turn in this world, that she was… that she was free.

That still developing brain of hers understood and she let go…

She didn't pass away at that moment.

Though it was shortly after.

I was in the room when it did happen.

Her tiny, beautiful little heart gave out. That sweet little face lay there like she was asleep. I used to watch her at night with that same face, thinking how lucky I was that I got something in this world that remarkable. But now that memory of the same sleeping face became morphed into a death mask, the final image I have for my daughter.

I had to not only witness but be an active part in the loss of my child. I knew I would hold that within me for the rest of my life. I always felt that, on some level, I was responsible for her death. Not just the telling her to let go part, but the whole disease saga was my

fault.

Like, it was my sins that brought about the heartbreak.

Something I had done that brought this on her. Either

because of the chemicals I had put in my bloodstream from partying

had passed to her, or karma from what I had been before her

childlike love had reformed me, I had somehow created what was

killing her.

And the words I said that had guided her to letting go, I

knew it was the right thing at the time to say to a sick and dying

child, and I still feel it was the correct decision to this day, but that

doesn't change my belief that she isn't here today because of me.

To me, she didn't diet from the disease.

She died from my words...

CHAPTER TWENTY-TWO

CLARK

After…

I make it to his dressing room first. I usually have too much

other shit to deal with before I can check in with him that he always

beats me here. But tonight, he has become top priority. I can hear

the other cast and crew outside the door enveloping Murphy with

accolades for his little performance. Of course, Vinny's voice is the

loudest amongst them.

"My god, Murphy, that was amazing! Where the hell did

you pull that out of?"

"That was something else!" I can tell from the elevated

pitch that that must have been Zoey.

"I just thought the kid was another snot sewer crying because they were scarred! How did you know it know it was something different? Do not tell me that was all staged!" Vinny again controlling the conversation.

"No, no, it was completely random. I don't know, I just kinda felt it. It was a deeper sadness coming from her." If it wasn't for the fact that Murphy's gravel churned voice is as distinct as a snowflake, I would never have believed that was him saying those words.

I mean, he has written some profound things with Bob for the show, but he doesn't really use his own words too well. He's one of those guys who can express himself through his art but can't string two coherent sentences together when having a conversation. Murphy can write a monologue where the character breathes truth and vulnerability in every word, yet when you ask him how he is feeling in person you receive a series of grunts.

That is why when he peaks his defeated face into his dressing room, dropping Digg Dogg's head onto the hook, I immediately come after him on the attack. This motherfucker, for years, would just stare at me, not saying a word when I tried to pry any type of emotion out of him. And now today, he spills out this incredible moment for some child. Not saying the kid wasn't deserving of Digg Dogg's love, just saying, where was this Murphy when the people that he knew and loved were trying to get this reaction out of him.

"Fuck you, Murphy." The first thing I say to him, and yet, he is not surprised at all by my greeting. "With everything going on surrounding the show, I was looking for an excuse to quit the tour. The brawl the other day was supposed to be the final straw. But then you pull some shit like that on stage…"

The asshole strolls past me and plops his fuzzy ass down on the couch. "Oh, please. If the Bob scandal didn't drive you away, a little furry fracas wasn't gonna make you snap."

I sit down next to him, making sure he is seeing me at eye level and that he is focused on my words. "No, seriously, that was a beautiful thing you did for that family." He doesn't believe my sincerity, so I press on, "It was. That mom took her daughter to see you to help during a devastating time in their lives. *You* were the comfort they were seeking. You should know you still matter to people."

He finally seems to be getting it through his thick fucking skull what he means to the world. And not in the how can I use this to make money, or get laid kind of way, but in a way that actually impacts people's hearts. Since he is in a proper, introspective place, I decide to leave him in that state. I get up to go deal with the rest of my idiots outside these doors. But not before leaving him with a final thought.

"Remember that when you're off doing your plans." I use my hands for extra quotations around "plans". I emphasize the word because I may not know the details of what he gets into at night between the hookers, the drugs, and the alcohol, but I'm sure it's not very family friendly. I'm not trying to tell the man to be a saint.

That wouldn't be true to the devil inside him.

I just want him to realize he's not all demon, and that deep down, deep, deep down. So, fucking deep down you're almost hitting core, that there is an angel there somewhere.

That's the fucking angel I fell in love with back when we were a "we".

CHAPTER TWENTY-THREE

CLARK

Before…

I can't really call what we were a "couple". We were more like two idiots fucking each other from time to time. We finally stopped slapping privates when it all imploded at Bob's housewarming party. He had just bought this bullshit palatial mansion with its own private acreage.

So, of course, Murphy convinced him to use his celebrity status to throw a Bacchanal gathering. It was basically a fine-dining catered orgy with fancy robes.

Bob had purchased an estate. And I mean an estate in every sense of the word. He had documentation of the house's

*lineage and shit. We rolled up through a security gate, not that big
of a deal as most of these giant mansions had fencing. But what
struck me as odd was that as we got to the main house, the windows
all had bars, like some crime ridden shack in South Central.*

Not exactly the California chic you'd expect.

*Still, even with Bob's metallic upgrades, the Spanish style
home impressed even the most jaded of high-class society.*

*I mean, you just knew it had a wine vineyard somewhere on
the property. It was that kind of sprawling set up. He even had a
valet service set up for us to park our car as we pulled up.*

*It got a little awkward as Murphy had a personal driver at
this point and the valet and driver didn't know how to handle the
hand off. But eventually they just agreed to let us go inside while
they worked out dealing with the car.*

*I didn't quite know what I was expecting when I walked
into Bob's mansion in my tight-fitting silk kimono. Underneath it
was just a lace thong and a matching black see-through bra.
Murphy had his arm around me, wearing the male equivalent of my*

*frock and nothing else. I was nervous because up until that point,
most of my sex life had been pretty vanilla by Hollywood standards,
while middle America would probably still think me a whore. We
entered the foyer expecting to see naked people grinding all over
each other under neon lights and throbbing techno music.*

What we found was an actual dignified affair.

*It was naked people everywhere, but they were milling
about like your average party, just conversing with each other. The
music playing was* Pursuit of Happiness *by Kid Cudi which didn't
feel out of place, but also should have been.*

*We were led into a ballroom that was centralized with a
long, giant table that barely elevated three feet off the ground.
Seated around the table, on copious amounts of throw pillows, were
the party guests. This seemed more in line with what I was expecting
as everyone was eating the extravagant meal laid out along the
entire twenty-foot-long table and downing glass after glass of red
wine while stretching out across each other on the floor.*

*The partiers were all dressed in scantily clad outfits that
made me feel better about my wardrobe selection. There was a sea*

of bodies groping and rubbing on each other, spilling wine into puddles on their flesh before slurping it clean and then feeding a partner food from the spread in front of them. I thought we would be greeted by Bob, but he was on the opposite side of the table, completely naked, dipping his entire dick and balls into a mountain of what I'm assuming was cocaine on a silver platter before having it licked up and rubbed off by a pair of women squatting next to him. I recognized a few of the people amongst the crowd, not as personal acquaintances, but as prominent figures in our industry.

Murphy could see the overwhelmed look on my face, so he pulled me out of the room to the hallway. We tried to muffle our laughter but couldn't help bursting out into a fit together.

We found ourselves wandering throughout the manor. We'd duck our heads into random rooms and found they were all dressed up in different themes complete with a safe word for those that enter posted onto the wall.

If you went into the jungle lounge, "Zazu" was the safe word.

Inside the underwater aquatic space, "Scuttle" stopped the action.

Back in the main ballroom, "Philoctetes" gave you a break.

Checking out the Asian inspired tearoom, "Mushu" ended the activity.

And as we passed the sheik's haram, "Iago" reduced the intensity.

In the hallway, we were finding most of the play areas densely populated and unappealing, so we were about to give up when Murphy pushed up against me and placed his lips against mine. It was a nice, comforting kiss that let me know I had an ally in this crazy place. My head bumped against a painting hanging above us. We stopped our make-out session as he pulled away to see the obstruction. It was a splash silk screening over a photo of a naked woman on her hands and knees wearing only a plastic sheep's head covering her face. A thought bubble caption with an Orwellian quote floating over her reads, "Four legs, good! Two legs, bad!"

We couldn't hold back our laughter then. This house and this party were so off-brand for Bob, and yet so ridiculously happening that we broke into giggle fits. Murphy asks me if I wanted to get out of here and I was about to take him up on that offer when we heard a familiar voice moaning in another room.

We didn't really have a choice but to investigate it.

Murphy slid a door open to a study filled with hundreds of books that I know Bob has never and will never read. A leather couch was flanked by two matching chairs in the center of the room, but the furniture was unoccupied. This was definitely where the sounds had emanated from, but it was empty now.

The room's safe word, "Lumiere".

That's when we hear the moaning again but coming from inside of the walls. We inched in closer and determined the area behind the far bookshelf must be the source.

Murphy looks at me before saying, "You don't think?"

He pokes at a few loose books before finding a solid one he flicks forward, causing the entire shelf to shift out of place and open

*to reveal a secret room. Of course, Bob would have a clichéd hidden
bookshelf room. I assumed it would be some kind of nerd den with
arcade games, geek memorabilia, and other entertainment systems
that would be right up Bob's alley.*

Instead, it was a full-on sex dungeon.

*An occupied dungeon at that, complete with a sound system
set up to create a mood as it steadily lets out the chorus of* Closer *by
Nine Inch Nails, only with a female vocalist. My eyes immediately
dart to the far corner, where I find Vinny and Ryan connected to
each other by a small man hanging from a swing between them.
Vinny was laying into the poor guy from behind while Ryan was
occupying his mouth. On the other end of the room were a few men
sticking their dicks into a set of obvious gloryholes drilled into the
wall. I don't even want to know what the rooms on the other end of
those holes look like. But the center of attention, bound at the wrists
and tied to a chain hanging from the ceiling, was Sunshine,
Murphy's future ex-wife.*

*They hadn't even hooked up yet at that point, but the look
in his eyes as he gazes upon his naked and blindfolded costar, I*

should have known then that he was going to marry that woman.

She's a skinny blonde that doesn't seem to have an ounce of fat on

her body outside of her C-cup breasts. I always said it was a crime

against nature for Bob and Murphy to put such a hot piece of ass

under a mountain of fluff and fur in that Chester Cheddar costume.

A separator bar connected to her ankles kept her legs apart

as a group of men and women took turns inserting appendages and

other objects inside of her. She keeps slightly bucking her back

every few seconds, and that's when I notice someone behind her

slowly and sporadically dripping wax from a long red candle down

her spin. There was a woman wearing only a pink, leather gimp

mask slapping at Sunshine's erect nipples with a riding crop and

directing the crowd on who gets to go next while holding the candle

over Sunshine.

Gimp lady lowered the chain that kept Sunshine aloft and

drops her to her knees. She then instructed everyone to bombard her

with their genitals. Sunshine gets flooded with dicks and vaginas in

her face. She tries her best to please them all, considering her hands

were still bound, but the moment she neglects someone, she would be met with the snapping end of the riding crop on her backside. It didn't seem like much of a punishment though, as each crack released a pleasure moan from her.

Murphy gave me an eagerly excited look that told me he was beyond turned on and that we couldn't help but join the fun. The crowd parted and allowed us to the front of the line. I dropped my robe to the floor and parted my panties to the side before I slid into Sunshine's awaiting tongue. Her mouth felt amazing, and there was something about her not knowing it was me, her best friend, that made it extra hot. But I found the most joy in seeing the excitement on Murphy's face as he stood next to me, stroking himself to attention. I step back and let him take my place as he slips his cock into her mouth. She enthusiastically sucked at his dick, and he let out sounds I hadn't heard from him before.

From what I'd observed before joining, most of the participants would occupy Sunshine's body for a few minutes before moving aside for another orgy attendant to take their turn with her. Common courtesy being that you don't selfishly monopolize the prize. But Murphy took longer than everyone else. You'd think the gimp lady would maintain order, but she was just rubbing herself, enjoying the show. He kept his dick in her face, and she kept sucking faster and faster. No one seemed to mind, though. In fact, everyone else starts pairing up to play with each other while they would watch Murphy move his hips back and forth to aid the blowjob.

I could tell what was about to happen next. Murphy's grunts had changed octaves, and he was about to finish. He grabs hold of the top of Sunshine's head, gripping at her hair. As he let out his final thrusts, the blindfold over Sunshine's eyes slips off and the two stared at each other as Murphy cums deep into the back of her throat. She pushes her face against his pelvic, taking him all in, matching his moaning, not breaking eye contact.

Her head snaps back, showing the audience that she'd swallowed his whole load. Like a magician revealing the disappearing act. This set everyone into a frenzy as they rushed her to get their own turns at her mouth. Murphy dipped back towards the door, and I meet him at the exit.

At the time, I was a little pissed Murphy wasted his first orgasm already, but I knew he'd be back in the game quickly. He always had a great recovery time, so I didn't make a big deal of it. We make our way back to the ballroom, not for the naked people, but because I was starving and didn't want that delicious looking food going to waste. Murphy makes up for cumming in my best friend by saving me the trouble of dealing with the crowd and agreeing to go in to retrieve me something to eat while I wait outside.

In the hallway I pass by a familiar looking girl pacing back and forth in lingerie. I couldn't remember her name, but I knew she was one of Bob's groupies. She was squirming back and forth on each leg like a child waiting for the bathroom. Turns out she was waiting. Not because a restroom was occupied, but because, as she told me, she was not allowed to use the restroom without Bob's approval.

I couldn't wrap my head around whatever domination game Bob was playing with this one, but she genuinely seemed scared of displeasing him. The worry on her face was not one of denied pleasure, but of terror filled pain.

I tried to get more information out of her, but the moment she sees Murphy emerge from the ballroom, her body goes ridged and she disappears through a side door.

That was the first time I thought something was not right with Bob. Looking back at this moment, I should have known. But how could I have? It definitely was an odd moment, but everything about that night was odd.

What could I have done?

What should I have done?

How should I have acted with only an uneasy feeling to go off of? If I had acted and was wrong, then I would have been blowing everything up over nothing.

Still, should I have done... something?

I feel like maybe I'm a bad person because I didn't do anything.

Am I a bad person?

Probably...

CHAPTER TWENTY-FOUR

MURPHY

After…

Who the fuck is she to judge my life? I know what I mean to people. I've had tons of women show me what I mean to them. Hell, I fucked half of LA in a giant fucking mansion because they wanted to be close to a star. That mansion and those fuck-toys, that's what I mean to people. At least… I used to mean something, be something. Just because some little lost soul reached out to me doesn't suddenly absolve everything I've done in the past. If I want to pay a woman to help me fuck the pain away, that is my business.

Whiskey.

Weed.

Coke.

Pussy.

It's how I heal…

And yet Clark is in my fucking head. I'm sitting in my
hotel chair, in the same black suit and tie, with another bottle of
tequila next to an empty snifter glass and an unlit cigar. My phone
sits on the side table next to the liquor and stogie. My leg won't stop
shaking as I try to think of anything else besides Clark's words.

Fuck her.

This is my life, and I'll destroy it how I see fit. I lose my
battle with decency and pick up my phone. I start to scroll through
the different ads for the local hookers, thanking God Chicago has
quality ladies of the night, compared to some other towns we've
been in. I have to click several pages deep before I find an
appropriate girl that I haven't already slept with. Each ad feature
photos of scantily clad women in provocative poses with phone

numbers plastered across the pictures. Some of the girls have blurred out parts of their faces or only show close-up shots of their ass or tits. That doesn't work for me, so I skip right by them.

It's not that I need their face to be particularly pretty, though I won't say I don't have standards. It's just that I learned in my travels with Bob that if you're going to pay a girl from the internet for sex, if she won't reveal what she looks like, she's not a real professional. Amateur prostitutes, the ones who are only in it for quick cash or drugs, or worse, are being trafficked, are too embarrassed to let the word know what they look like. The ones that let me see their identity, know what the fuck they're doing. And it's this one that I end up coming across.

A good five pages in and I finally settle on this girl, Deja. She fits the bill that I'm looking for: Skinny, but with a round ass, medium perky chest, and brunette. At least I think her tits are perky. It's hard to tell from a photo, but it's not a point of contention if they have a little sag to them.

I'm not a complete pig.

My finger hovers over the phone number in her profile, Clark's words still rattling around in the mush I pass off for a brain. Finally, I press down and the phone dials. The line rings for a few moments before it is answered by a sultry voiced woman.

We start with the basic formalities. I ask her if she's available for outcall, because I want her to come to me. She answers my question with a question, wondering where I'm located. I tell her I'm staying downtown, naming my hotel. Next, she wants to know how long I wanted to spend. I tell her just an hour and then she gives me the prices. I can't book her for the whole night because I got a book signing in the morning. I've got to be responsible. We agree on a number, and I tell her I'll text her my room number once she arrives. She's about to hang up, but I need to confirm something else with her before this can go down.

"Oh, one more thing. Are you a smoker?" I ask.

"I am. Is that a deal breaker?" she replies.

"Oh, no, actually the opposite. That's what I'm looking for. I'm going to be smoking a cigar and I want to be able to taste the nicotine on your body."

"No freaky talk over the phone." She stops me before I go any further into what I want to do to her. I apologize and let her know I just wanted to make sure I am getting what I wanted before we confirm our date and hang up the phone.

After the usual pacing and self-loathing, I walk to the hotel room's door and open it enough to flip the latch over, so it remains ajar. She said she wasn't far from where I was, so I figure I should get everything set up as soon as possible, when she already texts me that she's downstairs. I text her back with my room number and pick up my snifter glass and fill it up so it's practically overflowing the rim. I know you're supposed to turn the glass on its side and pour the liquor, so the bottom is barely full, but I'm by myself so I say fuck it and top it off. I have to sip the surface slightly to keep it from spilling over before setting it back down on the table. I ignite my cigar, surprised I didn't light the alcohol on fire as well and burn the place down, something I wouldn't be too upset happening.

Before I can even sit down in my chair, there's a knock at the door. I drop down into the seat before calling out that it's open and cue up *Flowers* on the stereo. The woman I assume is Deja, walks through the entrance to my hotel suite. She's in a very low-cut dress with a body that perfectly matches the pictures from her ad. Something I've come to find is not always the case. Her face is the woman I saw when I called, but this is not the woman I ordered.

This woman is blonde.

The next few seconds happen in a flash. I drop my drink and smoke and scream at her, "You're not the girl I called! I wanted Deja, the brunette!"

"Fuck off, I'm Deja! There's nobody but me." she replies.

"You can't be because Deja is not blonde!" I snap back, "I called the girl named Deja because of the picture in your ad, the picture of a woman with brown fucking hair!"

"Calm the fuck down. I just changed it recently and haven't posted new pictures yet." she tries to satiate me with this answer before continuing, "Don't worry, honey. I can still give you that good—"

I cut her off, "I don't care how fucking good you think your pussy is, that's not why I called you! I didn't sleep with the blonde!"

"Well, there's nothing I can do about it now. If it was such a big deal, you should have asked. Now, are we doing this or what?"

She removes the straps around her neck and lowers the top from her dress, revealing what turns out to be a truly perky chest. She doesn't pull it down in a sexy way, though. She flashes her nipples at me in a very matter of fact way, like she changing in front of a mirror or something. This is a business transaction, and she wants to provide good customer service, but I am trying her patience. I consider her for a moment, well my penis considers it, but ultimately, I know this isn't what I want.

So, my defensive ass yells at her, "No! You just fucking ruined my night! We're done here!"

I lead the still topless Deja out into the hallway. She doesn't rush to cover herself up, no, her main focus is on telling me off. "Thank you for wasting my fucking time, asshole!" She continues to yell out as she makes her way down the hall, clearly

226

trying to make a scene and call attention to the other guests. "Is this place full of assholes who jerk *hookers* around? Don't call a *hooker* to your room if you don't want to fuck her!"

She smacks her palm against random doors as I call back to her, "You can keep yelling all you want. You can't embarrass someone who doesn't have any shame!"

She turns around to storm back after me, screaming, "The fuck did you say to me!"

I step into the hallway to meet her. "Just get the fuck out of—"

As we meet in the hallway, I expect her to get in my grill and force me to experience some serious spitting and finger waving, but I'm met with a fist punching me right in my face, across my eye and nose, dropping me to the ground like a prizefighter out of his weight class. Ironic because I've got about a hundred pounds on this tiny woman.

"That's right, bitch! That's why you're bleeding! Fuck with me? That's why you're bleeding!"

I stay on the ground, nose bloodied, as Deja continues to gloat about her knockout and waits for the elevator. Now that the commotion has died down, several of the hotel guests find the courage to peek out of their rooms to find me still crumpled up on the floor.

"Yeah, it's fucking Digg Dogg! Tell this story to spice up your boring ass lives!" I bark at my onlookers as the doors shut.

I gather myself up and make my way downstairs to the hotel bar. I make it a quick exit through the stairwell before someone from security, who was no doubt called by one of my neighbors, shows up to deal with me.

As I stumble into the bar, I ditch my jacket and tie, opting instead to roll up my sleeves and unbutton the shirt. My disheveled appearance draws the attention of the bartender over to my corner right away. I wish I had known this trick earlier in life, could have saved myself hours waiting for a drink at all those crowded clubs.

Looking like you've just been run over by a truck gets you a drink faster.

Although it's not like this place is jumping tonight. It's a standard, inoffensive lounge type of place you'd find in most hotels. It's late enough might be about closing time, that there's only a few people still mingling about. Most of them already have half-full drinks in their hands and look to be tabbed out.

"I need a whiskey, neat. Whatever you think's good. Fuck the price."

The bartender, an older lady, probably been working here for some time, turns to grab my drink. She picks something from the top shelf, no doubt thinking that will result in a bigger tip. To be fair, she's not wrong. I may be an asshole who treats other people like garbage, but I am at least generous with my money when it comes to the service industry. I guess it's my way of making up for being a horrible person.

As she pours my whiskey, I suddenly feel the need to stop her. I ask if they have one of those big ass ice cubes or like an ice ball. She tells me they have big ice balls. She uses a bar spoon to drop it in and that fills up the entirety of my glass, pushing the brown liquor to the top. I charge it to my room, at least I think I did.

I had several of them and things started to get blurry by the time I paid out the tab. I would have stayed until closing, but I could tell I had some asshole filming me in my beleaguered state from the other end of the bar with their phone, no doubt posting it online instantaneously, so I decide to dip out.

The next thing I can remember is I'm walking down another hallway. I'm not sure if it's the right path to my room. In fact, I'm pretty sure it's the wrong floor since I took the stairwell and am not in good enough shape to make it to the top of the building. I wander aimlessly, both in life and in this physical hallway. The ice ball in my drink clinks from side to side, making an almost rhythmic noise with it.

Clink. Clink. Clink.

I take another sip, letting the ice swivel around some more in my glass as the color drains from the walls, enveloping me in a black and white reality.

Clink. Clink. Clink.

CHAPTER TWENTY-FIVE

MURPHY

Before…

Clink. Clink. Clink.

There's a phrase, L'appel du Vide, that translates to "the call of the void". It's that weird feeling you get like when driving a car and you feel a sudden urge to jerk the wheel and crash into a railing. Like when you see a flame and you have a thought to touch it. That brief moment when you want to do something dramatic and drastic but can't explain why.

Leaning forward against the railing of this high-rise balcony overlooking the city's skyline, I feel L'appel du Vide.

Can feel the call.

The call to go over that railing.

I imagine the rush and the thoughts I would have in the fall.

I look down and can see the city below has calmed down for the night, with only a few stragglers moving about. And what I thought was a single pigeon perched on the ledge next to me turned out was a random dove that must have been sticking around since we released them during the unveiling.

There's a glass in my hand with a large ice cube rattling around as I finish off the liquid. Most of the action from the semi-crowded bar is going on inside, while I'm taking in the peace outside by this ledge. The chill from the changing autumn weather has kept this rooftop patio unoccupied since it's hit see-my-own-breath temperature levels. I'm wearing a new black suit and tie while taking a puff from a cigar with my free hand, the alcohol and heat from the smoke keeping me warm enough. Still, I've got my shoulders practically touching my ears accompanied with the obligatory shivers. Bob walks over with two snifter glasses of alcohol and his own cigar balancing between his fingers. Bob is

232

wearing equally formal attire, almost showing me up with his effortless style. He hands one of the glasses to me before casually leaning his back against the railing. I discard the empty beverage to accept the new one from my best friend by setting it on the ground, even though I had an impulse to chuck it over the side like I was in an angsty movie.

Why am I thinking angsty teen thoughts? This is supposed to be a celebration. Must be some retrograding mercury shit.

"Can you see it from here?" Bob asks, referring to Franklin Avenue. A local street here in Chicago that was recently honorarily named after Digg Dogg.

Bob and I have just come from the unveiling earlier in the day and have continued the celebration into the night. The two of us have roots in this city, but Bob was the one who started a charity foundation that set up its headquarters in the South Loop. That charity ended up making a major impact on the gang violence in this city by aiding and educating the wayward youth. This dude, my co-creator, put my name in the founder's charter, giving me equal credit with him.

Who does that?

Just shares the credit with a friend? He knows I'm a fuck-up and he helps me karmatically align? Maybe that's why I'm feeling like a little goth bitch. Deep down, I know I don't deserve this accomplishment.

"I know we've gotten our fair share of awards and accolades, but having a street named after us in this beautifully broken city just seems on another level. We're fucking legends now, buddy! Icons!" Bob continues to wax poetic as my mind half listens. The two of us eventually clink our glasses together to cheers to our lifelong career success. Before Bob finishes the toast, I take a sniff of my drink, trying to determine what I'm about to ingest.

"What'd you get me?" I ask.

"I know you prefer whiskey, but they had a really good Añejo that went with the cigars." This is convincing enough to me that I decide to take that sip and I'm immediately pleased with this decision.

"When you're right..."

"Plus, the whiskey selections they passed off as top shelf here was completely subpar. Would have required a shitload of ice to make it tolerable."

"You know how I feel about ice in my whiskey."

"Mr. Purest!" Bob raises his hands in a mocking fashion before giggling over his clever jest.

All I can do is shrug it off before responding, "Purest? I don't hate ice in my whiskey. The little pebbles are actually the only way I enjoy a julep. It's those fucking large ice balls I hate." I kick the empty glass on the ground to emphasize my disappointment in my previous drink I was forced to order since 'that's the only way they serve their high-end whiskey.'

"Why do you hate on adding an ice ball to your drinks?" Bob asks.

"My dad, mostly."

"Oh, Mr. Purest Senior." He cracks a smile at the clever wordplay he just came up with in his head and was about to quip out, "Daddy hated the balls?"

"No, actually, the opposite. He always had it in his whiskey glass." I take another sip of my tequila before continuing the story, "Um, yeah, I remember growing up I would be trying to fall asleep in bed and could hear him wander the halls of our house to get a refill, holding his glass at his side... We had this shitty ice bin in the freezer, all of his ice cubes in that bin would stick together so he would take a big ball of these fused together cubes and he'd drop it in his drink. The clinking of the ice as he would stumble around more and more with each refill...

Just a clink, clink, clink.

Again, and again...

Those ice balls remind me of him. It's really the only thing I remember about him... He worked long hours that made it, so I never actually saw him much. Only heard the ice at night. He left when I was eight, and it wasn't until a couple years ago that I decided to look him up. Wondered why he never tried to contact me once the show took off... Found his obituary online."

Bob doesn't say anything.

He listens and lets my story sink in for a moment. He allows his friend to be comfortable in this vulnerability before holding up his glass to reply to me, "Fuck ice."

This is the profound wisdom that Bob imparts on his friend.

And I laugh.

A good hard laugh.

The kind of releasing, soul escaping, needed laugh that makes your eyes well up with tears in the corners from the sheer joy of deflating a painful thought with poignant comedy. I hold my own glass up to return Bob's toast.

"Fuck ice."

Bob adds on to his declaration, "And fuck the sins of our fathers. We succeed where they fail."

I can't help but love my best friend in this moment. I don't like to share things from my past. I don't like to expose the hardened inner child that I keep at bay inside myself. Mostly because when I do, I'm usually met with attempts to fix me, or to contextualize my trauma. But not with Bob.

I feel safe with Bob because Bob knows Murphy's soul.

I refer to my soul in the third person, mostly because my soul and I aren't on good terms. I keep denying it's feelings, and it tries to overwhelm me with them.

Souls can be real dicks sometimes.

Bob knows that his friend doesn't need help with dealing with his childhood.

His friend needs acceptance.

He needs to know he's going to be okay.

And Bob gives me that.

Bob also knows not to linger in the uncomfortable for too long. So, he changes the subject by bringing my attention over to a set of attractive women. The women, a blonde and a brunette, sit inside at the bar, slowly trickling away at their drinks and conversing with each other, but they keep glancing towards me and Bob out on the balcony. The blonde is wearing a short red dress that comes to a stop at her ample thighs, clinging to her backside that expands beautifully on the barstool. Her friend, the brunette, is wearing a silver two-piece skirt and top that shines on her slim, tender frame.

"Those two girls over there? I chatted them up while I was waiting to order this last round. They are huge fans of Diggsy. I was gonna have them join us to help finish off these cigars, but if you'd rather keep getting deep, I am here for you, man."

"No, no. That was just a memory that came to me. I'm good. Let's bring them out." I straighten, composing myself before taking a drag from the cigar. Bob waves to the women and they stand, walking out onto the balcony.

"Which one you want? Blonde or Brunette?" Bob inquires before we are joined by our companions.

"I'll let you have the blonde. I know you're not much for skinny girls."

As the ladies join us, their arms at their sides trying to warm themselves in vain thanks to their tiny outfits. Although that did give them the excuse to cuddle up to us immediately with the warmth defense. The blonde woman slips Bob's cigar from his hand

and takes a drag, while the girl with the brown hair opens her lips and wraps them around my smoke while it's still in my grasp.

"You remember when we first went on the air here?" Bob asks me.

"You mean when we took over the Ray Rayner time slot on WGN?"

"Who's that?" the blonde asks.

"He was a legend in Children's broadcasting in the sixties and seventies," he replies.

"Yeah, we had such huge shoes to fill, and we thought since they were just testing us out in the Chicago market that there was no way they would pick us up for national syndication," I say to Bob.

"And what did I tell you the day the pilot aired, and it reached only the greater Chicagoland area?"

"That even if this is the only thing that sees the light of day, we still made it to television. And eventually, we would have a street named after us."

"You're goddamn right I did! I fucking called it, dude!"
Bob holds up his glass, "Everybody get in here!" All four of us
bring our drinks together to cheers in celebration.

The rest of the night's small talk our group exchanged is
just gargled sounds inside my faded memory. I know we spoke to
each other about the show, they told us how they grew up on it,
because I distinctly remember making mental notes of the minimum
age difference there had to of been. But for the life of me, I cannot
recall anything else said in that little circle, the words floated out
into the Chicago skyline. I'll never forget taking that silver dress off
the girl later that night and tasting the cigar on her body. Hearing
her moans emanating from the back of her head as I watched her
straight brown hair sway with the rhythm of my strokes. Grabbing
ahold of that same hair as I thrust my cock into her mouth later that
night.

The call to Bob afterwards to discuss our experiences will
forever be implanted in my skull. But other details of that night, the
little, unimportant filler moments, have been lost to time. All I have
to look back on are the good times.

The happy parts.

I try to hold on to those times as the color returns to my world and I let the last drops of whiskey slip past the oversized frozen sphere and into my mouth while back at my hotel.

I am alone in this hallway.

Murphy's soul is alone.

The memory has faded and even some of the good times now have a haze, thanks to my drunken state. The edges of everything have softened away, yet I can still make out the details of my world, so life as I see it in my drunken state resembles something Sargent would have painted.

I sway for a moment, still holding the glass near my chin. I add to the sway with a jaunty tune as I sing *Chandelier* by Sia and let it echo down the empty hallway. Even though I'm drunkenly belting out the lines, "One. Two. Three. One. Two. Three. Drink," by the time I screech out the chorus, I'm still all alone.

No one has peaked their heads out of their rooms to see what's prompting this serenade. The fact that I'm not getting the attention my drunken outburst seems to be craving makes my balance go even more haywire.

As much as I try to center myself, trying to control my universe both mentally and physically. I've come to the realization that those faded memories will only continue to blur at the edges until the whole thing is unrecognizable and then fully forgotten. I've realized everything in existence will experience this same loss to time and this makes me angry. Not in an existential crisis sort of way, though that's kind of there, but because of the fact that Bob sped up this process. That the world forced the good times to end quicker than they should have.

I take that anger, that built up rage that has been sitting inside of me, waiting to get out, and I channel it all into the item in my hand. With a firm grip around the entire base, I chuck the ice filled glass across the hallway. It sails down, down the length of the hotel passage before the glass comes to a thud on the navy-blue carpeted floor.

It's doesn't break.

The glass just takes a few bounces before settling and rolling a bit as it comes to a stop. The ice ball had made a bigger crack as it was ejected out and onto the wall but hadn't busted either.

I wanted it to shatter.

I wanted that glass to crash and explode everywhere. I wanted my frustration to be transferred into a broken metaphor onto the ground. But instead, my temper is subsided by my own failures at a basic tantrum.

I let out a defeated sigh.

"Of course…"

CHAPTER TWENTY-SIX

CLARK

After…

I've long resigned myself to no longer give a shit what Murphy does anymore as long as he shows up and does his job.

No. Fuck. I'm lying to myself.

I want to believe I don't care anymore, but that motherfucker is still cared for, no matter how many times he breaks my heart. The bitch got so fucked up last night, he couldn't drag himself to even a mediocre turnout of a book signing. His picture book that was getting a reprint with Bob cut out was supposed to be a relaunching point. It was supposed to show us as a united show, unstained by Bob's scandal, but no one cares for our pivot. We had maybe ten families turn up. There's a bigger crowd of paparazzi

banned from the bookstore out front than fans inside.

Still… He should have showed up.

I put one of the background Plücker's in the suit and had

them stay silent while signing the books in exactly his handwriting.

A requirement for being an understudy of Digg Dogg's is learning

his signature and being able to duplicate it. I think the dude in the

suit is named Chris, but I honestly just picked the first name in the

call list and went with it.

'Chris' seems to be doing an okay job with the children, so

maybe it's better that Murphy passed out in the hotel hallway and

had to be dragged back to his room. I've had a security detail

following him all tour. I would say they're really good at their jobs

since he hasn't noticed them once, but it could be more to the fact

that he's such a self-centered prick that he couldn't be bothered to

notice his surroundings. Either way, the security team has been

reporting back to me and last night was quite a night for him.

Aside from getting punched out by one of his escorts, he

stumbled around the hotel for hours shouting about ice before curling up in a crying ball on the floor. Maybe if the hooker he upset had a weapon on her or took more shots at him, the team would have had to intervene and then he finally would have noticed them, but I'm guessing he was so black out drunk last night he still has no clue how he ended up in his own hotel room bed, cleaned up, and showed. They even stayed with him a few hours after to make sure he didn't choke on his own vomit. They tried reviving him in the morning to make it to this engagement, but he was in no state to even stand up, let alone be around children.

I guess I should be used to disappointment when it comes to Murphy. It's like how we had this amazing time at Bob's orgy. The experience rekindled our passion for each other. But that didn't last.

We were circling the drain relationship wise and thought if we attended another lifestyle house party, we could spark things back up again. Little did I know that the reason the first time was such a success was due to the fact that we were in a safe space with friends.

The second time around, we rolled up to this generic house in the sketchy part of the Los Angeles suburbs. We walked into low lighting and a dirty feeling, not the good kind of dirty either. Like a bad strip club, it had a seedy air about it that made you question your life choices. We walked from room to room, being followed by creepy guys lurking around, waiting to come across any kind of action. We'd come across a room with a group of overweight and unattractive people, and the creepers would start to swarm around like a beacon was ignited. It was all just so unnerving to be around that we left after less than fifteen minutes.

In the past, we would laugh and joke about it on the car ride home, but ever since he started to slip away from me and was lusting after Sunshine, we'd become so disconnected that the drive back to his house was total silence. It's not that I was mad at him or anything, though I probably should have been for bringing me to that place, but it was more that we no longer seemed to be on the same team.

And when you're no longer on the same team, you're no longer rooting for each other.

Needless to say, the breakup happened shortly after that. Just further proof that I should get this man out of my life. His tragedy is almost like a blackhole that sucks everyone in his orbit down with him. Sitting in one of the comfy reading chairs in the back of this bookstore, thinking about Murphy, reminds me of the time I ran into Andy Dick back when I was a young bartender in the Valley.

I had just finished up my contracted tour with *Sesame Street* and was looking for my next gig. My money had been running dry, so I took a part-time job at an Irish pub in Sherman Oaks, in order to still be close to the studios if I needed to pop over for an interview. It was almost too brief of a time to even be memorable. There was this one night though that he came in, Andy Dick. He had, by this time, already gained a bit of an urban legend amount of infamy in the area as a hurricane of terrible interactions. One fellow bartender told me of the time he gave him a ride home and he broke his side window before vomiting on the car dashboard. Another told me of his aggressively licking women's faces and grabbing at their chests. It wasn't hyperbole when you would ask anyone in a random Los Angeles bar if they had a personal story about Andy Dick making an ass of himself, and nine times out of ten, they would have a tale to tell.

So, this night he had made his presence known by stumbling up to my bar, drugged and drunk, and grabbing the drink from another customer's hand, before drinking it in front of them. He then had the balls to snap his fingers to get my attention to ask for another round and to put it on the customer's tab. I didn't get him another drink, since I didn't want to escalate things, plus he was a dick, and I didn't care about my job enough to deal with his shit. I didn't even really know how to bartend; I was just hired because the owner thought I was hot.

When I told him to promptly fuck off, he made a racist comment about my Asian nipples producing rice or some shit before stumbling back away into oblivion. I'll admit at the time it pissed me off, and I was a little shaken, but then I did some digging and got perspective.

Andy Dick's infamous scumbag star had already risen by the time two major life events took place in the same year, and in the same month. Granted, he already had some drug and alcohol run-ins at this point, but for a celebrity in the nineties, that was kind of par for the course. What happened ended up turning Andy from regular Hollywood douchebag to full on registered sex offender. In December, his AA sponsor and good friend Chris Farley died of an overdose. This event not only shook Andy and the whole comedy world, but it set off a butterfly effect we can now look back on and trace.

A no-longer-sober Dick then attended a Christmas party and supplied cocaine to a previously ten-year sober Brynn, wife to legendary comedian Phil Hartman. Five months after this, Brynn, high on cocaine, would kill herself and her husband. Blaming Andy for another person's action's is unfair, but when dealing with grief, many won't play fair.

His tragedy would continue.

Less than a year after Hartman's death, Andy and fellow actor, David Strickland, flew to Las Vegas for a weekend of strip clubs and debauchery. On March 22nd, 1999, an intoxicated Strickland committed suicide hanging himself from the motel's ceiling beam. A few months later, Mr. Dick would find his first of many run ins with the law. He currently has a longer rap sheet than IMDB page.

Learning of the tragedies and pain this man had gone through did not absolve him of his terrible behavior, but it did give myself some peace. I no longer felt angry at this lump of intoxication, I felt sorry. I realized that he was doing everything he could to take away his hurt and that sometimes others get caught up in the pain wave.

And that's what I had to tie back to Murphy. He's going to catch me with his wave and hurt me somehow. As sorry as I can feel for the bastard, I can't let myself get hurt for no good reason other than being in the wrong person's wake.

Snapping me out of my Dick trance, my cell phone goes off. It's our client relations manager at Live Nation, the company running the tour, my overlords. So, I don't have a choice but to answer and find out our fate.

CHAPTER TWENTY-SEVEN

MURPHY

After…

This isn't my first hangover.

And unless my life ends relatively soon, it won't be my last. But this one is definitely in the Top Five of shitty hangovers. I finished off all the little airplane bottles in my room as well as the remaining coke letters. Then had a service bring me more liquor and drugs, which made the rest of the night a bit of a blur. I'm pretty sure my words started drifting to the right, and then back and forth, but can't be certain with my foggy recollection.

I have a complete bingo card of ailments when it comes to symptoms right now. The slightest movement sends vibrations shivering throughout my skull, rattling my throbbing brain. My asshole is puckered and sealed so tight because if I relax my sphincter even a little, I'm positive I'll shit all down the side of my leg. Every fragment of light on the planet seems to be bearing down on me, eviscerating my tender eye sockets, the sunglasses yield no protection. And my stomach, it's the same story as with my backside, but with the combined nausea that keeps me in constant discomfort. Add to that the fact that my face feels so bloated and bloody, I'm fairly certain that the whore from last night is somehow related to Mike Tyson.

Not my first hangover but feeling for sure like the worst.

Number one with a bullet.

What's giving it the front runner status is that there is no one to share this pain with me. I'm generally a social drinker, so, in the past, when I've had too many, there's another person who was going shot for shot with me who's in equal amounts of hell as well.

But now that I drink alone… I'm hungover alone…

Which is why I am more than okay with Clark canceling

today's matinee. She said she had to call an emergency meeting for

everyone on the cast and crew. The entire tour company is sitting

either on the edge of the stage or in the theater seats. I'm in one of

the first few rows trying to play it cool, acting like I'm not trying to

fall asleep in my chair in order to relieve my pain. I strategically

wore sunglasses to hide my busted face, which is aiding me in my

sleeping ruse. I did not think through my seating arrangement,

though. I instinctively sat near Vinny and Ryan, as they're the only

two people on this show that I recognize or am able to stand to be

around for more than two minutes. Unfortunately, that girl who now

plays Chester came and sat down with us and will not stop

talking. The boys must have had a late night too, as they have

matching coffee orders in their hands, yet still look like fucking

models without a hair out of place. The girl is in a set of adult Digg

Dogg pajamas that must have been discontinued given they still

have Bob on them.

All three of us are ignoring her, yet she drones on and on as if not saying everything that comes into her skull immediately is a crime.

"I mean, I wasn't really a fan of the first season. They were really just trying to find the voice of the show at that point. And cause Diggsy kept referring to himself in the third person. Kinda like that Phil Collins guy. Oh, I am just so happy I can talk to you about being a fan now."

Vinny was dismissively scrolling through his phone, not giving her any eye contact. He would just give her a few cursory "Yeah's" and "Totally's" but suddenly he becomes interested by a nugget in her ramblings. "Wait—what? Phil Collins?"

"Yeah, you know how he has that one song where he sings about himself. It's that really epic one."

"Which song?"

"I can hear it, Collin, in the air tonight."

Vinny and Ryan exchange dumbfounded looks. They turn to me for confirmation of stupidity, but I am too paralyzed to acknowledge them.

"Do you think the song goes, *I can hear it,* comma, *Collin,* comma, *in the air tonight?* "

"Those are the lyrics."

"They are not." Vinny exclaims in the most incredulous way he can muster without having his head explode. Which just might happen because, as he is about to launch into a tirade, Clark walks up from the back of the theater, forcing Vinny to hold in his mountain of snark. She calls everyone to attention in order to make an announcement.

I suspect it has something to do with Bob's trial, some new information or victim coming forward, something to reignite the flames on this firestorm he's created.

"I am sure some of you were already suspecting this would happen, and I'm sorry for the uncertainty we've had to leave you with, but it just now came down as official. The holiday tour has been canceled." That set's off a ripple of discord. She lets that statement sink in before she continues, "Furthermore, the Detroit leg of the tour has also been cut."

This causes a bit more of an uproar in the group, stagehands and roadies wondering how this is going to affect their paychecks. I was under the impression these dates have already been locked in, but before I can bring up that point, Clark presses on, "The Fox Theater didn't feel comfortable hosting the show with the recent controversy surrounding it and pulled out. I know we thought those dates were locked in, but I believe due to low ticket sales, they decided it wasn't worth the hassle and added security we would require. They're using a morality clause in the contract to terminate the agreement."

"What about our contracts? Are we still getting paid for those dates we're losing?" A random crew member barks out from the stage.

"We have had to scale back on the budget. I'm sorry to say that per diem and lodging will be the area you see most affected by this. But we are not losing any dates, so you will still get paid your full rates since those shows will still be happening. We have been able to secure another venue and will be relocating production to an area outside of Detroit."

"How outside?" Vinny questions.

She hesitates.

"How outside?" he repeats more firmly, but with a slightly frightened anticipation.

She answers only with an apologetic look in her eyes.

"Not… Clark, no… Not there. Not that town…"

"I'm sorry. We're going to…"

"Don't say it!" Vinny pleads.

"Toledo."

CHAPTER TWENTY-EIGHT

CLARK

After...

Fuck Toledo.

I wish it could end with that, but unfortunately, I have to occupy this city. Back when this country was in its infantile formation, the state of Michigan and Ohio fought bloody battles over who got to claim this town as their own. I feel like if they'd have known what it would become, they would have killed each other to get rid of it and have the opposite state deal with it.

There's a single protester out front of this dilapidated theater. A far cry from the usual crowds of angry assholes who have been following us around. This one devoted dude wrote out his hatred for the show on the opposite side of a sign he must have used when protesting outside of an abortion clinic. Either that or he thinks Digg Dogg is a 'Fucking Baby Killer' as the white cardboard elevated above his head reads. We don't even have paparazzi since there's only one local newspaper still using a crank printing press and flash bulbs to take pictures.

I'm trapped in an open space behind the stage. It's setup as an area for the entire cast to get into their costumes. Stuck in uncomfortably close quarters, everyone keeps bumping into each other in a futile attempt to get their suits on in peace. The only thing in this orgy of fur and feathers that's not completely miserable is the glowing, smiling face of Zoey. Vinny scans the floor frantically, searching through the group for his frog head.

"Move, move, please! Has anyone seen my head? My god! Can I just get to my head? That's all I need!"

I try to calm everyone down, but this is such a disorganized mess that I just want to get them out on the stage for tech rehearsal to try to get some sort of semblance of order. I've kind of let the chaos wash over and let it sweep me away. I've become a Zen Yogi as the world burns around me. My soothing words do nothing for Vinny, who remains tense, but suddenly turns his attention to the grinning doofus.

"Why are you so happy, Zoey?" he snaps at her.

"I don't know. It's like that thing, if I can't have a dressing room, then no one gets a dressing room, kind of thing. You know? That kinda thing. We're all in this together."

"I'd slap you in the face if I wasn't worried you'd be into that."

Ugh. Why did he have to say that? Now I have this image of Zoey enjoying rough sex. I bet she's into some kinky ass shit, too. Wouldn't surprise me at all as I always suspected she was a closet freak ever since I saw her in that lacy little thong when I walked into Murphy's dressing room. Speaking of Murphy, I find him crammed in between a couple of male background dancers in chicken costumes as he tries to find some sliver of elbow room.

"How many—" He's met with a mouth full of feathers that he has to spit out. "Can I just get over? Thanks." He scoots by the background chickens before continuing, "How many shows do we have here again?"

I tell him, "You're not going to be happy with any number I give you, so what's it matter?" He is still wedged between several members of the cast when I see his face contort into a surprised and quizzical expression that he holds before squeezing out the question, "Who's beak is in my ass?"

On that note, I turn to walk away, exclaiming, "Five minutes to positions!"

Before I can get away though, I see the intrigued look on Murphy's face as he tries to wrestle with what he's experiencing. "No, don't move it. The beak is actually pretty smooth… It's nice…"

Five minutes later, I have the rest of my cast up on stage half-heartedly singing along as they go through the motions to rehearse their setup. They all know this routine so well they can practically do it in their sleep. I'm sure they can even do it intoxicated, because they have before.

But they still have to do this run through whenever we go to a new theater. Granted, it's always the same amount of space on stage, it's still good to get acclimated to the new environment. Plus, we have to make sure we test the audio levels each time. The crew is building the sets around them, creating an anti-rhythm to what we're trying to accomplish with their hammering and yelling as they string everything up. I'm alone in the stands, just near the back of the theater, so I can get a good look at the whole scene, but still close enough that I can see every detail.

I see Vinny squatting through the song, going full frog. He's got the thickest, muscular thighs that I sometimes imagine them wrapped around my face if I need some handheld motivations when I'm alone at night. Those tree trunks for legs help him bounce around for most of the performance. Any other mortal man would be crying at the end of the show if they had to do as many squats as Fab Frogg Freddy does, but for Vinny, it's just a light leg day.

Don't mind me. Just another straight woman objectifying a gay man.

I'm watching Vinny as he pushes down to try and hop up, but the ground beneath him suddenly gives way and breaks, sending his lower half falling through the stage. Luckily, the top half of the suit gets stuck in the floor, preventing him from falling all the way through.

"Seriously?" Vinny bellows as everyone stops what they're doing and rushes to help him out. I'm already out of breath as I reach the end of the stage, having come in at a full sprint.

"Shit! Vinny, are you okay?"

"Um, I just fell through the fucking floor! So, no, I'm not okay!" I set him up for that one with my stupid question. Murphy and a few crew members are helping to lift Vinny out of the floor as they check to see if he's hurt or broken anything.

"The frog suit cushioned most of it." Vinny tries to play off his accident now that he has recovered his footing, and the embarrassment of the crowd has started to settle in.

"Do you want to go to a hospital and get checked out?" I ask.

"I'm fine. It's fine. Can we just call it for rehearsal? I want to get checked into the hotel and get some sleep," Vinny pleads with me.

"Yeah, you're right. Cast, let's call it!" I yell out and let the performers head backstage to get out of their suits. I find some crew members willing to help fix the hole in the floor after they finish with the sets. But as I start to ask around, I'm met by a frustrated Murphy.

"Get the fucking theater to deal with this bullshit stage," he barks at me.

"Does it look like they have a maintenance staff here?" I gesture around, referring him to the decrepit auditorium we find ourselves in.

"Fuckin A." Murphy sighs. "Just… Are you coming with to get us checked into the hotel? More importantly, is my welcome basket set up?"

I tried. I mean, yes, he has a welcome basket. This hotel does not have the same level of hospitality we're used to. I attempt to explain this to him by telling him this one is a little more…

economical. I don't want him to ask the follow-up question, but he

does.

"How economical?"

CHAPTER TWENTY-NINE

CLARK

After...

If it wasn't my tragic lot in life to deal with these divas, I would find their shocked and downtrodden faces comical. Now this isn't some rundown, dirty ass hotel we're staying in. It's just not one of the boutique upscale glam resorts they're used to.

The place is fine.

The crew has no problem because this is the type of lodging they're used to. They usually get put up in budget-friendly, chain hotels like this one. My main cast, however, are a little more perturbed. The main offended, who I knew would be my biggest pain in the ass about all this, is pushing past the rest of the cast to make his way over to me. Vinny seems to think the show is still at its peak and able to throw money around like we print it at the merch counter. He doesn't grasp or really understand the razor thin margin lines we are operating on. We're a few more undersold shows away from having to sleep in the tour vans.

But that doesn't concern him.

He just wants spa treatments and king-sized beds for him and Ryan to fuck random groupies on.

I breathe in and out, centering myself before dealing with the hysterical actor.

"Clark. A word."

He's trying to pull me aside to not cause the scene everyone expects of him. Hell, I expected theatrics. As much as Vinny ends up playing the stereotypical gay sidekick role, he tries his damnedest to avoid the typecasting. I appreciate his restraint, but I'm still not in the mood to placate with him. So, I ignore his wishes and walk past him to the front desk. He's following me, so I call back to him, "This is the only decent hotel anywhere close to the theater."

I drop my clipboard with everyone's check-in information onto the front desk counter as Vinny leans against it next to me.

"You call this shithole decent?" Vinny exclaims loud enough that the stagehands near the entrance were able to hear him.

So much for not causing a scene.

The hotel clerk in front of us looks angrily hurt by Vinny's harsh words. Vinny is incredulous as he says, "What? If you don't want me to insult your backwoods ass hotel, clean it up and make it better."

I apologize to the attendant for Vinny's behavior, excusing his actions merely as the tantrum of a high maintenance, primadonna actor and to ignore him and focus on me. Vinny does not take kindly to this.

"Excuse me, I am high maintenance because I am amazing and need to be treated as such, not because I am an actor." He turns to the clerk now looking vaguely at his nametag. "Let me ask you something… Gregoles." The clerk interrupts him by correcting his name as Gregory, to which Vinny ignores. "Gregoles, does your establishment have a signature lounge or an elite club area? What's your in-house masseuse's training level? Like, where did they study? How many Michelin stars does your chef-driven kitchen have? Is the room service executive chef at least a James Beard award winner? Is there a cryo-chamber at the gym? How many followers does your Yoga instructor have? Are they Chopra center certified? Any other perks or amenities like that?"

Greg stutters with his response, "Um, we offer a continental breakfast?"

Oh, Greg. You should have just ignored him.

"Everyone has a continental breakfast!" Vinny snaps at him. "This is a hotel, not a fucking motel, yes? So, you're saying you have nothing here to offer me outside of a bed and a place to shit? You're telling me this place is only leveled up from a rat-infested truck stop, pay-by-the-hour-for-my-affair fuck lodge thanks to a platter of fucking bagels you call breakfast ala continental?

Congratulations. You just barely qualified as better than a box in an alleyway."

Vinny shoots me a glare before he leaves Greg a shattered man and storms off to go complain to his lover and Murphy. I can hear them bitching about their lodging as I press on and get everyone checked in.

"Fucking Ohio? Fucking Toledo?" Vinny shrieks in the background, "Why are the worst states always fucking swing states? Just pick a fucking lane!"

It's at least another twenty minutes of getting everyone their room numbers and keys before I can even focus on myself and where I will be crashing. I struggle with my luggage all the way to the elevator. I've got my overhead friendly rolling suitcase, but between my backpack of essentials and two duffle bags filled with the overflow crap that couldn't fit anywhere else, I'm left with not enough arms to carry it all. Everyone else has already made their way to their rooms, leaving me to fend for myself. I know I was giving them all shit about the lack of frills this place has, but I could really go for a bellhop right about now. After I exit the elevator, I

272

push my bags down to the end of the long ass hallway. It's just a series of empty white walls and row after row of bland green doors, with no accent lighting or distinctive artwork to be found. This hotel's whole aesthetic might as well be titled, "blank slate".

Of course, I wind up with the very last room on the far side of the building. My key card decides it doesn't want to work for the first five hundred swipes, but by the five hundred and first, it finally clicks the door open for me. The room is the standard double twin-bedded efficiency you'd expect at a midlevel hotel. I toss my crap onto the first bed, making sure not to crack the bottle of wine I have stashed away inside. Before the door even fully closes behind me, there's a loud pounding against it with a little pinky finger in between the crack, keeping it from shutting.

I open to find Murphy waiting expectantly.

How he figured out which room I am in is beyond me. I suspect Vinny told him. That bitch probably snuck a peek at my clipboard. I don't even get a chance to ask him what he wants before I suddenly find myself in his room.

We're standing side by side with our eyes locked onto the hotel's bedspread. On top of the blanket, just off the center near the foot of the bed, is a giant white stain surrounded by another larger red stain. I'm fairly certain that the white stain isn't cum, and the red one isn't blood, but I'm not positive. The red is a little too light, but it could just be the results of attempted cleaning. The white can't be sperm because it is way, way too big to be one person's load, although I can't rule out the possibility of multiple people/loads.

I try to play it off by calling Murphy a princess and to just not use the blanket. So, I yank at an unsullied corner to pull it down to reveal an even larger brown stain covering the bed sheets. And I'm talking dark brown, like nearly black in its darkness. There was no attempt at this thing to be cleaned up, that or housekeeping has just given up. Even so, I still have to ask, what the fuck happened in this room?

I go downstairs and explain to Greg that Mr. Harrison's room is unsatisfactory, and he sets us up with another accommodation. I help Murphy with his luggage and gift basket as we check out the new room.

And by help, I mean I carry his bags while he picks through the basket for anything he can ingest along the way.

We check the bed and find another dark stain on the blanket, but not as appalling as the last one. The sheets underneath appear clean, if we ignore the body shaped off-white coloring across the middle. Murphy can't help but to shrug as he accepts it for what it is and decides to start unpacking. I head towards the door as he opens the cabinet drawer. A loud rodent like screech erupts from inside it as he slams the drawer shut.

"What the fuck was that?" I spin around and ask.

"I don't know," terror struck across his face, "but it had babies."

CHAPTER THIRTY

MURPHY

After...

After a quick jaunt back down to Greg, we find ourselves
in my new room. I immediately flip the blanket off the bed, not even
checking to see what weird, unholy stain awaits me. Clark has
already given up on me and gone back to her room. I mean, at this
point, if there's anything wrong with this room, I'm just going to
have to deal with it. So, I take a roll of duct tape out of my suitcase
and strap down the cabinet drawers under the TV. If there's
anything alive inside there like the rodent infestation from the last
room, they'll be dying of starvation by the time I check out.

Luckily, I still had this roll of tape leftover from the Dallas leg. When we had toured Texas back before everything went to shit, I hooked up with this girl who was really into kinky BDSM shit. She was like a sexy little fuck toy for me the whole time we stayed in that city. I did some nasty shit with her. I'm talking, choking, spitting, slapping, all kinds of dirty. I probably could have called her up and she would have still been down to sub for me, but I couldn't bring myself to text her. I also had a hell of a time finding a whore who would let me do any of the things this girl had let me do. Only one hooker was okay with being tied up with the duct tape, but it cost a fuck load and we had to have a "normal" session first in order to gain her trust that I wasn't a complete psycho. And we only barely got through the session before she was using the safe word.

My Depression Playlist is playing *Try Walking in my Shoes* by Depeche Mode on my phone as I check out this piss-poor excuse of a welcome basket for more alcohol. I already cleaned most of it out during my room switching and the only thing left in here is a bottle of local wine (I didn't even know it was possible to make wine in Ohio), some coupons to some diarrhea, inducing a hot dog place, and a flesh-light molded after a Toledo pornstar named

Brandy Talore. Production always tries to lean into gift baskets

themed around the city we're inhabiting, and this one is fittingly

pathetic.

I grab the bottle of wine and thank God it's the twist-off

cap kind, although I should have expected that kind of quality.

Judging by the label, they're trying to say this young wine is a

Tempranillo, sure. The only glasses available in the room have

lipstick smeared on the rims. Something I only noticed after taking a

big gulp from one of them. Hopefully, the alcohol in the wine will

kill whatever Gona-Herp-AIDS I'm contracting from this rim,

because it's certainly not stopping me from drinking it. I figure I

might as well enjoy this, so I call up one of the production assistants

to run me over some fruit, Orange Bitters, and Mexican Coke so I

can make a Rioja Libre. I was also able to get a half ounce of weed

from the pimpled gopher, so I should be all set for the night, but I'm

still not in a good place, emotionally and geographically.

Maybe my phone will have some answers as to what this

city has in store for me. I Google, "Fun things to do in Toledo" and wait as the shitty complimentary hotel Wi-Fi takes its sweet ass time loading.

Search results: Zero.

I refine the search by removing the word "Fun" and get a few results for that coupon hot dog place and a single museum.

One museum.

Of course, none of these options are available to me this late at night. I didn't plan on hiring a call girl while I was in Ohio, mostly because we never really toured this state. We hit Cleveland one time back in the early days of the show, but I can't really remember any debauchery from that show. Since I don't have any memories with Bob tied to this city, I figured I'd just ride the depression out. But this hotel has a terrible cable package, and I am bored out of my fucking mind.

So I'm scrolling my phone again.

I've been trying to stay off the internet and social media since this all went down. This limits my screen time but increases my boredom. So, I guess I'll search for a companion for entertainment.

This time, I've got an array of pictures of scantily clad women. I might actually be able to keep up my initial plan of being celibate here since most of the women I am coming across are significantly less attractive than I am willing to pay full price for. But, again, I can't think of anything better to do, and don't want to be left alone with my thoughts. I start contacting a few of them. I'm using my burner phone, so I'm not worrying about cops trying to trap me, but still keep communication to text messages.

That still doesn't stop a few of the "girls" I hit up from being total scammers. They discuss pricing with me and even try sending me obvious fake pics then try to ask me to send them money first. They'll keep texting me saying they'll do crazy things to me if I just send them a Visa Gift Card number or send them money through an App as a "deposit" and then they'll "absolutely" come right over to my place. Which is always bullshit. That scam is run by a bunch of dudes that are easily sniffed out when you ask them to call you to voice verify. Oh, they still "attempt" to call you, but when you pick up there's a "bad connection" and you never actually speak to them. They'll keep pestering you to send them money and if you're stupid enough to do so, you'll never hear from them again. This bullshit doesn't happen in the bigger cities since the legit girls are flooding the market, but in this piss-poor excuse for a town, that's all I'm running into is scammers.

I'm about to give up, until I come across this one girl's ad. I can't see anything but a filtered selfie and when I click for more pictures, it's just more of the same pouty-lipped duckfaces. For some reason, when I look at her, I'm reminded of my ex-wife, so I say what the hell. Her details list her measurements as "Big Tits," which is good enough for me. We set everything up over text message and she is on her way for a fairly reasonable price. I'm going over which of the times with my ex that I want to recreate with her when there's that knock at my door.

That knock that send me knees weak. It's a sexy anticipation mixed with a dangerous unknown of what could be in store for me.

What I find when I open up my hotel room is a woman in her late thirties in a pair of sweatpants and a baggy sweater. At least I hope that it's baggy and not just comfortable snug. I almost close the door right in her face. She's coming over here to fuck a complete stranger, she could have at least put in a little effort to look good. Her hair is up in a messy ponytail like she just rolled off the couch and didn't even bother to clean the Skyline Chili staining her sweatshirt. At least I hope that's what's blotting her shirt; vomit and Skyline Chili are easily confused with each other thanks to their similar appearance and taste.

But I am a gentleman, so I lead her into my room and hand her a small wad of cash. I tried to hold it in but couldn't help but let out a sigh as we exchange money. She asks what's wrong and I say nothing at first, but she presses me.

"Your ad said you had big tits."

"Uh, yeah, I do," she says as she takes off her top to reveal she had left her house without a bra on. Normally that would be a sexy statement, but here, it just seems like more of a lazy excuse.

"You have fat girl tits."

"Excuse me?" She is rightfully offended.

"You don't have big tits. You have flaps sitting on top of your stomach. They look big because of them resting on your gut."

"The fuck is wrong with you, asshole?" I can tell she is about to slap me and leave, which, honestly, I would have more respect for her if she did.

"I really don't know."

I genuinely don't.

I should try to be kind, like I always preach on the show, but I've given up trying.

"I'm sorry," I spit out.

And I think she could tell I was being sincere because she decides to stay, that and the extra bills I slip her. She counts the money while still having a look of disgust on her face. It's at this point I realize I won't be able to use her as a surrogate for my ex and all the scenarios I had imagined go out the window.

"She totally fucking *catfished* you, dude."

That voice.

The words come from the corner of the room, but it's just me and the girl here. I slowly turn my head to find Bob sitting in the chair, drink in hand, but his entire body is in a black and white greyscale, like one of those old timey televisions.

"Like that girl from… from? Fuck, what city was that? She did the same thing to me. You have to remember. You said the same thing I said to you. The fat girl flaps line. That's what I told you I had said."

I try to ignore him. He's obviously a hallucination, since the hooker doesn't seem to notice him as I lay down on the bed. I glance back over and it's just an empty chair, as it should be. She takes off the rest of her clothes as nonchalantly as someone changing at the gym. I wait a moment, thinking she's going to undress me, but that doesn't seem very likely, so I remove my clothes myself. I get naked in such an unsexy way it's like I'm at a fucking doctor.

This whole exchange is just clinical and all business.

I pull out a condom and put it on as she crawls onto the bed, lying next to me. I prefer when someone is being paid on my dime that they do most of the heavy lifting in the sex position department. She's just waiting for me to crawl on top of her and get this thing over with. I half expect her to be checking her phone as I'm pumping, but I roll onto her anyway since I've already paid the piper. It's an awkward bit of fumbling around as I try to get myself inside of her and find a rhythm, but between her lady parts unwillingness to open up to me and the unsexy silence that's only filled with our bumping skin, we can't seem to get anything going at all.

Bob suddenly appears laying on the bed next to us, legs crossed, and arms folded behind his head. Still wearing his trademark suit and tie.

"Seriously, this is bugging me now. What city was that?"

I continue to bumble around with this Toledo hooker, still not getting any type of pleasure out of this, even when she finally lets me switch to her on top. I've grabbed her and we've rolled over imaginary Bob to make him disappear.

She barely moves her body up and down, and all I get is a slow thumping on top of me. I want to say it's because most of my attention is focused on ignoring the black and white Bob that's transported himself to my room to fuck with my mind more, but it's really just our incompatibility that's causing our struggles. I tell her what we both know, that this isn't working. She wants to know what I want to do then, and I tell her to just use her mouth. She says that she'll have to charge extra for that. I relent and pay her because I've already come this far, and I might as well attempt to cum. I'm still inside her as I reach over to the side table and fish out more cash.

"I also want to cum on your face." I tell her.

"That's another extra."

"Of course it is."

She tells me the upcharge price and I agree so she moves off of me and places her head between my legs. She yanks the condom off and goes to town on my dick. I didn't think it was possible to screw up a blowjob, short of not opening your mouth wide enough, but somehow this "professional" did.

Just like her downstairs parts, the upstairs is just as dry. There is absolutely nothing wet coming from her mouth. Judging by the smell of her, aside from being that of someone unwashed, she must also have cotton mouth from the weed she obviously freshly smoked. Granted, I had a joint waiting for me on the side table, but that was for the after-sex glow. Which makes the fact that she's mostly using her hand to do the majority of the work even more grating, since it's a dry rub. Still, the worst head is better than no head. So, I close my eyes and lean my head back, trying to enjoy myself.

But I can't.

He's still in my ear.

"Orlando? No. Miami? Nope. It was definitely one of those southern bum fuck towns."

I try to kill two birds by drowning him out and get myself closer to completion with a click of the remote. This hotel's tube television is so ancient it's still hooked up to a Pay-per-View network. I scroll quickly through the menu and find a satisfactory adult movie. The prostitute gives me an incredulous look for what

I've just done, but continues with the task at hand, lowering her head back down into my lap.

The film on the TV is something made in the late eighties, at least that's what I can tell from the grainy, pixelated, 4:3 ratio picture. The only way I can enjoy this is by saying fuck it and pulling out the joint from the side table and firing it up with a box of matches I found inside the drawer. I light it up and take a full drag while still focused on the bushy porn, all while Toledo's finest continues to bounce her head up and down.

None of this blocks out Bob's constant talking. So, I end is inquiry, "Atlanta. It was Atlanta."

"Fuck. You're right," Bob says.

For the first time I really take in what is happening. I notice a vase on a side table across the room. It's pattern contrasting with the tacky bamboo wallpaper. The sounds of sucking coming from the TV and from in front of me is out of sync as both live action and taped versions fill the room with slurping audio.

And in spite of all that… I close my eyes… And I cum.

CHAPTER THIRTY-ONE

MURPHY

Before...

There's nothing more existentially soul crushing than walking into a room with all of your hopes, dreams, and desires being held inside and you find that entire place is filled with assholes who look exactly like you, most are better looking and in better shape, with the same goal in mind when they walked in. What's worse is this is an almost regular occurrence whenever going out for auditions in LA.

It's actually become expected.

I'm now used to seeing Multiverse Murphys at these things. The first couple of open casting calls, I tried to be friendly and make conversation with my opponents, not realizing it was a 'me or them'

situation. After a while, I learned to say, fuck these guys, and focus

on making an impression when my name was called.

It was at a random call back that I collided with the

catalyst of my life.

I check in at the front and find a seat to focus on my lines,

my usual blinders up, and I'm completely thrown off when I see this

lanky fuck smiling at me from across the glass coffee table

separating the chairs. He's rocking this big, bushy mustache that

I'm sure he thinks makes him looks like Freddy Mercury, but

actually has him resembling Ned Flanders. I push my papers with

my sides printed on them up close to my face to block this schmuck's

glare, but I can feel it burning through the parchment.

I take a quick peek to confirm if he's still smiling at a

complete stranger and sure enough, I meet his gaze. My quick snap

behind the script to break the eye contact was not smooth or subtle

at all, so I relent and drop my barrier to let this random dude

continue to gawk at me. He does what I was dreading and moves

closer to introduce himself to me.

"Hey, I'm Bob. Is this your first audition with Alison?"

I'm pretty sure this guy was just trying to psych me out, making me think I came off like some bright-eyed newbie. But as I read his face and continued to reluctantly converse with him, I found he was genuinely trying to help me. Bob had thought that because I was so focused on my script that this was my first time going out for a part and was putting everything into it. He actually wanted to help me by legitimately offering advice and to calm my nerves.

He did it whenever he saw someone struggling.

Whereas I, and most hardened struggling actors, had become jaded to the process, Bob become more sympathetic. After going through the meat grinder that is Hollywood casting, this man did not give up and wanted to help others, knowing they were about to be devastated.

Who the fuck does that?

Even after I was super standoffish with him as he approached me, still thinking I needed help, he pushed and broke me down. We agreed to get coffee after we both bombed the

audition. I think it was a deodorant commercial, or maybe it was

some snack chips.

Not important.

So, we stopped at the nearest coffee shop and ordered the

cheap stale shit that had been rotting in their pots all day. Bob

insisted on paying. After finding seating, I let him know I had been

on the struggle for over two years and not some fresh off the bus

Midwesterner, as he had thought.

The conversation flowed pretty easily with him right away.

He kind of broke the ice when he got going on his

Apocalypse Debate. See, to Bob, he believed that all those movies

and stories about a single protagonist trying to survive during the

end of times was bullshit.

It was a fantasy.

Not the world ending stuff, we both agreed that was

coming, but the fact that we as the viewer are expected to see

ourselves in this person who is above it all, the protagonist that had morals and would go crazy like everyone else. Bob believed that everyone was the cannibalistic, backstabbing antagonist that our heroes end up coming across. He knew that deep down, when the order of society broke, we would all fend for ourselves and destroy anyone in our way to survive.

And it was really hard to argue that.

I don't know why he called it his Apocalypse Debate, when really it was more of his own personal theory, but I guess it was something he wanted to discuss with people. It would lead him into discussing why he uses that idea as a basis for he, himself to live a kinder more caring existence, in the hope that if all hell broke loose, he would go down right off the bat and not have to suffer, because he died helping people.

Kind of sweet. In a fucked-up way.

After the philosophical ice breakers were out of the way, we then started to reveal more personal stuff. Like where we grew up, surprisingly both of us in the Chicago suburbs, what we were currently doing to not starve and support our fledgling dreams, and then got into why we were here in the first place.

You see, the funny thing about Los Angeles is the feeling of possibility.

LA sucks. Plain and simple.

People who've never even been there knows how horrible it is. The traffic is famously horrendous, the wage gap is unattainable, and the everyday price on basic living is comically astronomical. Yet everyone still flocks to the city because there's something about the possibility of anything happening. You don't know what will lead to what that could suddenly turn all of the hardship into a fairytale.

Like how at a random audition, you meet a man who will set about changing the entire course of your life and the very DNA of your existence.

CHAPTER THIRTY-TWO

MURPHY

After…

"You know, common courtesy, you're supposed to give a girl a little head's up you're about to finish. So, she doesn't end up choking and getting cum all over her face. It went out my fucking nose."

I'm laying naked on the hotel bed with a wine cocktail in one hand and a joint in the other. The blankets are still crumpled up on the floor at the foot of the bed and I am glaringly watching the credits to the adult film I ordered roll across the screen, completely disgusted with myself. The Toledo hooker is in the doorway of the bathroom cleaning her face at the sink, still naked. She angrily trots back into the room and gathers her clothes.

"I'd remember that for next time," I say while still keeping my eyes locked on the TV. "But I don't think I'll be calling you again."

I pull out more cash from inside the nightstand's drawer and hand it to her, all the while not making eye contact, instead I'm still focused on the credits. She counts it in front of me, looking confused.

"This is a hundred? I said it was twenty for the facial."

"The extra's for... you know—" I finally remove my eyes from the screen and slowly turn to face her, "—not being courteous."

She stares blankly at me for a second, even more confused than before.

"For cumming on your face."

She finally understands what I was trying to say as I turn back to see my program has ended and has gone back to the welcome menu. She puts her clothes on and heads towards the door. She stops before turning the handle and cranes her neck back towards me. "So, was this some kind of fetish thing, where you act like a piece of shit to me, or are you just genuinely an asshole?"

"I really don't know," I repeat what I had said to her earlier as a bookend to our time together. I admit I kind of fat shamed her, even though her weight wasn't the issue I had with her. She wasn't even that big. I think it had more to do with her sloppy effort. She didn't seem to even care to present herself in a favorable light. She is going to a bunch of stranger's locations and getting naked and couldn't even be bothered to look presentable. I have a feeling she used her mangy attire as an excuse for her obesity. But I can't even call her obese, she was just sort of chunky, lazy. There are genuinely people who can't control their weight and I feel for them, but not this girl, she was just plain pathetic.

And I know pathetic because I live in Patheticville.

Fuck, I'm pretty sure I got elected Mayor of Patheticville.

No, I lost the election for Mayor of Patheticville.

That's how pathetic I am.

She leaves, and I remain just as dejected as ever. You'd think laying naked on a dirty hotel mattress covered in semen, saliva, and what I suspect is a bit of vomit, that I would consider this to be my lowest point.

Yet, it gets worse.

A commercial for the tour comes on.

And it's not even a recent one. This fucking spray fart of a city couldn't even get the correct advertisement when they aired it on their local channels. The TV is playing one of the old ads that still features Mr. Bob, front and center. The station interns don't even put in enough effort to screen what they put on the air. They just throw in any old tape and assume it doesn't matter because people will come out to the event center anyway since there's nothing else to do in this should-have-been-aborted town.

An appropriate groan escapes my mouth as I grab the remote and make it stop by turning off the television. I get up and stare out the window, not caring who's seeing my junk. It doesn't really matter though since there's only a barren parking lot for me to brood at as I sip on my wine with its subtle notes of lipstick.

He's still there.

He's a blurry, out of focus grey blob on the bed, but he's still there.

Still talking.

"So, have you officially lost your mind or is there still going to be some wacky hijinks where you accidentally talk to me in front of people in a desperate attempt to hold on to your sanity? I'd look forward to a hilarious moment where you scream at me something inappropriate and then awkwardly try to explain it to confused onlookers."

I keep trying to ignore him, knowing it's just my subconscious speaking to me as I run my hands along the edges of the window, looking to open it.

"Good luck jumping out the window," it says.

"I don't want to jump. I just want to hang over the edge and contemplate jumping while brooding. Because I want to think I'm dark and brooding and not some middle-aged fossil."

"Hotel windows don't open. They don't want people accidentally committing suicide on their watch."

I sigh. "Of course."

"Are you sure it was Atlanta? I feel like I fucked a fat chick in Milwaukee."

"You did, but the flaps line was from Atlanta."

"Oh, yeah, that stripper from the Claremont Hotel."

He goes on to tell me in graphic detail what he did with this stripper. And it's here that I actually wish the window would open, not because I want to be dramatic and act like a rock star dangling on a ledge. I want it open because I want to end it all. I have been circling this drain for so long now that my self-destruction needs to finally come to its completion. I need to reach the end of my journey. He prevented me from going there before, but now he is the reason for my will to die.

CHAPTER THIRTY-THREE

CLARK

After...

There was a moment this morning, brief as it was, where all was right with the world. I didn't know who I was or where I was, and my problems were just as distant. Then I moved slightly, and my cognitive memory flooded back, and I was back in reality.

Such a beautiful moment.

As I rolled out of bed, I felt a stiffness in my neck. I was pretty sure it would go away, but it's stuck around all day, and I can barely swivel my head around while I'm directing everyone backstage. I'm at the point in my life where I have to contemplate every pain or discomfort, I get as to whether it will be temporary or that it'll become chronic. Of course, I don't have time to worry about this or focus any attention on myself for that matter, because I know it's coming.

And there it is.

Like clockwork, another tantrum coming from one of my actors. It seems like every other show has one of *them* on the floor crying about how much they hate it here. This time, it's Murphy. I hear him screaming, "I can't! I can't fucking do it! Someone go and get Clark. I refuse to get back into that sweat-soaked monstrosity again! I am done!"

As I make my way backstage to Murphy, I see Vinny and Ryan have already made their way over to try and comfort him. "Hey, I know we're all a little frustrated right now, but this is the last day. And then it's on to New York. You know, a good city."

Vinny's words do little to calm him as I assess his mental state. I assumed it was just another case of boredom and exhaustion that everyone has been feeling rise to the surface here, but this seems to be something different coming from Murphy. He's not just burnt out. He's straight up fried.

"I can't do this anymore, Boss. I just can't fucking put that suit on again." Even though he is having a full-on melt down, that doesn't deter the rest of the background dancers from preparing for the show around us. We continue our conversation as they bump into us while putting on their costumes and stretching their limbs. I decide since he's in hysterics, the best tactic is subversion.

"One must imagine Sisyphus happy."

His tantrum subsides with a momentary pause of confusion as he blurts out, "Huh?"

"One must imagine Sisyphus happy," I repeat.

"Is she talking about the Greek rock guy?" Vinny whispers to Ryan.

"Yes, the story goes that Sisyphus was cursed by the gods to push a boulder up a hill for all of eternity, only to have it roll down every time he got to the top and start again. It's supposed to be a cautionary tale about the tedium of work, but if you imagine he is happy to do the task, it changes the whole dynamic of the story."

The three morons stare at me, dumbfounded for a moment before I get a response from Murphy.

"What does that have to do with me putting on a fucking dog suit?"

"It gives meaning and purpose to your tedium. A story thought to be about suffering can be seen as a routine. There are unknowns out there, but Sisyphus has his role known. Come on, Murph, it's just two more shows. Let's just get through these two and then it's New York to close out the tour. You're almost done." I use the tactic of laying out small steps in front of him to try to get him to ignore the bigger picture, but he doesn't bite.

"I am trying. But I cannot find the will to shed what little self-respect I still have and get back into that thing." He points at a crumbled-up ball of fur on the ground that was his Digg Dogg costume.

"Wait, when did you gain back your self-respect? Can I have some of that?" I joke with him, badly.

"I am being serious, Boss."

"What about this?" Vinny interjects. "Clark, if you're okay with it, Sunshine's new tour is opening in Windsor today. We can get the understudies to do the matinee so we can go see her perform. We'll be back for the show tonight and be refreshed, having lost all that pesky self-respect."

I tell them I can make that work if they want to take one of the tour vans. Sunshine and Murphy have only really spoken to each other through their lawyers since their divorce. There's no bad blood between them and they really should work out some closure with each other. They also have been radio-silent since Murphy's world fell to shit. I know I'm supposed to stick by my guy friend and call her a bitch, but I really can't call her that. They went through a hell together and frankly most couples would not be able to survive such strife. And, unfortunately, they were most couples.

"Why the fuck do you guys think that would be something I'd want to do?" Murphy asks a valid question, throwing his hands up in the air like he's tossing the idea off out the window

"Because you need to talk to her." Vinny responds with his finger softly pointed back at Murphy before it comes to rest at his shoulder. Vinny's right too, and Murphy reluctantly knows and accepts it. But before we can all come to an agreement, we're interrupted by Zoey popping up from behind a chicken.

"You guys aren't going to bring Sunshine back, are you? If she comes back, do I have to be a Plücker again?"

I should string her along and make her sweat, but I assure her that she is our Chester Cheddar for the time being.

"Yeah, Sunshine is never going back into that rat costume." Vinny snaps at her, completely negating my progress.

"Okay, it's a mouse. And why not?" Zoey pokes the bear.

Vinny replies in a tone so sharp it could cut glass, "Because she left for a reason, Zoey! Her reasons are her reasons! Don't worry about it!" He turns to me and politely asks, "Keys?"

I direct the boys away and leave Zoey devastated as she's left behind. I shouldn't have gotten as much joy out of that as I did. I'll figure out a way to make it up to her. But first, one crisis at a time.

This may be our last night in Toledo, but I'm gonna need a whole bottle of wine to ease my neck and forget this town. I can already see the ambitious understudy grabbing Digg Dogg from the ground and knocking the dirt off it. Vinny and Ryan have already shimmied out of their costumes and thrown them to their backups.

I'm surrounded by these half-naked men, and it's almost like back when me and Murphy dated.

CHAPTER THIRTY-FOUR

CLARK

Before…

You ever have one of those moments at your job where you realize your bosses are morons and yet still dictate the majority of your life? That's a moment I am in as I sit in the back of this rented theater watching as Bob and Murphy drool over backup dancers doing everything but offering lap dances in order to land this new gig.

Sunshine's pregnancy with their first kid makes it impossible for her to fit into the Chester outfit. And really, she shouldn't be dancing and on her feet for hours at a time just for the sake of a third-rate children's show. She's completely over the moon

*about the prospect of becoming a mom. Murphy on the other hand,
seems to be retreating into himself. I want to get in there and try to
talk to him about how he's feeling, but the closest I can get is when
he cracks self-deprecating jokes that hold the kernel of truth about
where his mental state is at.*

*So, instead of working that out, we're auditioning for her
replacement on the upcoming tour. The boys just keep asking the
same dumb questions about "flexibility" and "willingness to go the
extra mile" that I swear any HR department would deem
inappropriate to ask sweaty, skintight clothed girls. Yet, these
dancers seem all the happy to be demeaned if it means a steady
income on a hit show.*

*The plucky little one at the front of the crowd, showing the
most enthusiasm, is this blonde girl that I swear just got off the bus
from Bumfuck, Middle-of-Nowhere State. She keeps repeating her
name, Zoey, again and again in some attempt at a psychological
trick to keep her name fresh in our minds. I honestly might have
them hire her just for the fact that I can see the crazy twinkling
behind her eyes.*

And I like crazy.

But I should be more selective in our search. Especially when I already know my morons are just thinking with their dicks right now. This one is a little more important because it includes a stint on a cruise. If the test run on the boat works out, we can use it as a template for the entire cruise line with hired stand-ins. A cruise deal would be massive in terms of pushing our show to a new level, not just monetary, but in terms of global impact. These shows would be touring internationally all around the world, simultaneously reaching an even larger audience than we already have.

If we land this, that would be the final step in cementing the show's legacy as an icon of children's television.

They've broken the news to the dancers not moving on to the next round of call backs to leave. And have now gotten the individuals standing center stage as they grill them with the real questions for determining who they hire to fill Sunshine's mouse shoes. They all stand back as each girl takes turns stepping up to answer or to one up the previous girl like this is a goddam beauty pageant.

I immediately dismiss all of the airheads with racks bigger than their brains when they can't answer simple questions on interacting with children. I'm finally sold on the Zoey chick when she mentions very casually, not casually, that she has a degree in child psychology.

I don't let her know this and simple belt out from the back row, "We've all got child psych degrees, honey! It's a pre-rec."

I don't know why I'm being mean to her. She's my favorite of the lot. There's just something about her calculated innocence that sets off alarms for me. Like it brings out a form of female misogyny from deep inside.

It's interesting because Murphy would always compare me to a Nagel Woman. The subjects from the artist who did those iconic eighties paintings of women with the jet-black hair and completely white skin, all art deco minimalist with pastel coloring. Which is funny because the women that Nagel painted were seen as elegant, chic, and powerful, characteristics that I am certainly not known for.

Whatever let's just hire this Zoey. *Maybe she'll become my new best friend. She can replace my Sunshine in that role as well.*

"One last question. Which superpower would you want: The power of flight or invisibility?" Murphy asks.

CHAPTER THIRTY-FIVE

MURPHY

After…

There's really no comfortable way to sit on a folding chair. It's like they were designed with the exact opposite of the human body in mind when they were created. You've got your back arched so all your weight doesn't go on the fat of your butt cheeks, but on the point end of your spin and tailbone. Not to mention the height has you low enough to the ground, it's enough to make anyone's knees pop from the force of the angle as they're practically placed against your chest. Why we insist on using such medieval devices when arranging temporary group gatherings is beyond me.

And yet here I am.

Destroying my body in a way I didn't think was possible. And for someone as self-destructive as I am, that's saying something. The fit Adonis's next to me seem to be having no trouble keeping up their postures, but I am dying. We're trapped in these torture seats under a large white tent that was only built to be torn down quickly, like the roving band of gypsies that they are. I'm glad we decided to grab our coats before heading here as the tent is barely even a shelter to the point the autumn wind is blowing leaves inside of it, gathering a pile at my feet.

A group of choir singers, dressed in floral print gowns, are up at the front altar singing. The song is about "Jesus going down on me" without a hint of understanding about the possible double meaning. They're trying to stress the notion of Jesus coming down from heaven and bestowing his love upon them, but with the chorus about him "going down on me" they've un-ironically created juvenile comedic gold. Vinny and Ryan smile and giggle like school children next to me, trying not to laugh too loud and cause a scene.

At the center of the group, she emerges to finish the song, Sunshine, my ex-wife. Her radiant gold hair gives credence to her namesake. I had wished for her to not remain the goddess of grace and beauty that she had been during our time together, but she still disappointed me by gaining more of these attributes. It's like a cruel trick that after breaking up with someone, they suddenly become more attractive.

The song concludes, and she wraps up the service. "Thank you all for coming out today! That wind may have chilled things down, but you gave us the warmest of receptions! We want to praise you as much as we praise him! And don't forget to stick around for some of our homemade *Jesus Juice* and *Body of Christ Bread* at the *Last Supper Table*. It's so good, it'll make you want to die for all of man's sins!"

The congregation disperses, and we make our way outside. The offering table is getting swarmed with hungry church goers, so it looks like instead of getting a chance to linger, we're going straight to Sunshine; right after the other worshipers' finish congratulating her on her performance.

When I finally get an opening to approach her, Sunshine is standing outside the tent area, thanking the last of the audience members. But Vinny beats me to the point and gives her a great big, warm hug.

"Oh, my god, Sunshine, that was so great. Just great. Soooo great."

He releases his grip on her, making way for Ryan and myself to embrace her next. I try to speak to my ex, but Vinny interrupts me.

"But seriously, though. Jesus going down on you? Is that how he got you to follow him around in a tent?"

"Only you would turn it dirty. Oh, how I've missed you, Vinny." She gives him a playful punch to his bicep.

"How could I not?" He glances over at me, already knowing his social cue. "Okay, listen, I have to get some of that *Jesus Juice* before the heathens drink it all, but I want to catch up with you, okay? Seriously, it was so good to see you."

Vinny takes Ryan by the hand and leads him over to the food table. And with that, they leave me and Sunshine by ourselves to awkwardly stand in front of each other.

"Hey."

"Hey."

There's a moment as we simultaneously avoid eye contact and at the same time seek it out as we try to find the words that we both know will fail us.

"Care to take a walk?" She eventually gets out.

"Sure."

The task of walking to a destination, as undecided as it may be, is enough to relax us. We take a stroll away from the tent and the crowd, the uncomfortableness between us still apparent though. We head towards the edge of the field, making our way to a row of trees leading into the forest. She tries to broach safe subjects by asking my honest opinion of her god show. I tell her she really doesn't want to hear what I thought of her performance, but she persists, telling me she's trying to reach a younger audience.

And no one knows how to speak to kids like Digg Dogg.

"All right fine. I'll give you the obvious stuff." I finally acquiesce, "It was a little preachy."

"It's a church summit. That's kind of the whole point."

"I know that, but you could have a little more fun with it. You're being too heavy with the Lord. Just use His teachings as an example and then bring it back to the fact that He came up with them. Kids are more about emotions than philosophy. Teach them about what they're feeling."

"Okay, okay, I'll take that."

"Just… remember you were once a child, too."

We finally reach the tree line. That walk felt like it lasted hours when really it was only a couple seconds. We stop by a random willow tree, circling it—the plant and our issues. I stick with innocuous questions like, how she's doing, how's she liking the new gig, how's life? She gives me the stock answers of good, fine, and great, respectively. I knew she wasn't going to let me off the hook, though. She had to turn the conversation to my world.

"So… How've you been? With the whole…" she asks.

"You mean with the whole Bob thing?" I reply.

"Yeah. The Bob of it all."

"I'm doing…" I let out a sigh as I can't find the words, just repeat, "I'm doing."

She can tell I don't want to talk about him. I'm repeating myself like a broken record and she doesn't stop it, just lets me let the subject die. I sometimes feel she knows me better than anyone else in this world outside of Clark. Plus, we have enough things we need to resolve between us, my current crisis can be put on hold. I kick at the roots of the tree, focusing my attention on it while keeping my hands in my jacket pockets.

"If you can't talk about him and all that stuff going on, can we finally talk about Rey?"

I knew she was going to bring her up. I fucking came here because we needed to talk about her, but that doesn't mean I'm ready for it, or even fully want to. I shoot my head up and look back at Sunshine while I'm pleading, "Please. Don't."

She takes a few steps backwards, back towards the tent. I can tell she's over my bullshit, as she won't sit here while I say nothing anymore. Because that's what I did that lead to our divorce. We would have these arguments, one sided really, I would not say a word. She would plead with me to say something, but I would be too overcome with emotions to have any words come out of my mouth. I'd have an entire depot of trains of thoughts in my head, but not a single syllable would escape me.

There's practically a world of distance between us as she calls back to me, "Look, Murph, I still have to help with tear down and I have to try and get donations from the—"

"Sunny," I spit out her name.

My stern tone stops her in her tracks. I've never had an authoritative manner, so the fact that I added some bass to my voice is enough to bring her back to me. But she doesn't come back in a submissive way. She comes back with fire in her heart that she has been wanting to let out. Not helping the hippie flower child look she has going for right now.

"Are we going to talk? Are *you* going to talk?" she spits out.

"You know I can't talk about her." I sheepishly curl back into myself.

"See, it's shit like this that lead to me leaving you."

"I thought it was because I kept cheating on you?" I quip back.

Why did I try to make a joke? Did I think making her angrier would be helpful? How did bringing up my infidelity improve things at this moment?

"If you want to go on believing our marriage ended because you kept sleeping with other women after I left the tour, go ahead and believe that. I didn't really give a shit about what you did on the road. All I cared about was who you were to me. Who you were when we were together. And the fact of the matter is, I was broken after losing our daughter and you refused to help me through it."

"How could I help you when I needed help myself?" I yell at her. I mean, not so much at her, more at the universe. She's not taken aback by my sudden willingness to share though.

"You could have talked to *me* about it!" she snaps back. "We could have worked through it together. Instead, I had to turn to my faith without you."

"Fuck off with your Born-Again shit! I never was a religious guy, and I certainly wasn't going to turn to a god that took my toddler, my daughter, away from me!"

We're screaming at each other enough now that the crowd back at the tent surely must hear us, but those repressed assholes just ignore us as if we're a couple of animals in the woods.

"I don't care that you couldn't pray with me! I just needed you to be there for me! Be there for us! Be a man for me!" She cut deep with that one. "But instead you let Bob save you and you went on without me."

"Well, I'm sorry! I wanted to be a better man, but I couldn't be! I was hurting, and Bob seemed to be the only one who could help me. I didn't know how to deal with it on my own! I still don't!"

"That's the thing." She's suddenly calm and even. "You didn't have to deal with it alone. We should have had each other to lean on." I can see the tears in her eyes being fought back. "You *have* to deal with it. There's no right way to handle grief and pain. You kinda just have to do it. Denial isn't an option if you want to move on."

How did she do it? How does she go from blindingly upset with me to logically nurturing? She could have kept kicking me while I was down. I had pretty much admitted that I was to blame for the disillusionment of our union, and she could have used that to get out all her pent-up rage. But instead, she used the moment of my weakness and vulnerability to help me heal. Why couldn't I have done this when we were still an "us"? She was in just as much pain as I was.

Fuck, what am I talking about?

She lost the little girl she felt grow inside of her. She went through the constant discomfort and pains of pregnancy and the trials of childbirth, only to lose it all. I can never know what that connection was or how she felt when she lost her. And I was too self-absorbed to realize any of that.

"You really are a great person. I really fucked up by letting you go." I make this statement not as a ploy to get back with her, but because I am vulnerable enough right now to speak truths that need to be heard.

Again, she can throw back these words and use them to hurt me, but she chooses a kindness I do not deserve when she speaks to me. "No, you didn't. It was the best thing for both of us."

She says that not knowing what my world has become since she's left it. She may have a new fulfilling life, but I am a husk of a human with no hope on my horizon. If she knew, she wouldn't have said what she thought was a compliment. She grabs my hands and makes sure to look me directly in the eye as she lays out her parting words.

"Just because someone is a great person, doesn't mean they are great for you."

Sunshine kisses me on my cheek before letting go of my hands and turning to walk back to the tent.

"Did Bob ever… to you?" I ask as she walks away.

She doesn't turn around to reply, "No. But that doesn't mean he's innocent."

"That's not why I was asking."

"He's not getting out, Murphy. He's not going to be there to help you through this."

CHAPTER THIRTY-SIX

MURPHY

Before...

I don't understand how someone can buy alfredo sauce

from a jar. Now I'm not trying to come from some place of an

Italian sauce gatekeeper. I'm more baffled by the fact that it's so

easy to make your own, and a fresh sauce always tastes better than

something hermetically sealed. Plus, you get to customize to the

types of flavors you like.

I start mine by not making the sauce right away.

First, I season and cook some chicken breast, and then I'm

frying that up in a pan. Once the chicken is done, I dice it up and set

it to the side as I sauté my shrimp with some sliced kielbasa sausage. Now that my meat is cooked, I can start on the sauce. I drop half a stick of butter on the pan I used to cook my meat to get all the seasoning and meat juice to mix in with a fuck-load of crushed garlic. After that butter's all melted and the garlic is sizzling, I had heavy whipping cream and parmesan cheese with my favorite seasonings. My secret ingredient is red chili flakes and Jerk spice. Obviously, the standard pesto, black pepper, and seasoning salt goes in there as well. Throw the sauce with the meat mixed back in on top of some pasta and you got a mother fucking masterpiece on your plate!

A masterpiece I'm creating for myself...

Only myself...

Just me and a big ass pot full of pasta that I'll be crying into the reheated remnants of for the next few days. I feel like someone online could help me figure out how to make pasta for one, but that's a sad corner of the internet I don't wish to dwell in.

I take my plate of fresh food to stare out the window of my luxury apartment like a brooding Batman. If Batman ever got back on carbs. It's fitting that I'm here at this moment in my life. New

York never felt like home, but then again, neither did LA. But being on the East Coast, trying to be closer to my soon-to-be ex-wife in an attempt to hold of the soon-to-be divorce.

She wants us to go to counseling.

It's not that I don't believe it will help us. It's the opposite, in fact. I feel it will mend what's broken between the two of us. But I don't know if I want that fixed. I know I love her, but she reminds me of my hurt. Her simple act of being is a constant reminder to me of our loss, and I don't know if I'm strong enough to not end up back at my own personal rock bottom. So even though I want to be near her, and I want to continue to be her husband, I have to let her go.

It's what's best for both of us.

I'm all sad and mopey without the alcoholic assist. I need to make myself a cocktail to go with my culinary creation.

I leave my Batman windows to cross back through my apartment that I don't even recognize as my own. I didn't decorate this place at all, some trendy interior designer created everything in here. It's furnished in a cold style that doesn't appear to be lived in, like it's set up for a magazine shoot. Chic white furniture, stone and marble features exude elegance, but is void of any uniqueness. No personal photos on the walls, no clothing dropped in random places, nothing in this home tells you that a person lives here. It might as well be plucked directly from a showroom floor.

The stereo plays Good Life *by Francis Dunnery as I pour myself a glass of whiskey from a matching crystal decanter set. I probably shouldn't make a cocktail with such expensive whiskey, but I'm not gonna be a snob about my alcohols. I've decided tonight calls for a Chicago Kiss, a cocktail I used to order back before I got famous. So, I add some lemon juice with some pomegranate syrup and whatever opened Malbec I have lying around before mixing it all together with the whiskey and some egg white before typically straining it into a coupe glass. But I pour it into a rocks glass, with a big ass ice ball inside it.*

Before I can take my fist sip, there is a knock at the front door.

I wanted a place where the elevator opens right into the apartment, but according to Clark, that is just another thing that looks cool on television but is a pain in the ass in real life. She let me in on how noisy they actually are and that I'd end up hating it and I reluctantly relented to her advice and ended up with a regular door, like any other regular guy.

I open my not-an-elevator-just-a-plain-old-door to reveal the tall, slim figure of Bob, who walks right in past me, grabbing the glass of whiskey from my hand along the way. His dark hair is slicked back like he's an eighties Wall Street douche bag. He tries to look the exact opposite of "Mr. Bob" any time we're not on tour or shooting new episodes.

"Good to see I didn't have to break down a window." He smells the brown liquor before taking a sip. "No bleach this time?"

"Fuck you, man," I reply to his back as he continues to the adjacent kitchen.

I follow as he leans against the marble-topped island, letting the drink slide across it over back to me. "No, seriously, how you are doing?"

"With my wife leaving me?" I sigh. "Great. Just great. Great." I let the exhausted sarcasms escape my lips like a deflated airbag.

"I mean, you seem to be holding it together," Bob says.

"Sunshine is a hell of a woman, but it's tough for any marriage to survive when you go through what we went through."

I shift my eyes and head around, trying to focus on objects in this apartment in order to take my mind off of the lingering thoughts of loss. It's made somewhat easier by the fact that I have no idea what all this stuff in my own apartment even is or where it came from. I didn't even want to mention her, Rey, but it slipped out. Now I have to put all of this effort into suppressing the emotions reaching the surface at the mere mention of my daughter.

I fight back at the tears attempting to build in my eyes.

It's not that I can't let my feelings be known to Bob, it's that I don't want my feelings to even be known by me.

"That's true. I just hope you're doing all right." Bob sees my struggle, and tries to be a friend, but also doesn't want to push me any deeper into a depression that he knows I'm already circling.

"I'm doing as well as I can be. I really just need to forget about all this and move on."

"Okay, buddy."

That's all the confirmation he needs. If he was truly concerned, he wouldn't allow me to change the subject.

"Perfect! Well, I got a tub of Vaseline and a giant bag of cocaine. How about we find something fun to do with it?" I shout at him.

Bob turns his head, looking all around, bringing attention to the fact that we are alone in the apartment before saying, "Not just the two of us, right?"

"You think you've known pain? Bend over, sweetheart. You're about to experience a whole new world of hurt." Bob laughs as I let out a few jabs at his sides. He contorts his body to move away from my poking before he props himself up on the counter and

grabs the glass from me again, taking a sip before exclaiming, "I'll make some calls and get some girls to join us."

The two of us share a laugh as I pour a drink for myself, so we're no longer sharing.

"Can we get some girls that are at least well into their twenties? I'm sick of talking to these nineteen-year-olds that can't hold a conversation."

"What's wrong with young girls? They're from our demo. That's not illegal."

"Dude, it's starting to get gross. Plus, I'm just not in the mood for vapid little girls. Bring someone mature. Someone who knew life before the internet. Who remembers when Facebook updates had the "is" preface."

"I'll see what I can do, but most of my booty call contacts weren't even alive when we started the show."

"You realize that's gonna get you in trouble."

"Don't worry about me. I'm Mr. Bob. I'm America's dad."

CHAPTER THIRTY-SEVEN

CLARK

After...

My cast starts trotting off the stage and begins to get
undressed in the open area behind the curtains. They don't even
remotely have a trace of celebration in their demeanor, having just
finished the last show, wrapping up Ohio. That's not gonna stop me
from wheeling in the big black cart with a rectangular bin on top
filled with ice and boxed champagne. I usually try to close out each
leg of the tour with celebratory bubbly, procuring the finest
sparkling wine I can find from the area. And the best I could come
up with here came in boxed form. Vinny is, of course, the first to
notice my treat and walks over to grab one.

"I didn't know they made champagne in boxes." He looks at the squared drink. "And apparently, they don't. This isn't champagne. This is—" he reads directly from the box, "—Carbonated fermented grape juice."

The wine snob, Murphy, chimes in, "For it to be considered champagne it has—"

"—to be made in Champagne, France," Vinny cuts him off. "Sorry, I meant Prosecco."

"Actually, Prosecco is Italian. Anything outside of those two regions is considered sparkling wine." Murphy counters.

"Can you just not? Just let me enjoy my carbonated fermented grape juice in peace." Even with his eyes closed, you could see Vinny rolling his eyes as he spoke.

"Toledo's finest." I try to play it off like this isn't a complete disaster. But Vinny is having none of my optimism. He sighs as he and Murphy grab a few more boxes to take to Ryan. I abandon my cart and join them with my own carton. The three sit on folding chairs as they drink their "champagne" and take off their costumes.

"Can I ask you guys something?" Murphy says to Ryan and Vinny.

We're all a little puzzled by this question as Murphy is usually the last person to start up a conversation. He's more at home with a snide remark and watching everyone else speak around him. That doesn't stop Vinny from coming back with a quick-witted quip, "I think you already know which one of us is the top."

"Yeah, obviously that's not my question," Murphy presses on. "Did you guys have any idea Bob was capable of? I mean, that he was… you know."

Another question that takes us all by surprise. Murphy asking about Bob in a group setting, as casually as if he's asking about the notes on our wine.

"Murphy, you made us sign an NDA about all of this. We're not supposed to disclose anything regarding our interactions with Bob" Vinny replies.

"*I* didn't make you sign it. That was the lawyers. And that was meant for not talking to the press. This is for me."

"Look, Murph, you and Bob were super close. Don't beat yourself up for not seeing it." Vinny places his hand on Murphy's leg and tries to comfort him.

"Are you saying you knew?"

"No, not exactly, but I can't say that I wasn't surprised. I know you liked hanging out with him and he was "Mr. Bob" for a lot of kids growing up, myself included. He always just kind of gave off an energy that didn't feel right to us. I mean, Ryan never really liked him."

"Really, Ryan?" Murphy directs his questioning to our cool silent friend, who just replies with a shrug and a nod.

"And that was all I needed to know about someone," Vinny continues. "Ryan is like a puppy that way. If he doesn't like someone, there's got to be something wrong with them."

"Are you hearing this, Clark?" He turns the attention to me, trying to save Bob's reputation. But I can't come to his rescue.

"It was kind of this widely known secret around Hollywood. I mean, nobody knew for sure, but we had all heard stories." He doesn't take my response very well.

"You had heard stories about him? Why didn't you tell me?"

"They were just rumors. And I thought you already knew about them."

"So, you're just like the media, thinking I covered up his crimes all these years?" Murphy's starting to get really angry. He tucks his chin to his chest and furrows his brow like a toddler. When he gets this way, I know he's about to storm off and stew in his anger. I can't let him do that because I know it will only lead to his self-harm. His unexplained black eye and bruises from Chicago had finally started to heal, and the last thing I wanted was for him to end up with fresh ones.

"I'm not saying that. We're not calling you Joe Paterno or anything. I'm just saying I thought you knew the same whispers that I knew and dismissed them as bullshit like I did."

"No. I didn't know about him. I didn't know anything. I was kept in the dark like a naïve child."

Murphy takes a big gulp of his boxed wine, finishing it off and chucking it across the open area, narrowly avoiding hitting a backup dancer. As he sits up and walks away, still half in costume, he cracks open another box that had been shaken up from his movement and sprays all over the ground.

I know exactly where he's heading.

Well, not exactly, but I know the type of place he's heading. He's going to go to a strip club. He's going to go to a place where he can guarantee he will have women flirt with him and make him feel good about himself. He needs to have his ego stroked and then he'll pay some stripper to stroke his cock in the VIP room.

I'd chase after him, but I have too much to do with tear down and getting us shipped for New York. We're on our way to the final leg of this tour and frankly, at this point, we could finish this show with his understudy. If he ends up face down in a gutter, choking to death on his own vomit, at least we would be able to cancel the rest of the show. His tragic, untimely death would tie a little bow around the tour. We could run retrospectives of his career in a kinder light, only hinting at the fall from grace near the end. True Joe Paterno style. I'm going to go deal with my own shit and let him run off and sulk like a baby with the whores he wants to throw his money at.

Have fun with your strippers, Murphy.

I'm going to go ahead and take care of me.

CHAPTER THIRTY-EIGHT

CLARK

Before...

The single lane road, barely wide enough for a car to fit all four wheels on it, winds around, hugging the side of the mountain. Blind curves just asking for a head-on collisions from cars crossing fateful paths. The snow still covers everything in sight, excluding the tracks from tires hitting the street. And, of course, I'm the one behind the wheel, praying I don't steer too far and the van slides down the hill. The rest of the cast is in the back, holding their breaths so they don't disturb this driver's concentration.

And just as we round the last corner, the mountains part and they open to the city of Vail, welcoming us for a weekend of skiing and debauchery.

I park the white fifteen passenger van in front of the lodge as the party unloads and stretches their legs. We've pulled up to the luxury cabin with its giant bay windows overlooking the grand scenic view. Murphy and Bob are the first to enter and select their master suites, leaving Vinny, Ryan, myself, and the rest of the hangers-on that came with them on this trip to fight over our own rooms.

I end up right next to the lovebirds, Murphy and Sunshine. Just what a girl needs on a nice relaxing vacation is knowing she's going to have to sleep with a pillow over her head to block out the noise of her ex-whatever-it-was-we-were/boss fucking his new girlfriend all night. I tried getting the room next to Vinny and Ryan, because I already know their sex sounds, and I can't say I wouldn't have enjoyed hearing that, but a couple of the background dancers that the principles actually liked enough to invite beat me to it. I'd be upset with them, but since they're the only ones joining me in singledom this trip, I give them a pass.

I pop my head into the lovebirds' room as an exhausted Murphy flops down on the king-sized bed, letting his legs dangle over the wooden log bedframe. The rest of their suite matches the bed with its wooded rustic feel. Sunshine drops her suitcase next to him, playfully throwing her white winter coat over Murphy's face.

"So, straight to the hot tub?" I ask as Murphy's pulling the jacket from his head. "I need to relax asap after that drive."

"That actually sounds amazing. I nearly had a heart attack coming up here. I don't know how we're supposed to get back down, because I'm not taking that road again," Sunshine replies as she continues to unpack.

"You had a heart attack?" I snort. "How do you think I felt? My whole body is still in an intense knot! There's no way I'm driving that rig again!"

"I guess we live here now," Murphy jokes.

Sunshine pulls her shirt off and changes into her swimsuit. She's one of those girls that has no qualms about being naked in front of another girl. Even if it's a girl who used to bang your boyfriend.

I don't have any ill feelings towards her. She didn't take Murphy from me or anything like that. She was just the woman who came along and received his heart. A heart that wasn't mine in the first place. And to be honest, I was kind of happy to see him happy. I leave them to go back to my room as I can already tell that once Murphy gets up to change with her, the two of them are going to fool around a little bit.

Hey, they're in love and on a romantic getaway. I can't blame them for giving in to appropriate urges. I just need to make sure I'm not there to witness it. I do a quick change to avoid the forthcoming noises from the other room and head out to the deck, where the heat from the Jacuzzi sends out a cloud of steam welcoming me in.

It's already waiting for me, waiting for me to submerge down to my neck in the hot water and wash away all of my small world problems.

I must have been in the water a good ten minutes before I'm joined by the lovers, assuming my knowledge of Murphy's stamina to still be correct. Sunny sheds her shawl and braces against the cold before diving into the hot tub for warmth. She has on this little bikini with little neon sunflowers all over it.

"That's a cute suit, Sunny." I would totally ask to borrow it if I thought I could pull it off. I mean, yes, I'm wearing a two-piece suit as well, but I am not rocking mine like she's rocking hers.

"Thanks! I got it just for this trip."

"You knew there was a hot tub here?" I asked because I had picked up my suit at the airport, with all its fun inflated prices, as Murphy only told me about the jacuzzi after we landed.

"No, I thought we were going to Thailand for the break. Murphy changed the plans to join you guys at the last moment."

"We'll go to Thailand someday. Next break, we'll go."
Murphy defends his choice by pointing out the beautiful sights we
are taking in from the deck. The lodge we are staying at is adjacent
to a cross-country skiing trail that leads right to a mountain slope
with fresh powder from the recent snowfall. We're able to see it all
thanks to the breathtaking one-hundred-and-eighty-degree view of
the valley that lays before us.

We all sit in comfortable silence for a moment, soaking in
the sight as our bodies soak in the water, letting the stresses of the
drive and the world fade away as nothing but the awe of nature
matters right now.

The heat from the hot water hitting the cold air creates a
steam cloud enveloping our heads, and we have found peace in the
contrast of temperatures.

And, of course, all that is interrupted as Bob drops in with
a splash, holding an opened bottle of champagne against his chest
and four filled glasses in his hands.

"Holy shit! Anybody else have to change their diaper after
that drive?" Bob settles in and dishes out the drinks. I should wait

until I see Bob take a sip from his glass before indulging myself.

Something about a secluded cabin in the woods and my general

distrust of accepting a drink from a guy without seeing if it's been

safely made always makes me hesitate. But I'm amongst friends, so I

let my guard down and just enjoy the company.

After we all finish marinating, and a quick, tiptoed run

back inside the cabin from the cold, Murphy helps towel off

Sunshine and Bob attempts to help me, but I playfully, yet seriously,

push him away. Vinny and Ryan pass by us in full ski attire, letting

everyone know they are about to either hit the slopes or just needed

to show off that even under heavy coats we can still see their

phenomenal physiques. I take the mountain fashion show as my cue

to go back to my room to finish drying off and change into my winter

wear to join the boys.

After finally getting a moment to relax, I can take in the

room I have ended up with. And it is like a full-on forest cemetery.

The walls are made of timber trunks stacked and stained on top of

each other with sealant in between the cracks. The bed frame is

various sized logs cut up into rows and screwed together to support the mattress with a side laddered headboard perfectly spaced for the pillows to prop up against. The nightstand is a literal stump that's been epoxy coated with a branch wired lamp sitting on top of it. The dresser is also made of wood, but at least it had been shaved down to boards before being constructed and not just a tree trunk with bark that swings open, but it still adds to the wooded aesthetic.

As I exit the forest funeral and head down the hallway, I pass by Bob's room. The door is ajar, and I can hear a small, muffled crying coming from inside. I peek my head and can see a large, brown leather suitcase propped up on the corner of the bed. I inch in a little closer and swear the crying is coming from the luggage, but the bag is just slightly too small for any person to be inside it, but that crying is almost certainly human.

I've now made my way fully into his bedroom, which is in keeping with the cabin's tree massacre theme, and am at the edge of the bed, staring at the crying bag in disbelief. I reach my hand out to touch it and then suddenly it starts to move ever so slightly, rocking back and forth.

"What are you doing in here?"

At that same moment, Bob has suddenly emerged from the adjacent bathroom and is standing over me like a towering, immortal horror monster. Except, he's wearing a bright red ski jacket that makes him look like a winter lifeguard.

"Nothing! I thought I heard you crying—"

"And you were checking up on me?" The anger in his face has my mind racing and looking for an exit.

"Yes! Well,—not really—I…" My eyes dart from him to the bag that's still moving and crying to get out.

"It's a doll." He snaps at me before unzipping and flipping open the top flap of the bag, revealing several boxes of toy babies. A few of the voice boxes on the dolls let out computerized cries, while others have mechanical arms moving back and forth. "I picked up these donations from the charity event from the other night and have to drop off the donation once we hit Denver."

Understanding the anger in his eyes now makes me cling for the exit even more.

"What? Did you think I had a body in here or something?" *he asks.*

"No! I don't know what I thought."

"Why would I stuff a body into a suitcase and then bring on a trip to a cabin that I'm sharing with a giant group of people?" The more he lays out the foolishness of my snooping, the more I crumble into an embarrassed puddle.

"I don't know! I heard crying and investigated—"

"Investigated? Okay, Carmen San Diego, I guess you're a world class detective, danger following you everywhere!"

"Carmen San Diego was actually the villain; the contestants were the detectives. That's why they were called Gum Shoes." I don't know why I felt the need to correct him after invading his privacy, but I did.

"Get out." He barks.

"Yup!"

I still can't believe I wasn't branded the nickname Gum Shoes for the rest of my life after this incident. But Bob never mentioned it to anybody that weekend. I don't think he ever told anyone about my prying, not even Murphy.

I'm now trudging through the trail, huffing and puffing with each effortful pass of the skis, still mortified by my behavior, when I reach the clearing and gaze out at the mountainside. I can see Ryan, Vinny, and a few others from their party already at the bottom, so I push myself with the poles and glide down the hill.

The fresh, pure white snow billows up as I cut back and forth from side to side, taking care not to go straight down and gain too much speed and lose control. I'm about halfway down when my path is suddenly crossed by a bright red blur. The blur cut so fast by me that it forces a drastic change up in my trajectory.

Unfortunately, I am not the most experienced of skiers and the sudden shift has me lose my balance and tumble. I fall and roll, and fall and roll, and roll some more as I fall for what seems an agonizing and terrifying lifetime before finally coming to a stop, mere inches from a skull-cracking large spruce tree. Covered in a sheet of snow and dirt, I just lay on the ground for a moment, hoping that the reason I'm not feeling pain is because I'm genuinely not hurt and it's not just due to the adrenaline making me numb.

Once I'm sure there's nothing seriously injured on my person, I start to sit myself up. The rest of the party must have seen my crash and have kicked off their skis to run up and check on me. After a few worried remarks and assurances of my physical state, everyone calms themselves and decides to call it a day and head back to the lodge. We all go as a group, finding a nearby ski lift to take us back up.

The rest of the trip was uneventful, though. Aside from the expected drinking, fucking, and general party atmosphere. Murphy did set a pillow on fire when he stuck it in the oven, thinking it was a pizza, but it was quickly put out when we threw it into the snow. The "pizza pillow" would be the main story that emerged from this vacation, that everyone would recall when reminiscing about the good times.

As I look back on that weekend in Colorado, the forgotten moments being lost in my brain and only the highlights remaining, I don't even recall the faces of some of the people who were with us.

These acquaintances who would swim through our lives and then float away into nothingness in our minds. No one commented when one of the girls who had joined us on the vacation had left suddenly near the end. She was one of the attractive women brought to add to the environment, but never really made an impact on the mood or left an impression. It wasn't questioned when she was gone because her absence didn't affect the core party. Hell, I couldn't even remember her name.

Of course, prosecutors who had subpoenaed all of us over the events of this weekend would make sure we remembered her name…

That woman would be the one to set all of this in motion…

She was the first one to come forward.

Her name was Jada.

CHAPTER THIRTY-NINE

MURPHY

After...

I tried finding a strip club, but the few they actually had in

this shit hole town were so depressing, I immediately turned and ran

away after I got a good look at the "talent" inside. You shouldn't

really call them clubs as it was more like a bar with naked ugly, girls

talking to overweight boot and jeans wearing motherfuckers,

complete with neon beer sign lighting and sad country music

blasting. As much as I love *Neon Moon* by Brooks & Dunn, it's

hitting a little too close in this building. So instead, I ended up in

this bar that's supposed to pass for trendy around here but would be

considered a dive anywhere else. It's basically a glorified college hang out with the smell of cheap liquor and chemically cleaned up vomit floors.

I have my shot of whiskey to accompany my beer while I sit and sulk on the farthest stool. I didn't even attempt to look at the selections since I already knew their "top shelf" liquors should be considered crap for the rail at any decent establishment. I wish I could say I was by myself, but a black and white tinted apparition in the form of Bob appears sitting next to me.

"You know what? Fuck Ryan! Who is he to judge me? He doesn't like me? I don't like him! How about that?" The figment of imagination on my right screams as it takes a swig from the fake drink in its hands.

"And what's with Clark the Cunt not having my back? I thought we were buddies? No wonder I never stuck my dick in her," it continues.

I try in vain to ignore the hallucination my grieving mind has created. I take a quick scan around the bar to try and continue to avoid the fact that I'm losing my grip on reality and focus on something, anything else. I spot two guys at the opposite end of the bar talking up a pair of girls and decide they could be a welcomed distraction. The group appears to be in college or at least of that age. Shorts and t-shirts are worn by all like it's practically s uniform.

I down the rest of my expensive-for-Toledo whiskey and stumble to my feet. I don't recognize the song playing over the speakers, but the song coming through in my head makes me dance to my own rhythm as I make my way down to my new friends, beer in hand. I'm hearing something like a choir playing just for me. I'm pretty sure it's that gospel song *It's Gonna Rain* from a Reverend Milton or something like that. It's a standard drunk white guy shuffle happening down here. I've got a strut in my step that the good lord has put there and I'm dancing away my demons.

Unfortunately, Bob, said demon, is still following behind me as I shimmy my ass down the line. A server with a tray full of drinks walks by me so I deliberately flip the tray out of her hand to try and take him out as I keep walking on by, not breaking stride.

And yet Bob is still behind me.

"You really think some broken glass makes me go away?" My subconscious yells back at me as I reach the group at the end of the bar. They've turned to face me thanks to the commotion I just made on my way over to them.

"You two—you two are buddies, right?" I bark out at them, spraying a light mist of saliva from my mouth all over everyone.

"Not tonight, guy," Douchebag Number One says to me as they try to turn away and dismiss me.

"You're sitting at the bar. You don't want to be hassled sit at a table. Everyone knows that." I'm approached angrily by the bartender who just came from behind the well to deal with me. He is a fairly large man in a shirt that is so tight it must have been sized for a small baby. "The fuck is wrong with you? Get the fuck out of here!" The barkeep screams at me as he gets closer.

"Slip the dude a fifty and it'll be fine." Imaginary Bob whispers to me.

I raise my hands up in surrender, so the bartender doesn't accost me. "All right, okay, I'll find some other shithole to get drunk in. There's plenty of terrible places in Toledo." I scoot past the massive man in the tiny t-shirt who served me my beer and make my way towards the exit.

But Douchebag Number Two decides to chime in, "Wait, aren't you the guy in Digg Dogg?"

"Holy shit, he is! That's Digg Dogg!" Douchebag Number One adds.

"Oh, man, how's Mr. Bob doing? Does he miss his old pal Diggsy?" The mocking from Douchebag Number Two stops me in my tracks, and I turn back to the frat bros.

"Now they done fucked up! They don't even know they fucked up, but they about to find out they fucked up!" A now hyped-up fake Bob power walks in circles around me like a break-dancer about to jump in on the next beat.

The musclebound bartender stands in between me and the dickheads, but I put my hands back up as a signal that it's all right and that I'll be harmless, hoping he'll let me pass to talk with them. I pull out the sharpie that I always keep in my pocket for occasions such as this. I mime a signature, so muscle-head gets that I want to give the Douchebag Twins my autograph. Which he accepts and steps out of the way. These common bitches always start to bend over backwards once they realize I'm famous.

"Who the fuck are these two Ohio frat fucks to talk shit about us?! Show them who we are! Show them!" Black and White Bob has now gotten into the asshole twins faces, but they can't see him, obviously, so they pay him no mind.

I approach the boys calmly.

"I wanted to show you something. You probably weren't expecting to see the star of a children's program covered in tattoos, right?" The shit-squirts just smirk, their only response when not understanding where a conversation is going. "You see this one, on the top of my right hand? This one says, 'Be' it's really a continuation of the ink on my knuckles. These letters that start on my pinkie and go all the way down, 'K-I-N-D'. It's a reminder for me to not choose anger with my hands, but to choose kindness, to always remember to *Be Kind*."

The dumb fucks crack some lame joke about me trying to spread rainbows or some shit, but I don't let them deter my lesson.

"Now. Here." I point to my eyes and make them focus on my pupils, "I want you two to look at me right here, okay? Right in my eyes. Because when reporters ask you, and they will ask you what happened, I don't want to hear any bullshit stories. I don't want to hear anything about me sucker punching you."

And with that, I slam my kind fist, wrapped around the sharpie for maximum impact, right into the face of Douchebag Number Two, knocking him to the ground. *It's Gonna Rain* has now been replaced with Wu-Tang Clan's *Ain't Nuthing Ta F' Wit* as the song playing in my head. Number One gets over his initial shock and attacks me as the Goliath liquor slinger behind me grabs us both and tries to break us up. Douche Two gets back up and joins into the scuffle.

I want to believe it all looked like one of those cool bar fights in movies where beer bottles are broken over skull and the entire place erupts in fisticuffs, but it turned out to be more like a couple of drunk white dudes flailing at each other while a bigger dude pulled us apart. Whatever swollen bits from my black eye had healed were now back to bulging after baby t-shirt manhandled me while throwing me out of the front door.

After being chucked outside, tripping and scrapping the side of my face on the concrete sidewalk, I slowly pick myself back up off the ground. The Douche Brothers have devolved into the form of the "backing away and yelling" kind of tough guys as they escape down an alley, asserting their Alpha male dominance by running away. This seems like the best place to remain seated with my elbows on my knees, contemplating how I ended up outside an awful bar in Ohio, of all places.

Bruised, bloodied, and not nearly drunk enough, I know there's only one person left in my life who hasn't completely given up on me yet.

The one person I can still turn to…

CHAPTER FORTY

CLARK

After...

Funny thing about updating your resume, when you've

been doing the same job for the last decade, you'd think you'd have

plenty of things to say about said job. Yet when it comes to my CV,

I have to dance around the fact that I have to explain what I did on

the show without actually naming or giving too many hints as to

what it was.

I'm seated on this questionable hotel bedspread, glaring at

a blank screen on my laptop, with a glass of red wine to accompany

it on my nightstand, as my music plays from the computer. I was

going for light background songs, so I put on The 1975, it started out right with *Be My Mistake* and *When We are Together*, but then it went to *If You're Too Shy*, and right now *I'd Love It If We Made It* is playing. Great songs, but the opposite of background music. So, I switch it over to a shuffle and see what comes up.

I've ditched the blanket and thrown it on top of the adjacent twin bed. I shouldn't be wearing my black tank top and pajama shorts on sheets likely dyed white from all the semen it's accumulated over the years, but I don't have many other options for sleepwear on this trip. I usually only pack the bare essentials for a tour, and shorts and a wife-beater shirt take up minimal space in luggage.

I'm about to give up and drop my computer in my bag for the night when a sudden loud knocking on my hotel room door makes me get up to answer it. Murphy immediately bursts through with a bloodied lip and freshly bruised face to complement his bloody knuckles.

"You carry a first aid kit with you, right, Boss?" is all he gets out as he moves right past me.

"What the fuck, Murphy?"

He rifles through my bags, throwing my unsexy underwear over his shoulder after a quick inspection. I try to stop him and get some kind of explanation out of him, but he just keeps rummaging. He finally comes across the first aid kit and pulls out some bandages that he applies to his knuckles while sitting down on the second bed.

I ask him again what happened to him.

"Just the usual bullshit that comes with being Digg Dogg… Mr. Bob's best friend" Is all I get from him.

I sit on my adjacent bed as he grabs for my bottle of wine situated next to my half full glass.

"What varietal is this?" He looks at the label on the bottle. "How did you get Orin Swift in this shit hole?" he asks before taking my glass and finishing it off. He wipes away a small trickle of wine that spilled onto his chin with the back of his hand. "I'm trying to hold it together, Clark, but I just can't here." He used my real name. He only uses my real name when he's really gone off the deep end. I sit on the edge of my bed as he takes out some gauze from the kit and tries to clean up his face before continuing, "I have no memories here."

"What are you talking about?" I can't understand what he's trying to say, as he's rambling now. But I let him keep going, hoping to get some kind of coherent thought out of there.

"My Bob memories! I am trying to hold on to my life before all this shit hit the fan. I had a great life. We'd shoot some episodes in LA for a couple months, then hit the road and bang our way across the country in a nonstop party."

"So classy." I deadpan as I slowly close my eyes and reopen them in lieu of giving him an eye roll.

"I mean, yeah, gross, but that was my life. For the past twenty years, that was my life. And then it fucking ended. That life was ruined, and that bullshit made it all a lie. Not bullshit. I mean, yes, it was a horrible fucking crime, if it's true. I'm just saying the situation I'm in is bullshit. I'm not even that drunk, what the fuck am I saying?"

"You're not the only one affected by Bob's crimes," I chime in. "I have been with you guys since the very first tour. You don't think I had a life ruined by that asshole?"

"Huh?"

"You don't have a monopoly on fucked-up psyches. Bob was my friend, too. I feel just as betrayed by him."

Murphy stands, looking at me judgingly. "You blame Bob? You think he's guilty?"

I shoot up to meet his face. "Of course, he's fucking guilty!"

"But it's Bob." He pleads with me, but I can't hold in my real feelings about this scumbag anymore.

"Yeah, Bob, the guy who was so creepy, he gave Dahmer a hard on."

"Creepy? How was he creepy? He had women draping themselves all over him!" he replies.

Murphy genuinely didn't see Bob for the pervert he really was. I tried to not see it for a while too. I tried to dismiss what I had heard from others about what he was up to. I feel responsible for not coming forward or confronting him when I could have. But what was I supposed to do? I had no evidence, just feelings. And you can't accuse someone so powerful and influential of something that could destroy their life and reputation on just a feeling. It doesn't matter if the feeling turned out to be true.

"He skeeved on every desperate single mother looking for a father figure for their children. He was the scum of the earth on tour and now the world knows he was scum off of it!" I scream at him, trying to get through that thick skull of his, to make him see the light.

"If he was scum, then why did you stay with the tour?"

Why did he have to ask me that? And why can't I just lie to him? He knows the answer. He's going to make me say it.

"Because of you, you fucking prick!" I grab him by the shirt. It's already in pretty rough shape from whatever mess he had gotten himself into earlier in the night, so I don't care how forceful I have to be. "Murphy, you're the reason everyone loved the show. It's called *Digg Dogg and Friends*, not Mr. Bob's fuck house. You made this show fucking special. You made it a safe place. He fucking ruined it. He did that. And you're too much of a beautiful soul to recognize how he did that for all these years and for what he

367

did to you." His eyes start to well up as he fights back tears, but I keep going. "You keep chasing these memories from a poisoned past. Make some fucking new ones."

I had forgotten about the music still going, even though it's the only thing breaking up our silence. I had ignored most of the song's playing, but *Dark Times* by the Weeknd has started emitting from my laptop now. I don't know why that song stuck out to me, I think it had been playing all of his songs, but that one I remember.

I've said what needed to be said. I finally laid it all out there. As it lingers in the air between us, I can't help but feel a pull. All his talk of memories and who we used to be; I'm reminded of a younger Murphy. Yes, he had abs you could just lick, and a jawline chiseled from marble, but he also wasn't beaten down. He had hope in his eyes. Those memories pull me to him.

So, I pull back.

I pull him by that tattered t-shirt and bring his face to mine, wrapping my lips over his. Our brief affairs in the past never amounted to any kind of passion, just animalistic urges.

But this is different.

We have seen each other's flaws and still we want this.

We never really kissed much during sex before, but now we can't remove our faces from each other's for a second.

My yanking of his shirt is an invitation to take it all the way off. I continue to pull him back against my bed as he grabs the front of my shorts with one hand, clutching them by the fistful, before shoving it with my panties down to my ankles.

I can barely kick out of my bottoms as he lowers himself down and grabs me by the hips, fingers wrapping around to the top of my ass. He pushes my pelvis into his face, and I can feel those same lips that were just on my mouth now tasting me as I grip him by his hair.

He spins me around and we fallback onto the bed, all the while never removing his mouth from my clit. We slide further down so we are fully across the mattress, and I position myself so I am sitting on top of his face. His tongue working its magic as he devours me, and I can't help but grind across that mouth as my pulsating heat forces the rhythm.

His hand slaps my ass just enough to add a sweet sting before grabbing onto my hips again and really pushing me down. The stubble of his scruffy beard rubs my thighs raw. Those hands then slide up and under my shirt, caressing my breasts and lightly rubbing my nipples.

I want more, though.

I want all of him.

I stick my hand down his pants, expecting to have to bring him to attention, but he is already there. His shaft is quivering it's so hard and I marvel at how each stoke of my hand on it brings a pleasure moan from him that vibrates from his mouth to inside me.

He pulls his pants down and I get a good look at it for the first time.

We had always been a little drunk and fumbled around in the dark before. So, I never really got a chance to stare at his cock, but now, with the bedside lamp illuminating our lovemaking, I watch as his foreskin slides up and down between my fingers.

Like a piston from a well-oiled car, the head of his dick emerging from under his skin only to drop back with each stroke. His hands are back down on my hips, using them to throw me down onto my back. He climbs on top of me, and I prepare to take him, but he hesitates.

His dick hovers just outside my pussy, teasing it. He rubs his head on my clit and then pulls back. He slips just the tip inside before pulling back out. He does this again and again, just playing with me, until I can't take anymore, and I grab him by his hips now, wrapping my legs around his ass and I push him deep inside me.

Our Black Hearts pressing against each other.

I let out a gasp as the shock of his full length is enveloped by me and his body hits against mine. I regain my breath, but it's racing to keep up. The heat inside me is boiling over and I need more of him.

He responds with long strokes, taking himself almost all the way out before thrusting back all the way in. The power he puts behind each thrust as he smacks against my thighs practically sends me through the wall.

He grips the collar of my tank top, his fists pressed against my chest before he can't help his desire and tears the shirt down the middle, ripping it right off me and plunging his face into my chest. He's like a rabid animal tearing open its meal as he can't simply take my shirt off, he had to get me naked as fast as possible and went directly after it.

He slides his head back and forth, sucking on each nipple, rotating from one to the other, giving them a slight bite before switching sides. Each tender yet direct nibble, with its pinch of delight, releases a little whimper from my lips.

He slips his hands underneath me, resting at the small of my back so he can roll me over and I'm now on top of him, leaning back and gyrating back and forth.

Those hands start by rubbing my thighs before making their way to smacking my ass again. Each slap sends my slightly startled body to the tip of his dick before sliding back down. Those hands make their way back up to massage my breasts again before reaching the back of my neck.

He grips my head, bringing my face down to him and we kiss again. My ass is bouncing up and down, getting to a fever pitch as our mouths don't dare separate from each other's, aside from the occasional moan and exclamation of 'fuck'.

We finally release our mouths, and my hands are now on his face, holding his head so we stare into each other's eyes.

We really look at each other now. Between the panting and passion, we finally see each other.

I position my legs, so my feet are under me, and I use my thighs to really move along his shaft. Our eyes continue to stay locked as I move faster and faster. The rhythmic smacking of our bodies growing louder and louder, matched only by our moaning.

He slips his hand under my legs and his thumb rests right on my clit, playing with it ever so slightly. His other hand grips around my neck. He's trying to tease me by not applying any pressure, but I'm too far gone to play around anymore, and I press my throat against his palm and choke the air out of myself.

And that's when I feel it.

My whole body begins to quake.

I've had orgasms before. Most of the time, I brought them on myself with a little battery-operated help.

But this is different.

I'm still bouncing, bringing it more and more as I reach my climax and can feel his dick throbbing along with me, building to release. I strain as my legs start to give out and burn from exhaustion, but I can't stop.

My eyes start to water from lack of oxygen, but I love it as the rough grip of his hand around my neck tightens and my hands squeeze his face even tighter.

We lock eyes and see the determination within each other as we keep thrusting, working.

And I can see into his soul.

He sees mine.

I can't take anymore, and at the last second, I pull out from on top of him. A rush of water pours out of me.

I have never cum like this before.

It is a fountain coming out of me, covering his stomach, as he unloads at the same time, shooting his cum into the air and hitting my shaking pussy. I squeak out a few more moans while still half arched over Murphy and am shocked at the sight of the soaked sheets. I don't have time to give a shit, as every inch of me is exploding with delight and twitching muscles.

But I know the afterglow will soon wear off.

I've collapsed with my stomach over his face and my shivering vagina pulsating against his chest. My arms resting on the sorry excuse for a headboard, still gasping from the workout. Plus, having deprived myself of air, all we can do is pant like dogs in heat as we try to recover.

With some time, I've finally caught my breath as my senses start to rush back to my head and I take everything in. The nasty ass sheets we're laying on made dirtier by what we just did.

His probably diseased dick having just gone in raw. Not to mention

how many countless prostitutes and groupies before me passing the

same fluids.

All this and more are hitting my skull as I prop myself up

by my hands on the headboard. My brain is thinking this, but my

body is still on fire. As I look back at that dick, still hard and

glistening from my wetness, I realize I might as well enjoy tonight.

Whatever happens tomorrow won't change by going

another round.

So, I slide my body down bringing my mouth to lick at his

dick's head, just to tease him enough to keep from passing out. I've

never tasted myself on another guy's cock before, but the sweet

stickiness of my juices makes me wish I had done this before.

That's a new degree of narcissism.

On my knees, with my ass in the air, and sucking down to

the base of his body, my lips wrapped around his dick, I open my mouth wider to let my tongue out. Gagging on the head of his cock hitting the back of my throat.

He grabs the back of my head, gripping my hair as he fucks my face harder and harder. I was doing this for him because I want to make sure he stays awake, even though we nearly fucked each other into a coma, but his enthusiastic moans and my guttural noises has me worked up so much I have to slide my fingers between my legs and play with my clit.

Once I'm sure he's not going to fall soft on me, I climb past him and back to the edge of the bed to grab ahold of the headboard, bending back so my ass sticks out for him. My pussy still sticky from where he just shot his load onto it. He takes the invite and crawls up, sliding his cock back into me.

I hold on to that shoddy piece of wood for dear life as he rails into me from behind. He starts with powerful, deliberate thrusts, pulling almost all the way out of me again like before as he's ramming his hips into my ass with solid thwacks.

But he can't help himself and starts to pick up the pace.

He's pumping so fast now.

Faster and faster.

It's like he's hit overdrive and is racing for the finish line with a constant thrusting. I push back against the wall and try to meet his frantic pace as my backside slams against his dick at a furious level.

Between the intermittent ass slapping, hair pulling, and his thumb playfully tickling entry into my asshole, my legs start to shake uncontrollably while my pussy explodes from cumming again. We've completely soaked the hotel sheets now and he pulls out his cock, attempting to shoot his load all over my back. I don't know what compelled me in the moment, but I felt I needed to taste his seed.

It was a split-second decision.

I wanted his cum inside me.

I flip around to bury his dick in my mouth. My face gets hit with the first shots of seamen before I envelope his entire member and take in his load all the way down my throat. The quick change in momentum knocks him backwards onto his back with my face still attached to his waist, all while my pussy still dumps my own cum down in a steady stream onto the bedspread.

He's got his hands at the side of my head, fists gripping me tight as he releases an orgasm that was built up over a lifetime.

His first load may have been the main event, but this second one was the much-needed encore.

Each pulsating ejaculation throbbing past my tongue sends a direct line to my cunt to squirt out its own equal stream as the taste of his pleasure keeps me erupting with each pump.

His shoulders and head dangle over the edge of the foot of the bed. I'm laying with a cum covered face against his hip as his dick spasms against my cheek before going flaccid while our breath returns to us.

I'm giving the side of his fluid-soaked penis gently kisses as my rational brain starts to come back into focus. I realize that even though I am in love with what I am doing, that doesn't mean that I love him.

Or that I ever could love him.

I have love *for* this man.

This man very well might love me. But that doesn't mean anything.

Because as great as tonight is, it can only be tonight…

CHAPTER FORTY-ONE

MURPHY

Before…

I'm sat behind a folding table, clean shaven and trying to look all presentable and shit. As if I wasn't still smelling like the groupie that sat on my face last night. Next to me is Bob wearing business casual attire in order to make one of us look professional. Seeing as his partner's outfit could only be described as 'homeless chic', since I'm in a tattered hoodie and stained sweats with my black painted toenails visible thanks to the flip-flops I got on.

Hey, at least I shaved and combed my hair.

Across from us, seated in a plastic chair, is an eager looking young woman in a violet business casual pantsuit. We're all inside a nondescript, white walled room. It's one of those shared space offices that are rented out for temporary purposes. We pass back and forth her resume, glancing over her credentials as we try to appear like we know what we're doing. When in the reality of this interview, she's the one we're trying to impress. We need her to take the job because we need her more than she needs us.

"I'm sorry, I am extremely white, and I don't want to further wave my Caucasian card by butchering your name. How do you pronounce it, miss?"

"It's Caihong, but you can just call me Clark if it's easier for you honkies." Her eyes go wide as beach balls when she realizes we're not close enough yet for insults. "I'm so sorry—"

"Don't. You'll find out quickly we like to bust each other's balls here. Jokes will get you far." I shoot her a side smile to put her at ease.

"And you were an assistant tour manager for Sesame Street? *How was that experience?" Bob throws out the obvious question.*

"It was a wonderful time for me," Clark answers with a genuine smile as her face lights up at the mention of her previous employment. "I started working at the Children's Television Workshop as an associate producer in the production department for the broadcast and when the position on the touring company came up, I jumped at the chance to take another step in my career."

"So, what makes you want to leave The Street?" I ask.

"The Street? I like that." She shoots back a side smile to me before continuing. "Um, well, I don't actually want to leave. Working at Jim Henson Studios, they all hold this special reverence for the job they're doing because of what it means to people. But, for one thing, I want to lose the 'assistant' title and really get a chance to run my own tour. And everyone's been there so long they're kind of entrenched in those roles." A few strands of her long, straight black hair fall in front of her eyes. She tucks it back behind her left ear, struggling to decide if she wants to express her next thought. "To be honest, the opportunity to work for you guys is the real reason why I want this job."

"Us?" I'm taken aback by this. The show has only been on for two seasons now, and even though it has been a solid success so far, I wouldn't consider it anything special. I'm still not used to anybody complimenting my creative side.

"I feel like Digg Dogg is going to become one of those legacy children's programs. Those shows that live on with us from when we're kids to passing it on to our own children. Like one of the few generations spanning programs. It's something I would love to be a part of from the beginning."

"Flattery will get you everywhere." I make the quick quip in order to deflect the positive attention. "One last question. If you had to choose a superpower, would you want flight or invisibility?"

Clark just smirks as she thinks to herself for a second.

"I know you have a degree in child psychology. I've done my research on you guys. I should answer flight going with Maslow's theory of self-actualization to make myself look good, but I honestly would say invisibility."

"Why's that?" Bob asks.

"As most assume, choosing invisibility, you're embracing your shadow, but I see it as a way to simply not be seen. I don't care if I come off as conceited, but I understand that I am an attractive woman. I'm sure you two, as celebrities, can understand the desire to be able to live your life without eyes fixed on you."

Bob and I are so taken aback we can only simply nod our heads in agreement.

"Do you have any questions for us before we finish up?" Clark doesn't have anything to add to follow Bob's question. So, we all stand and shake hands, sporting the usual, "You'll hear from us" line that is said at the end to leave interviewees unsure of their standings after the process.

Clark exits the office, as me and Bob sit back down to discuss her as a candidate.

"So, what do you think of her?" Bob throws it out there first.

"Nice dumper. Tits are pretty solid, too," I passively exclaim as I pretend to study her resume again.

Bob snatches the paper from my hand. "We're looking for a tour manager. Not someone to stick your dick into."

"She can't be both?"

"This is our first tour." Bob turns serious. "We get this one right; we'll be doing them every year and we're set for life. The show could go off the air and we would still be able to make a fuck load of cash on the road. So, we have to pick a tour manager that's going to ensure the clocks run on time and we don't end up in the wrong city."

"I mean, she has the credentials." I state.

"She does. But I don't want her on the tour if you're going to keep trying to fuck her. That's a lawsuit waiting to happen."

"I'll behave." I give him a condescendingly sheepish look.

"I don't know. Let's keep looking." Bob shuffles through a stack of resumes, perusing each one. "She's a front runner for sure, but let's see who else we got before we decide. I'm not certain a nice pair of legs you can't stop drooling over is going to be the one that works out for us."

"Honestly? You don't have to worry about me and her."

CHAPTER FORTY-TWO

CLARK

After...

Why would they install a headboard this uncomfortable?
Better yet, why would they even make a headboard that's
uncomfortable in the first place? You'd think the whole point of a
headboard is to provide a comfortable spot for your head. Of the
millions of questions rattling around in my dense skull, this is the
least important and yet the most persistent. I try to adjust as much as
I can, but with a naked tattooed man sleeping on my lap, it's kind of
hard to move my neck off this slab of wood resting between the wall
and my head. The only respite is how his slow breathing kind of

calms my mind. For the slightest of moments, I am actually able to concentrate on the white noise his body is making.

But those moments don't last long as I'm back to the regrettable thoughts of what I've just done.

So fucking stupid.

On so many fucking levels.

I need another distraction, something to help me sleep.

I trace my fingers along his tattoos. I remember he told me a big reason for getting so much ink was because he had heard a rumor that Mr. Rogers had his arms tatted up from his time in the military, that's why Fred always wore long sleeves.

It turned out not to be true, but that didn't matter to Murphy. He preferred the story. I'm guessing because he wanted to find some kind of flaw in his idol. Not that getting tattoos is a flaw, but that he had a secret that he hid from the world. Murphy has always felt inadequate when it came to his place in the world. After all the years of success and accolades, he still always felt like a fraud. Like any minute, he was going to be found out. Turns out it wasn't him with the secret.

My fingers slowly slide over the mural on his back. A giant sun, swirling in a Van Gogh style of reds, yellows, and oranges, as the line of each ray stretches across his body. My index finger follows the path of a single ray as it flows over his shoulder and disappears into our pressed flesh. I know where that particular line ends over his heart as it curls into a cursive "R".

I wasn't there for him when she died. The season's tour had ended, and I was back in New York while he was filming new episodes in LA. I should have been there. I should have flown out and comforted him in his time of need, but I was so caught up in getting the venues and dates locked up for the next tour.

I was- fucking hell- I was looking into long-term understudies to cover in case he couldn't bring himself to do the show before I even offered condolences.

I'm such a good friend...

I make my way back to the tattoo's central circle before branching back out with a line that follows around to his hip. I can't reach any farther, and frankly, I shouldn't with that ray. That one continues down towards his thighs and I've already gotten into enough trouble in that area. That ray ends up circling around the small bleeding blackheart inside his hip. I think about the matching one on me. The ones we got together a while ago, back in Chicago.

Back when we were happy.

I make the mistake of grazing my finger over the path on his ribcage. The one that morphs into a portrait of a Boston Terrier. Not the cartoonish kind that Digg Dogg is, but a real life canine. It must have been the inspiration for the character. All these years knowing him, and I never asked about where this creature came from. His body shudders lightly from the soft tickling I've unknowingly elicited.

Murphy slowly starts to stir awake. His shaggy brown hair that contrasts with his hazel eyes, I hoped to get that smile of his, the one that he used to have that would show across his entire face. But now he's sat up in front of me, no smile to be seen, just a million thoughts in his own dense skull. I rack my brain to come up with what I'm going to say to him once he's fully coherent. I have to let him down gently so we can still maintain some sort of professional relationship.

Do I want to let him down though?

That's the smart thing to do, right?

But then again, I haven't really been making smart decisions lately. This is what I've been struggling with for the last few hours while he slept hard and peacefully on top of me. And I still don't have an answer to any of it, but I run through it at a million miles an hour as he starts to move back to life and props himself up.

He rubs the sleep out of his face as he sits up to face me. He must have forgotten about whatever fight he had gotten into last night that made his face all swollen because he winces from accidentally rubbing a tender spot. After his pain subsides, he stares at me.

We're staring at each other.

It feels like this moment drags on forever and yet it's also a split second as I try to find the words that need to be said. Instead, we continue to stare at each other, not saying anything. He breaks the silence first with a perfect eloquent thought.

"Hey."

"Hey."

That's all I can muster back at him. In one word, we express all of our love and hurt. With a single word, we acknowledge what has happened and where we are now. That one word meant everything and nothing all at once.

Am I fucking high?

Can you get a sexually transmitted contact high?

What the fuck am I thinking?

I should be saying everything I have had on my mind since he last pulled his dick out of me and came all over my stomach. If it wasn't for the crusted cum on my chest, I wouldn't believe we had sex that many times before passing out from exhaustion.

I should be unloading my thoughts onto the one person

who needs to hear it the most. But instead, we stare at each other.

Letting a single word do the talking for us. He moves in to kiss me. I

don't know if it was a kiss of love or a kiss goodbye. I will never

know because I stop him, gently grabbing his face before resting my

forehead on his. My body has betrayed me in so many ways tonight

and now it's doing it again as the tears start to well up in my eyes,

letting a few streaks out down my cheeks. I bite my lower lip to

fight them back to no avail as the only response I can give Murphy

is a strained headshake, letting him know I can't.

He can only look down, dejected, but eventually he gets up

from the bed.

I sit up, cradling my arms around my knees, my chin

tucked under them. I watch as Murphy gathers his clothes and gets

dressed in silence. He grabs another roll of gauze and some Band-

Aids from the first aid kit, holding it up so I know he's taking it with

him before heading towards the door.

I grip my legs tighter, holding myself back from leaping off

this bed and telling him to stay. I don't see him leave. All I catch is his body disappearing down the bathroom hallway. I hear the door open, but I still haven't heard it close. It's gone past the normal delay that comes with it swinging shut behind him.

I know he's standing in that doorway.

I don't know if he's turned around or is still facing the hallway, but I do know he's standing there. I know he's struggling to walk away because I'm struggling with letting him. I honestly can't say that if he were to walk back into my room, take me in his arms and try to kiss me again, that I wouldn't let him. I'm about two seconds away from chasing after him, not caring that I'd end up in the hallway completely naked.

But then I hear it…

The door closes.

I wait…

Still wanting him to come around that corner. That he stayed in the room. Wanting him to come back and talk to me, kiss me, be here with me. I want him to come back and get his shit together, to stop destroying his body, mind, and reputation, to go back to being the Murphy I knew.

But he doesn't.

The door remains closed.

And I'm alone.

Alone in a garbage hotel room.

In a garbage place, physically and mentally. I am alone and so I stop holding back. The tears flow freely now. I let it all out because I am by myself and can full-on ugly cry.

And then there's a knocking.

I don't want to answer, but there's another knock.

My hesitation is over, and I spring up from the bed, going directly to the door and throwing it open…

And I find Vinny standing in front of me as Ryan leans his back against the far hallway wall, looking effortlessly cool as always. There's a pause as we all stand frozen in shock at my naked, disheveled look. They're both dressed in nice suits that are a little rough for wear since they must be coming back from a night out having partied straight through to morning.

"So, I was about to give you shit about seeing Murphy leaving your room…" Vinny trails off, speechless for the first time in his life, I'm sure. He wants to get the dirty details, but my tear-soaked face breaks through our shallow surface friendship and makes him consider my feelings. Ryan pushes himself off the wall and slides off his suit jacket, slipping it around my shoulders to cover me up as we all step back into my hotel room.

I sit back down on my bed while they take seats next to me on the mattress. I should throw on my own clothes and give Ryan his coat back, but I'm too distraught to do anything sensible like that.

They let me speak first, when I'm ready, and I tell them everything I should have said to Murphy. How complicated everything is and how it can't work between us. How last night was a mistake that shouldn't have happened.

How it was so. God. Damn. Good.

The connection between our bodies was unlike anything I had ever experienced. We have become such close friends, having talked so much about our sex lives over the years, that when we finally got back together, we knew exactly what the other wanted done. But that fucking asshole is such a piece of shit right now that I can't get sucked into his world any more than I already am. And that really fucking sucks because we could really be awesome together.

When I finish, I expect to hear some kind of advice, but I get nothing. Ryan turns to Vinny and just gives him a look. Like some kind of secret code, that apparently only they know.

My two boys get up and pull me to my feet. We each hug tightly before they leave me with a kiss on the temple. I should feel abandoned, but instead I feel comforted, heard. I got all I was feeling off my chest and got the release of emotions I needed.

Plus, Ryan left his jacket. Free coat!

I sigh.

Fuck my life.

CHAPTER FORTY-THREE

MURPHY

After…

Is it possible to be both suicidal, depressed, and mind-numbingly horny at the same time? In the age of the internet, I'm sure that's pretty common. I woke up, and all I wanted to do was take her in my arms and hold her tight. I wanted to just stay there, inside her. Clark has always been a safe place for me, but I didn't realize how good it felt to be even closer to her. I'm not bragging when I say I've had more than my fair share of sexual encounters with different partners, but nothing compared to my time with Clark. This woman is stunning. It's the little things, like the way she will turn down her chin making her eyes get closer to you, so she can really look at you, connect with you.

Whatever that was that ignited between us could not be put out, at least that's what I thought. All I wanted was to see her get more and more pleasure. My own ego got off on how she enjoyed what I was doing.

Yes, my ego was placated by her arousal, and I genuinely cared that my friend was satisfied.

None of that matters anymore.

I seem to be saying that a lot lately.

It was all just a moment that didn't mean anything in the end. A great highlight of my life ruined by events after the fact. At least the figment of my imagination in the shape of a black and white Bob had the decency to keep its mouth shut as it followed me down the hallway after leaving a beautiful, naked woman alone in her bed. We walk in silence for a good hour because I can't bring myself to be alone in my room yet. We circle the hallway, imagining that the people on the other side of the walls are walking with us. Almost by accident, we end up back in front of my own room, met by a waiting couple. Ryan is sitting on the ground crossing his legs as Vinny lays with his head in his lap.

I don't know why they're here, and frankly I don't care. These boys have passed out in front of my hotel door plenty of times thinking it was their own, frustrated because their incorrect key wasn't working. But this time they actually look relatively sober, almost like they were expecting me.

"We're going to have to talk about this on the road," Vinny says as he pushes himself up off the ground. "Grab your shit. We're going to drive to New York."

"Why do we have to go now?" I ask. I knew we would be driving; we've taken vans everywhere this tour since airports are a paparazzi hotbed that are off limits to me. But I figured we wouldn't hit the road until at least late afternoon, Clark usually schedules around my expected hangovers.

"Because we have to take a quick detour along the way." He replies.

I ask what kind of detour because when it comes to these two, it could mean anything from a quick snack at a gas station to jumping out of a plane over Milan before it crashes and then landing at a midnight mansion rave hosted by a fake Middle Eastern

Princess with a coke and pill problem while her jilted lover's

security force is trying to kill us, and we have to escape through a

set of underground tunnels, only to find ourselves hiding out in a

local's yurt being served pancakes, but still make it back in time for

curtain call.

Both are probable possibilities due to the fact that they've

already happened multiple times. Though not in Milan every time.

We somehow meet in the middle and end up in Pittsburgh, PA. I'd

never been to the city, so I didn't know what to expect, but as we

shot out of those bridge tunnels and the skyline opened up with the

sun's reflection shining off the river, I couldn't help but brighten up

my spirits, if only for a minute.

We park in a large structure, and they take me down a set

of sidewalk turns until we reach the destination. A small,

nondescript museum with no real indication of what kind of exhibits

it holds inside. I'm able to infer by some of the bold lettered signs

hanging around the arched doorways that it's a children's museum.

Because I am very observant when it comes to the obvious. I pay for

the three of us and expect to find some kind of introspective on my career, with the Bob sections edited out. I'm not sure if I approved

of anything like this being displayed, but I probably signed off on it

when I was coked out and grieving.

Yeah, that's not what this is.

This is Mecca for someone like me.

I mean, aside from Amsterdam's Red-Light District. This is

a *Mr. Roger's Neighborhood* exhibition that has been here for

longer than I've been around. I can't hold my emotions inside at the

twist of expectations and start to choke up un-ironically. We split up

because I have to take in the displays through my own journey. I

pass by plaque after plaque after glass structure after video message,

each one shedding more light on the man that shaped myself and so

many others in immeasurably positive ways.

I'm observing a framed photo of Fred and a black

policeman dipping their feet into a little kiddie pool and read about

what this televised moment meant in educating racial equality, when

Ryan walks up next to me. We don't have to exchange eye contact

to appreciate the picture while we both examine its relevance.

So many feelings about this place run through me that I finally have to share them with my friend. "This man." I point to the smiling Mr. Rogers. "Can you believe Mr. Bob was supposed to be based off of him?"

Ryan just gives me a smile while still focused on the display.

"Of course, our version never even came close to doing the original any type of justice with its homage. We were just a cheap imitation. And now…" I can't keep going without letting out a sigh. "I don't even want our show associated with Fred. I don't want to tarnish him with our bullshit."

"Did I ever tell you how I used to work as a wrangler on *Sesame Street*?"

I have to look around and behind him, to double check that wasn't somebody else's voice coming from Ryan. I can't actually recall ever hearing his voice before, so I'm a little taken aback. I've heard him say his lines and sing songs, but those were in a Kitty Kelly voice that sounds nothing like the silky baritone coming out of this tiny man.

I try to play it cool, though. "Yeah, I think I remember. Clark brought you in, right? She worked with you there."

"Back then, I got to know Carroll Spinney pretty well." Ryan is still focused on the photo and hasn't given me even a cursory glance.

"Shit. What was it like working with Big Bird?" I ask.

He smiles, thinking of a pleasant memory before slightly turning his head to me. "He was a sweet soul. He knew what he meant to children all around the world. It's something you need to understand again."

"It doesn't matter what I meant to people, Ryan. I don't mean anything to anyone anymore. It's all been ruined." I let out the huff that always accompanies my little rant.

"Art cannot be ruined."

I want to let his profound sage advice wash over me like a gay Dalai Lama, but I can't let it be. "Sure, it can. I mean, what do you do when the art you love was created by a monster?"

"It's still the art you love. It might have an asterisk now. You might see it in a new light. But it is still the art you loved. It still had an impact on you."

"So now my whole legacy, my whole career has an asterisk by it? How am I supposed to love that?"

He doesn't give me the answer I'm looking for. He takes a moment to let me sit in my self-hatred as his attention is back on the plaque that we've been focusing on for the last twenty minutes.

"Carroll used to tell me stories about working with Jim Henson. And how he didn't just leave one show as his legacy. How he kept pushing to put more of his creative self out there."

Ryan points to the display next to us. I hadn't noticed it before because I was distracted by my own self-pity. I don't get a chance to study it as he's already reading it out loud to me.

"Fred Rogers wrote a reply to every single piece of fan mail he ever got. A personal letter to every piece of mail. Every. Single. One." He turns and points his finger right at me. "Digg Dogg is only a small part of you, Murphy. You still have so much to give to this world. Keep pushing."

Ryan walks away, leaving my devastated with my attempted comprehension. Vinny walks up to observe the crumbled human being left in his lover's wake. Although he doesn't pay me any attention as he approaches, being just as aloof and looking at the display we were just observing.

"You look like you had a little talk with Ryan."

"I don't think I've ever heard him say more than two words."

"Yeah, he doesn't say much, but when he does…" Vinny smiles to himself before turning to walk away, leaving me, like everybody else does, but he stops to turn back for a second. "Have we ever talked about why I loved Digg Dogg? Why being a part of this tour, all these years has been my dream come true?"

"This is your dream?" I look around befuddled, then realize we're not at our theater and the looking around gesture meant nothing.

"Yes, dream come true. Sure, *The Digg Dogg Show* was always entertaining, and the songs were catchy. But it was this one episode..."

I can see a sincerity from Vinny that makes me uncomfortable. I'm so used to straight snark coming from his mouth that something genuine scares me.

Vinny continues, "An episode with a message of love and equality, teaching children that gay people are just as normal and that they deserve to love and be loved just like everyone else. You had people from the Keith Haring and Ryan White Foundations on to teach everyone about AIDS and, in doing so, pushed not to be afraid of gay love. I can tell you I am not alone when I say that was something special you did. You let every little queer child know that they weren't confused, they were true and valued and loved..."

The narcissist in me should be doing back flips, but the weight of my actions keeps me humbled. I hadn't realized the impact I had made. I knew we had fans and made money, but when something like that hits you, your soul becomes full.

Too bad my soul is made of dogshit.

"You didn't have to, but you did." Vinny's still going. "You fought Bob to make that episode at a time when it was almost guaranteed to cause backlash, but you did it anyway because you knew it was a message that needed to be heard. And then the season after you lost your daughter…"

I want to cut him off.

I want him to not say a thing about my dead child.

I want to punch him in his fucking face for bringing her up.

He can sense this and chooses his words carefully. "You were going through something most could never recover from. And despite all that, you went out and you continued to care for those that looked up to Diggsy. You wouldn't let them down. Everyone knew you weren't continuing for the money, but because helping others helps you. It's the same reason why this tour is still going, not for your own good, not so you can keep whoring around, but because *you have* to do good for others."

He finally completes his path and turns to leave me. I want to follow and argue that I was so fucked up on OxyContin during the aftermath filming, but that would ruin his point.

Well, that's not completely accurate. I mean, I did kind of throw myself into work to distract from the pain I was going through. It was some of the most rewarding work I had done during that stretch, too. But fuck him for thinking I had risen above adversity. I just got through it is all.

I wasn't a fucking hero.

I'm barely a survivor.

I wait for him to turn around and give me one last jab, but he just keeps walking, letting the shot ring out without even looking back at me as he says, "I mean, we can all see it. Every time me and Ryan forced you to perform something other than the same ten songs you've done twice a day for the last two decades, we'd see that spark in you. The spark that made us fall in love with you in the first place."

And with that, he leaves me to stare at a nearby plaque with the simple, yet perfect quote from Fred…

"Look for the Helpers."

CHAPTER FORTY-FOUR

MURPHY

Before...

Boom. Boom. Boom.

The pounding comes quick and loud.

Boom. Boom. Boom.

It comes again with even more urgency.

This time, it's accompanied by muffled yelling from the other side of the door. The glass panel directly to the right is shattered by a bloodied fist breaking through and clearing out the debris around the edges. The hand belongs to Bob as he reaches in and unlocks the entrance. Bob calls out for me as he explores the empty house. It used to feel inhabited. It used to be a happy home for me... .

For Sunshine...

For our daughter.

Now it's in such a desolate state that it only houses a few random pieces of furniture that were left behind as trash along with the actual garbage on the ground.

I watch as Bob grabs a random dish towel he comes across on the counter and wraps his bloody hand. He's still unaware of where I'm at so he yells out again for me, this time expressing Sunshine's concern. She had flown back to New York to arrange the funeral. We'd wanted Rey to be buried at the cabin we'd owned upstate. We'd actually had many of the arrangements set up prior to her official death.

Already had the funeral announcements printed.

I had gone almost catatonic though. I couldn't bring myself to get out of bed, so Sunshine left with a promise to check in. But

*I'm guessing since she hadn't heard from her husband in days,
dispatching Bob to check up on me became a priority.*

*Bob's still scanning the house before stopping dead in his
tracks when he finally comes across me. It's like when you enter a
room so filled with emotion it's like a wall hits you. Like when you
come home to an angered spouse and their rage sucks the air out of
the room. My emotional wall is emanating from my pathetic body
sitting on the floor, my back against the far wall. I'm not looking at
Bob. I'm staring, painfully, at a whiskey glass filled with a clear,
yellowish liquid, too light to be alcohol.*

Next to the glass is a bottle of bleach.

*Bob sits down on the floor next to me, leaning his back
against the wall. "I can't—I can't even begin to know how hurt you
are right now—"*

"She's gone," I blurt out.

*These are the first words I have spoken since the loss of my
daughter.*

414

Bob nods, trying to listen. He had tried to call and sent a text the moment he had heard of Rey's death, but this is the first time he's been able to come face to face with his best friend since the tragedy. I had pretty much shunned any attempts at condolences from anyone. I had secluded myself away and had silenced my phone for the entire week. And by silenced, I mean I threw it into the ocean after the hundredth 'So sorry for your loss' text.

"I... I was the one man in this world who was supposed to protect her... Fathers are supposed to keep their little girls from harm... I failed her." I can't hold back the tears that streak down the sides of my face. Not that I was trying to. I'd long given up on controlling my liquids.

Bob turns to look at me but says nothing.

I continue to shout. "I failed as a father! I couldn't even be a dad for more than three years!"

"You didn't. There was nothing you—"

"She's dead because I—"

"You can't blame yourself for this. It was—"

"Stop saying that! That's what everyone said! I don't need to hear that from you!" We keep interrupting each other. Bob trying to comfort his friend, but I just keep trying to justify my next move.

I lunge for the whiskey glass. I know what it will do to me, to my body. The bleach in that cup will burn through my throat and erode my stomach. I'll choke on my own blood and bile and die a slow, painful death. It's what I want, what a piece of shit failure deserves. I can't bring myself to continue with the rest of my life after losing a part of it already. My raw, exposed nerve was destroyed and now I want to do the same thing to the rest of me.

Bob dives after me, knocking the glass from my lips and pushing the plastic jug out of the way. The two of us wrestle on the floor as I continue to try to get my hands on the bleach. I scream for him to let me go, to let me relieve my pain. He finally gets a firm hold on me by hugging my arms to my sides and locking his legs around my knees. He grips me tight from behind in order to calm me, blood from Bob's hand spilling all over us. He may have me trapped, but I continue to fight. As I squirm, he starts to sing to calm me. He sings in a low whisper, barely audible over the struggle.

416

"Sunny days, sweeping the clouds away. On my way to where the air… is… sweet. Can you tell me how to get… how to get to…"

It's at this moment that I breakdown into a full sob. Whereas the water coming from my eyes before was slow streams, now I've let the dam break free and am in full on ugly cry mode. The struggled fight I was putting up has faded.

Bob continues, "Come and play… Everything's A-Okay… friendly neighbors, that's where we'll meet… Can you tell me how to get… How to get to *Sesame Street*… How to get to *Sesame Street*."

I've turned so that I can embrace him back. He's holding me like a newborn baby, which is fitting on many levels, from my crying to the fact that I will emerge from this encounter anew.

Still the same old piece of shit, just new.

We come into this world as screaming little balls of pure emotion and that's what I am now.

Pure emotion.

Bob loosens his grip since I've stopped fighting, but I cling to him as I start to hyperventilate from crying too hard and not breathing.

Bob holds me tight again.

The two of us lay on the floor, in each other's arms as the blood and tears smear between us. Nobody gets to know what kind of bond that forms. To be unafraid to be that vulnerable with another human being, let alone between two hetero men.

Two friends.

One needing the other.

One being there for the other.

Two friends. A moment.

For only us.

CHAPTER FORTY-FIVE

MURPHY

After…

The thing that most people don't get when frying Brussel sprouts is you have to over season the fuck out of them. This little plant will not absorb the seasoning unless it is overloaded with everything you've got. I usually cut out the hearts and then place the leaves in a shallow pan with olive oil, garlic, and a shit ton of spices. After they're all cooked up, I drizzle a nice balsamic vinaigrette and some shaved parmesan, and then I've got a bomb ass side dish.

I'll work on the sprouts after I finish dropping the chicken in the oil, which is still heating up. I've battered and breaded the chicken breast with its own complimentary seasoning, making sure

not to get any excess flour on my marble countertop. A quick slide
into the pan so I don't splash the hot oil everywhere and we are
cooking now. I would normally make some russet potatoes to go
with this dish, but I'm trying to cut back on the starches. I've got
Colin Hay playing on vinyl through the speakers that are wired all
over my apartment, and right now it's on *Waiting for My Real Life
to Begin.*

As everything cooks, I fix myself a cocktail. I usually
prefer to make myself a Manhattan when I'm back in the city, as it
seems so apropos, but I decided to switch it up with an Old
Fashioned. I start by dropping a single sugar cube into my glass
mixer. After a few dashes of bitters, I drop two brandied cherries in
and muddle it all together. Now after that is when I add the whiskey.
Some people don't like a muddled Old Fashion, but I strain it out, so
that it's not like a fucking salad in a glass. I stir it all up with a bar
spoon before pouring it over a big ice ball resting in my highball
glass. You have to use ice in an old-fashioned, so the big ice ball is
the only time I'll accept it. I use the spoon to stir it up again to chill
the drink and then grab an orange from my fruit bowl. I peel off part

of the skin and take out a lighter from a drawer. A few flaming orange zests over the glass, followed by a rim wipe and it's ready to go.

With my greens and chicken breast finally done; I sit at my table in my New York apartment. The first big thing I purchased for myself with the Digg Dogg money was this apartment overlooking Central Park with its giant windows and posh interior.

I thought a glass of whiskey with my meal would help me to eat in silence, but my own thoughts seem to keep me from peace.

"Yeah, I made my fucking fried chicken," I yell out into the void of my empty space. I try to distract myself by playing some music on my speaker, switching out the vinyl.

It doesn't work.

I'm still agitated.

"Just leave me alone!" I scream.

I can't see him, but I feel his presence. That black and white imaginary version of my friend, saying everything he would normally say to me about how pathetic I am right now, eating alone in my giant penthouse all by myself. He'd make fun of me for having all my wealth, yet there's no one here to share it with.

The conjuring does not appear.

Probably because the lock on the front door starts to turn instead, and it opens to reveal Clark walking in.

"Wh-When did you get a key to my place?" I ask.

"I've got all your keys. How do you think you end up with gift baskets at every hotel?" she snaps back at me. She's wearing the same black tank and jeans she's always in on tour along with the ponytail, but it almost seems like she's got makeup on, more so than her regular base. Her features are softer, her edges look to be glossed over.

"What are you doing here?" I ask.

"I know we're going through our whole complicated thing right now, but can we just put a pause on that? There's something I need to show you." She takes out her phone and hands it to me. I never noticed she has the same phone as me. It's frozen on a bright image with black all around it. A singular sideways triangle at the center lets me know this is the start of a video. I press play on the screen and see a shaky display move itself into focus.

"This is the video of you comforting that kid on stage in Chicago, the one that had just lost her dad. Somebody in the audience caught it on video and uploaded it a few days ago. It's racked up almost three million views already." She's explaining to me what I am already watching, what I've already experienced, but this feels different. It feels like this profound moment between me and the child, with only the sparse audience in attendance, is now out there for the world to see.

As I continue to watch, Clark walks over to a chair and sits across from me. She takes her thumb and index finger and picks at my food, eating small scraps. She has an upbeat, almost bouncy quality to her that I haven't seen in over a decade. It's like a new energy has been poured back into her soul.

"I think it's time you talk about Bob," she tells me between bites.

"I thought you wanted me to stop thinking about him. Now you want me to talk to you about him?"

She meets my gaze.

"Not to me. You need to do an interview with someone, some news outlet and get your side out there. You could do network, cable, internet. Hell, even a podcast could be cathartic. Everyone wants to talk to you. You can have your pick, but you have to do it if you're ever going to move on."

"I thought the studio lawyers wanted us to all plead the fifth on this one?"

"That was back when the media was out for blood. This video has swayed public opinion back to your side."

I take a drink of my whiskey to buy myself time to think. What she's saying is almost exactly what I have in my head. It's what I feel I need to do. Hearing it come from Clark, though, is just the validation I was looking for.

So why am I hesitating?

I guess maybe I'm scared to finally let the truth about Bob be spoken. The last sliver of hope that I have that this was all a big misunderstanding, and thar my friend will come back through my door any moment now. But I know, deep down, that's not going to happen. Because, as much as I don't want to admit it, I know he's guilty.

"I'll call the lawyers and then have my publicist get something set up."

She's happy with my decision and keeps picking at my food. "This is some pretty good chicken."

"I know," I say with complete confidence in my own culinary skills. "Since we're still on pause and we're not going to talk yet about *our* whole complicated thing, can I just ask you something as a friend and get an honest answer?"

"What?" She looks at me sideways.

"Dude, the sex? I mean, that was so good, right?" I blurt out.

"Right?" she agrees. "I mean, yes, it's a super complicates thing with us even more—"

"Completely complicated!" I concur with her.

"—and we'll get into all that, but damn! What was that? It was never like that those few times before. We both laid it down." Clark holds her fist out to me and I return the bump.

"I know! I'm sorry I ripped your shirt, though. I'll buy you a new one. I just got caught up in the moment."

"That was so hot. I don't even care."

The two of us share a laugh.

A good laugh.

The kind of laugh that tears up the corner of your eyes because you can't breathe, but also you needed to get it out kind of laugh. I use the tips of my fingers to pick at some of the food, like Clark. My face is turned down, focused on the plate, but I'm looking at her out of the corner of my eye as I probe her with the next question, "So… are you going to stay the night, Boss?"

"I got a hotel room," she responds immediately.

"And?"

Clark moves her head, scooping it under, so I'm forced to meet her gaze. I bring my head up, so her neck is craned awkwardly. She's smiling a playful smile.

"Chicken's not *that* good."

CHAPTER FORTY-SIX

MURPHY

After…

Clark is laying in my bed, naked as I am.

The elegant curves of her body grab hold of my gaze, and I can't look away from them. She runs every day to keep herself in shape, so the muscle and tone from her workouts shows off the beautiful figure she's maintained. I'm slightly sat up with my head against the comfortable pillowtop headboard while she sleeps on her side with her head on my stomach.

It's peaceful.

The rest of the world outside my bedroom's floor to ceiling windows has faded into a blurry background. I am here with her and that is the only thing that matters to me now. I've got my Bluetooth speaker quietly humming out tracks from the Weeknd. *Often, Earn It,* and *Call Out My Name* cycle through, one after the other, as I lay in peace and sync them with my night with Clark in that Toledo hotel.

My phone goes off with a vibration that luckily doesn't disturb Clark's slumber. I check the text message before I am forced to slowly nudge her awake.

"Interview is all set up," I whisper to her.

Clark just lets out a negative moan as she tries to continue sleeping. I don't think the negativity was directed at the news of my upcoming interview, more at the fact that I'm interrupting her REM cycle.

I still press her, though. "It's in Times Square on a morning show in a few hours. You want to go get some brunch before I go in?"

She releases another moan that seems to indicate that's the last thing she wants to be doing right now before stretching and rolling over to the other side of the bed, off of my stomach. Now that she has released me from her cuddle hold, I'm free to get up and grab my clothes. I don't know what compelled me, but I decide to look back at her for one last glimpse of that perfectly round jogger's ass.

Except…

Clark's not there.

I am alone in my bedroom.

Well, not alone.

He comes and stands next to me. The Black and White Bob somehow appears at my side again.

"I think you may be losing your mind there, buddy."

Dejected, I turn away and walk towards the bathroom to clean myself up.

Did she leave this morning before I woke up? Did we even have sex last night? Did she even come over to my apartment?

"Dude, you know the answer to that," BW Bob says to me.

And he's right.

The same way I know he's not the real Bob. That he's just a manifestation of my subconscious taking the form of my former best friend. He's really just saying what I'm thinking because he is me. I'm apparently sane enough to realize all this, but not sane enough to make them stop.

I ponder these thoughts as I sit at a cafe table, alternating sips between my mimosa, coffee, and water. Why are there so many different glasses to drink from at brunch? It's like you need every type of beverage possible in order to enjoy eggs benedict. I could have rounded out this stereotypical meal with a Bloody Mary, but I hate tomatoes, and everything associated with them. I pick at my poached eggs smothered in a passable bearnaise sauce as my manifestation sits across from me. Obviously, no one notices him because he doesn't exist and I'm not going to let him get to me, so I continue to ignore him, yet he still keeps talking.

"You have been just a rip-roaring ball of fun this morning." The sarcastic tone coming from my delusional brain's creation cutting deep. I watch as the city streaks by in the flurry of activity and note that, even at eight in the morning, New York City still doesn't rest. Continuing to ignore fake Bob, I suddenly recognize one of the waiters walking around carrying a pitcher of water.

He was one of the child actors on the show.

His name is Connor.

A featured player.

He would get regular speaking parts in different segments until he aged out. I thought for sure he would be one of the Dogg Gang members that would end up going on to success in the acting world, but judging by his server uniform, I'm guessing fame and fortune eluded him. We lock eyes and the recognition on our faces pulls him over to my tiny table at the edge of the patio. We exchange pleasantries before I ask him the obvious rhetorical question of how he's come to work here.

"I mean, yeah, gotta pay the bills… After those royalty checks stopped…" he says, avoiding eye contact as he's clearly embarrassed by his new position in life.

"You're not getting royalties?"

"No. Murphy, they pulled the old episodes off syndication. I'm not getting anything from the show anymore."

I'm a little dumbfounded by this. I mean, I knew production had been halted, and we probably weren't going to come back for more episodes. And the syndication deal going down the drain, thanks to a bullshit morality clause, meant the little kids that looked forward to re-watching the same episode a thousand times, were now deprived of that. But, for some reason, I thought they still paid out the contracts for the talent. I really should have checked my finances to make sure I have any kind of income coming in. I honestly haven't looked at my bank account in decades. The money has just kind of always been there for me whenever I wanted to buy anything.

"Oh, man, that sucks. And you haven't been getting any other gigs?" I ask.

"Kinda hard to get booked when the most prominent role on your resume is playing a kid on a blacklisted show. Can't even get booked for conventions anymore."

I apologize to him for this. I really feel bad for him. If I could cast him in a new series, I would in a heartbeat. Connor was such a great kid to work with. Most of the time, the other child actors would forget their lines, or run around knocking over set pieces, or piss themselves.

Not Connor.

That kid was a professional out of the womb. Now this twenty-something standing in front of me, probably not even old enough to drink yet, is struggling and isn't able to live out his dream of performing, or his parents dream. Not sure if he had a crazy stage mom or not. Shit, I actually might have slept with his mom in his trailer now that I think about it. Either way, he is being deprived.

So again, I apologize.

"I'm sorry the show gave your career a big old black eye."

"It's not your fault, Murphy. You had nothing to do with that Bob stuff. Just sucks that he ruined the show for everyone. And don't worry about my career. You know the funny thing about black eyes?"

"What's that?"

"They heal."

I'm a little shocked by his pious attitude. This kid has been chewed up, spit out, and had the ground beneath him salted by the entertainment industry. Here I am, the face of the thing that destroyed his life, and he should have every right to scream and dump that water pitcher over my head, yet he absolves me?

Or maybe this isn't all about me?

Maybe he's just a better person than me and can just move on with his life, not getting dragged down by his past. I don't get a chance to investigate his inner workings further as he swivels his head to look around.

"I gotta check on my section, but it was good seeing you."

"Yeah, you too, Connor."

He turns and goes back to attending to his tables, being the charmer that I remember him to be in order to earn better gratuity from his guests. I grab whatever cup is in front of me to take a sip, not caring which beverage it is. Bob is looking over his shoulder at Connor before turning back to me.

"My fault? I made our show relevant. I made him relevant. And that's the thanks he gives me?" Imaginary Bob screams at him for only my sad skull to hear, "Dickhead doesn't even know the difference between royalties and residuals."

It's weird because I didn't think that was a thought in my head, but I guess it's what my mind feels Bob would say in this situation. How he was always taking credit for the show, even when he knew it was a collaborative process that was more my hard work than his. That doesn't stop him from making one last declaration before I grab the check.

"Fuck that guy."

CHAPTER FORTY-SEVEN

MURPHY

Before…

The stubble on my face is noticeable, but not the sexy

rugged kind that usually grows into a full beard.

It's like a starter stubble.

It's like, yes, I grow facial hair, but it's a young man's

facial hair that only has to occasionally be shaven down to clean up.

A step up from a puberty mustache.

At this time in my life, my skin is almost completely barren

of tattoos. And my belly still hasn't pooched out yet. So, the six-pack is still the main attraction on me, distracting from my terrible personality.

Bob sits on our secondhand couch, in our modest apartment, mid conversation. I'm standing in front of a white dry erase board that's covered in half-finished ideas.

"Did you know that Captain Kangaroo was actually an angry old man who would accost every one of his employees? And before he would step out on stage, he would pull his pants down and wave his dick at the announcer, Green Jeans?"

"What does that have to do with anything?" I sigh out as I cover my face with my hands in sheer exhausted disbelief that he is talking about some random old guy's dick.

"The man was an asshole but made a great show. We're assholes. Why can't we make a great show?" he responds.

"We do have a show, Bob. We just have to finalize it."

"We can't finalize it until it's great."

"Jesus Christ, it's good enough!" I yell through my hands, still covering my face.

"I don't want just 'good enough'. And we can't even call this 'good enough' yet," Bob replies.

"We have the bright colors and silly characters. That's all we need to keep these little diaper-fillers' attention. Let's slap some goofy names on these assholes and call it a day." I exhaustedly chuck the dry erase marker across the room.

"And we'll last maybe three seasons like every other kid's show."

"Three seasons will get us paid." I try to convince Bob, but he will not be bent.

"Three seasons will get us forgotten. Listen, if we want to make a show that will last, we have to put our hearts into it. We're going to have to actually fucking care."

"Fine!" I relent. "I'll give you fucking heart. I'll give you a heart-on. *But this all seems like tedious crap for a bunch of bedwetters that won't know the difference between milked out shit and our heart crap."*

"If we treat them like bedwetters and create pushed out shit that doesn't challenge them, then they'll treat our show like said pushed out shit. If we treat our audience like human fucking beings and respect their developing intelligence, they will reward us with loyalty."

"Respect their intelligence?" Even though I've relented, I'm still unconvinced. "Most of them will be literally releasing a dook as they watch us."

Bob stands up and grabs me by the shoulder reassuringly.

"Childhood is a fragile and fleeting time. If we are invited into the homes of these families, the least we could do is put a little more effort into shaping their young minds. Because we also have to make a show that the parents aren't going to want to kill us over since they have to watch us as well, a million times on repeat."

"The parents aren't going to be watching us with them. We're keeping the snot leakers distracted and stuck on a screen while they go sneak off for a quick bang."

"We are not gonna make just a distraction." Bob picks up the dry erase marker I discarded and rubs his face as he approaches the board and studies our chicken scratches we call notes. "We have an opportunity to make an impact on an entire generation."

"An entire generation?" I chuckle. "We don't even have a show yet. But now we're children's programing legends? Icons of the industry?"

"What we do here could affect the world moving forward. Maybe it's not iconic like our wildest dreams are leading us towards, but it can still end up making some kind of difference. Do we want to leave this world a better place or do we just want to make a quick buck?"

"Can we do both?" I quip with a coy smile.

Bob just shakes his head before replying, "Okay, then, so pushing forward, I don't like calling the group the 'Backyard Gang'. It leaves us open for parody already sounding like a porn title. Plus, it makes no sense if we're going with this dinosaur idea for our MC. Why did you want him purple?"

"Because every dinosaur is green. I wanted to look different," I reply.

"You're so fucking weird, dude. If we wanted it to be kind of a group of animals in a backyard, let's stick to one's that are currently not extinct."

"What about a pig? It's a sloppy animal, but I could classy it up by doing the voice in British," I try my best English accent when I spit out the end of that sentence, but Bob doesn't bite.

"That was supposed to be British? You sounded Australian?"

"What's the difference?"

"Let's go back to the idea of a dog for the mascot."

"A dog? That's so lame. Let's do some one eyed fucked-up looking creatures that can rap and dance."

"What? No. It's not lame. Everyone loves dogs. Grandmas love dogs. Kids love dogs. They're classic."

"Can we do a weird color for the dog, then? Like blue?" I ask. "You think anyone will watch a show with a dog that's all bluey?"

"Let's just keep the simple Boston Terrier design for now, but we need a different name. Dave the Dog isn't going to work. It's lazy and uninspired. But I like the ideas we've come up with using an alliteration for the animal character names. What do you think, stick with rhymes?"

Bob's eyes go wide as baseballs as a lightbulb goes off in his head after I utter my reply:

"I can dig that."

CHAPTER FORTY-EIGHT

MURPHY

After…

I think I ruined the carpet.

My tiny repetitive circle I continue to walk seems to be wearing a track in the floor, wrecking the fibers. I don't know what to do with my hands, so I just keep them fixed at my side in my pants pockets. Of the million thoughts inside my head right now, the one that keeps popping up, even though it is in no way relevant to my current situation; why do they call it the *Green Room* if it's not actually green? I'm sure I'm not the first person to have thought that. I'm sure because I'm already a pretty unoriginal hack as it is.

At least this news studio's green room followed my rider and got the right kind of bottled water for me.

I just prefer Ozarka water from Texas is all. I've been all around the world and that's my favorite tasting water.

I'm a douchebag that has a favorite water.

The playlist is humming from the speaker I hooked up and, fuck, now it's got *the* song on. It's the one I put on there because it hits so close to home but skipped every time it tried to play.

This time, I finally let it play.

I See a Darkness by Johnny Cash.

It starts low with his simple guitar strumming. But as it builds and each note hits harder and harder, recalling the troublesome lives of two close friends and how they must separate in order to heal. AT least that's what I get from it. This was from one of the American Recordings albums Johnny put out near the end of his life, doing such beautiful covers of these songs that he's surpassed the original versions and most consider them his now.

The Man in Black finishes the song and I avoid letting my tears stain my blazer. At least the new suit I just bought over in the fashion district fits like a dream. It still needs to be broken in, it's a little too fresh off the tailor. The studio's hair and makeup department cleaned up my beard and styled this dead plant on top of my head. For the first time in a long time, I actually look better than I feel.

It's a nice facade.

Because as presentable as I appear, I'm still watching as a black and white version of my former partner sits on the couch across from me counting the circles I've been walking in and mocking my pacing.

I can ignore my mind's mockery, but I can't ignore the vibrating coming from my pocket. I check the ID on my phone and see it is again, an UNKOWN CALLER.

Bob and I exchange looks before I click the green button.

"Hello," I answer.

BW Bob disappears.

An automated voice kicks in. "This is a prepaid call from an inmate at Carlton County Corrections. *Robert Hale*. To accept these charges, press one. To—" I tap on my cell and hear a tone before some rustling on the other line. That's when I hear him…

"Damn, Murph, it's about time you picked up."

It's Bob.

I mean, I knew it would be him, but hearing his voice, for the first time since he blew up my universe, talking so casually to me, I'm still shook. He continues as if we've just come back from a long hiatus. "Man, how have you been? How's the tour going? You gotta be wrapping up in New York about now, right?"

"I can't really talk at the moment," is all I can squeak out.

"I get it, I get it, man. You're all busy with your freedom and what not. Can't really say I know what that's like, though." He lets out a sad chuckle.

All I can do is respond with the same hurt laugh and solemnly agree.

"Listen, Murph, the reason I've been trying to get ahold of you is I need you to unfreeze some of my residuals. My lawyers have tapped me dry, and I need some cash flow to float me while I'm in here."

"Bob, that's not really something that I control. You gotta take that up with the network. They set up the morality clause in the contracts. It's kind of their discretion."

"I know, I know. Hell, the Feds would probably seize it, anyway. They've seized everything else already. I was just wondering if you could talk to them. Plead for me a little."

I tell him I don't know.

I tell him that maybe I'll see what I can do. He thanks me and then says he appreciates me as I rest my forehead against the non-green room wall. For just a moment, I take in a deep breath to collect my thoughts before speaking.

"Bob."

"Yeah?"

"Just… Be honest with me, man, be honest… Did you do it?"

Silence.

"Come on, man… You know I can't answer that," is all he can muster.

"Bob. It's me."

"This conversation is being recorded by the prison. The DA can use it. I seriously can't answer that."

"There it is."

A knock at the door as a production assistant with an impeccable sense of timing interrupts us and says they're almost ready for me. I tell them okay and then let Bob know I have to go. He understands, but before hanging up, he slips in his motives one more time and tries to remind me to talk to the network, to help him out.

He destroyed my life and wants me to help him.

I hang up the phone and take another deep breath before my subconscious brings the black and white Bob hallucination to reappear behind my back.

"Was that me?" It knows it was, yet it still asks, "Why didn't you yell at me?"

I turn around to face it.

For the first time, really looking at it in its imaginary eyes. This whole time, I knew this thing wasn't real, but now, staring at those grey pupils, I succumb to my madness and treat it like the real Robert.

The next song has started up on my speaker, *Face To Face* by Sevendust.

With all that, I still can only formulate a one-word response, "What?"

"Why didn't you yell at me—him? Why didn't you tell me off?"

"I wanted to. I should have." I look down at the phone in my hand, give it a long glance, almost inspecting it. "I wanted to tell you that you ruined my life. I wanted to tell you that you ruined the life of everyone that ever came into contact with you. I wanted to tell you that you are a FUCKING CANCER! You are a FUCKING VIRUS!"

With those last words, I've now brought myself to look at fake Bob in the eyes again, yelling to his face. "I should have told you that you deserve to rot in that piss and shit filled jail cell! But I won't because you fucking ruined that too by being my fucking friend! You weaseled your way into my heart, you piece of shit! And now all I'm left with is second guessing everything we ever had, everything I've ever known, wondering if I'm just the biggest schmuck on the planet for having not seen who you really were this whole time! This whole time! This whole time I fell for your bullshit! You were just lying to me, to everyone! Fuck that! I was your best friend and you kept this from me! The fuck?! I let you into my world, my whole fucking world had you as the fucking centerpiece and you had me on the fucking outskirts! I never actually, ACTUALLY fucking knew you!"

My arms are flailing around at this point, and the volume of my voice has filled the room. The perfect level of sweaty and manic energy for me to turn and see the news studio's producer standing in the doorway, shocked, having watched me yell at no one. The producer checks their notes on the clipboard in their hand, two seconds away from radioing into their earpiece microphone to call the whole segment off.

I compose myself before turning to them.

"Ready for me? Yeah."

CHAPTER FORTY-NINE

MURPHY

The Moment.

The sun seems to hit differently when you're on vacation in another part of the world. It's like it knows your problems are time zones away and shines extra sweet for you. That's what my only thought was as I woke up in my bungalow with three beautiful naked women in my bed.

I thought about the sun.

The bungalow sat in a small lagoon perched on top of crystal-clear blue water, welcoming me as I left my companions to sleep as I enjoyed an early morning swim in the ocean, naked as the day I was born. The water baptizes me as I emerge from dipping below the surface, only to rise again with renewed energy in my body and spirit. My previous night's debauchery still replaying what I can remember as I float back to my bungalow. I emerge from the water walking up deck steps leading into my room, not bothering to be quiet or conscience of my slumbering concubines. I towel myself off and pour a wake-up cocktail of coconut rum and pineapple juice, there's a knock at my hotel room door.

Figuring it was just the concierge dropping my bill, I ignored the first knocks. But the persistence makes me throw on a robe and answer the disturbance.

What I find when I open the bamboo door is a small troop of federal agents in typical navy-blue jackets with the yellow print across the backs. My face goes white, and my brain goes numb. I can't do anything but grip the door handle and pray that the three girls in my bed had somehow taken the money I had paid them the night before and escaped out one of the windows…

*   *   *   *

Before…

I had never been to Thailand. I'd never even really had much of a desire to travel there other than knowing it as an obvious vacation destination. To me, there were plenty of other places I could relax, beachside or poolside, while we took a break between filming new episodes. But Bob had insisted this was the place for our next getaway. He had looked into getting a private jet, but the cost of a transcontinental flight was too exorbitant when we could just book first class private cabins and sleep the whole time.

Bob booked the hotel, too. He found these private villas that sat on top of perfect blue ocean water next to a cavernous lagoon with walls that lit up when it got dark. Perfect for a night swim, he told me. We had to board a small luxury boat that would portage us from the main hotel lobby across the water to our rooms. A small deck system connected the separate bungalows that allowed you to look over the edge and watch the fish swim by. Inside my room, I threw down my luggage (well, the bellhop did) admiring the glass floor panels that meant I didn't need to go outside to enjoy the sea below. I thought about using the outdoor shower to wash the plane ride off of me, but instead decide to opt for a dip in the bay. A set of steps out the back of the room lead right down to the waist deep warm water. I stripped down to my underwear and approached the first step, but before I could dip even a toe in the water, Bob walked straight through the door.

"What are you doing? Get some clothes on. We're going out!" Bob exclaimed.

"Dude, we just got here. I need a moment," I replied.

But Bob would not be swayed. After getting dressed for a night out, we were met by our handler, James, who took us into Patpong's more... interesting districts. Bob has taken me to various ends of the world: Tripping our brains out and watching live sex shows in Amsterdam, big wave surfing in New Zealand, barreling whiskey in an Irish castle, and the various escapades on Brazil's nude beaches could fill a tell-all book, but nothing prepared me for what I was about to experience on this outing.

First of all, there was James. We had met him in Auckland as our surf instructor and he insisted on being our guide through the city during our stay. Apparently, he frequented Thailand enough to be considered a local. His heavy accent, leathery, sun-kissed skin, and bleach blond hair made him stand out wherever we went. Every other word out of his mouth was either 'fuck' or 'cunt', and he tried to start a fight with every security guard at every bar we went into. It was like his short stature made him need to fight above his weight class.

The very first place James took us to was, of course, a strip club. The sun hadn't even gone down yet when we slid into the semi crowded building. As soon as we got inside, James brought us right up to the front of the stage, which had just started its cattle call, bringing the entire staff of scantily clad strippers to cram onto the small platform and present themselves.

There must have been at least fifty girls standing shoulder to shoulder, slightly swaying to the beat of the bass thumping music, up on that little ledge. Eyeing the talent that was displayed to us, I felt a little uncomfortable when I came to the realization that some of the girls were on the younger side. James had disappeared as soon as we found our spot to watch the show, but instantly reappeared with drinks for all of us. Standard vacation concoctions with tropical fruit and alcohol blended together.

"Is this place legit, James? Like, are these girls legal?" I leaned into yell in his ear over the music.

"Of course, they're legal." James took a sip of his drink before looking away. "Thailand legal."

"The fuck does 'Thailand legal' mean?" I pressed him.

He rubbed the back of his neck. It seemed he had misread his companion's intentions. "Sixteen is the legal age here."

"Seriously? I am not okay with this!" I set my drink down by the stage's railing and take Bob's as well. "We're out of here."

"Come on, mates—"

"No! Do you have any idea how fucked we would be if it got out that we slept with underage girls?" I yell at James with my stern finger pointing in his face, but Bob calms me down.

"They're not underage here, Murph."

"It doesn't matter because; first of all, what the fuck? That's so wrong! And second, the internet back home doesn't care and will still say they're underage! This could ruin us, Bob!"

"Nobody said we had to sleep with the young girls. We can find some older ones if that works better for you," Bob replies.

"Dude, what did I tell you about coming to Thailand? I didn't want to go to a place where I had to pay for sex as the main form of entertainment, and you promised me that wasn't going to be why we chose Thailand. Yet here we are, discussing the moral implications of child prostitutes."

He offers up a compromise to me, which hesitates my retreat. "Can you find us someone age appropriate, James?"

"I mean, yeah, you could hire a girl that's like, maybe twenty-five. That's about as old as you can get around here, but that's tough to find and they may be a little damaged goods if you get my drift." James replies.

"Damaged goods? Why is that hard to find?" I ask.

"Hookers aren't exactly built for long-lasting careers, mate," James replies.

"Fine. Can you give us eighteen, at least?" Bob asks, trying to salvage our evening.

"Oh, hell yeah! Those are your perfect girls. They've been around long enough to know what they're doing but are still new enough to the game that they still have the enthusiasm you're looking for."

With James' assurance, the three of us turn back to our drinks to find the stage has cleared out and is occupied by a single dancer, who is already down to wearing just her neon thong and matching high heels. She's got this sexy self-confidence to her, it's almost like she doesn't give a shit that everyone is watching her naked body, like this is actually boring her. The woman dances her way over to me and Bob at the edge of the rail that separates us. The platform is raised high enough that it comes all the way up to our chests, forcing the woman to start gyrating on her hands and knees to reach eye level with her potential clients.

Bob pulls out a wad of colorful bills from his pocket and tips her. She proceeds to stick Bob's face in between her fake breasts and shakes them back and forth, their size helps with the smacking on each side of his ears as they sway. I take a stack of colorful paper from my own wallet and throw it in the air over her to award her vigor. I assumed the amount must have added up to maybe twenty dollars, but judging by the stripper's reaction, it apparently was much more than that.

The stripper leans away from Bob and crouches down in front of us, balancing on her impossibly narrow heels. She starts to rub her nipples with both her hands but let's one slide down her stomach and slips into her panties. Her palm rubs underneath the neon fabric as she maintains eye contact with me. Her shoulders arch up as she appears to dig her fingers in deep for a moment before pulling her fist back out. Her balled-up hand hovers over our drinks for a second before opening up above each one. With a clink and a splash, she drops an item into the two glasses before blowing us a kiss and collecting her cash as the song ends and she exits the stage.

Bob and me, stunned at first, finally come to our senses and look down into our drinks. Floating at the top of the liquid is a small metallic sphere. The little ball glistening and gleaming in the glass as the club lights reflect off of them. She had a pair of Ben WA balls inside her for the whole performance and had now dropped one into each of our drinks.

"I didn't know you could drink an STD," I joke.

Bob picks up his glass and toasts his friend. "I ordered Chlamydia, but I think they brought me Herpes."

And with that, Bob downs his drink, letting the metal ball slip into his mouth before spitting it out into his hand and smiling at me while he holds up his souvenir.

*   *   *   *

Before...

We'd been on vacation for over a week now. Bob has taken a different girl to his room every night. And as much as Bob had insisted, I refused to pay a girl to come back to my cabana.

Instead, I would relax at night in the infinity hot tub connected to my room. In the morning, after a quick swim, we would have James take us to some beautifully scenic sight-seeing locations, then get lunch at various local eateries, with dinner finding us at some of the best five-star restaurants Thailand had to offer. The nights would still end up with us in crowded clubs with seas of girls on display for Bob to peruse before purchasing. He would have to pay the bar in order for the woman of his choosing to leave with him, then pay the girl after he got them back to his room. James explained the double paying system to us. It was how the girls could be accounted for and considered safe. The bar would have a record of who took a girl.

Kind of like a library book. But with sexual implications.

On the last night before Bob headed back to Los Angeles

for some promotional photo shoots, he turned it up when it came to

his pursuit of my nightly activities, or lack thereof. He tried to

convince me to at least bring home a girl while he was still there.

Since the photo shoot didn't require it to be me in the Digg Dogg

suit, I had elected to let my understudy take up the mantle and stay a

little longer in my luxury suite.

"Come on, how can you not get laid while on vacation?"
Bob goads me.

"Because you keep taking me to strip clubs. Kind of hard to

find a girl here you're not paying to go back to your hotel with

you," I reply.

"Then pay them!" Bob laughs.

"I've never paid for sex. It's so transactional. I just can't

find it sexy."

"You're missing out. Like James said, they know what

they're doing and are very, very enthusiastic." Bob nods in the

direction of James, who's being held above a bouncer's head, flailing as he gets thrown about. Bob and I are unfazed by the commotion, as it's happened nearly every evening so far. James had an uncanny ability when it came to pissing off security.

As I ignore Bob's insistence and return to my drink, a small metallic ball drops into it before I can even take a sip, splashing liquor into my face. I slowly raise my head to find the stripper from our first night towering over me, pulling her underwear to the side so I am now staring up at her shaved-down-to-a-stubble vagina.

"You want to go searching for the other one?" she says in a sultry tone.

I just continue to stare in awe as the woman steps back to continue her dance. She rolls her hips and drops down to the platform, grinding to Darling Nikki. *An odd choice of song to strip to, considering its non-contemporary status, but the rhythm works as every Prince song does and she is showered in colorful bills when the song hits its crescendo.*

As soon as she steps off the stage, I invite her to sit with me and Bob for a drink. She introduced herself, but I couldn't hear her name over the sound of the club's throbbing bass. I expected when she sat down that my infatuation would be exacerbated by her surprising conversational skills, but, sadly, the chemistry did not translate. Bob tried to keep the momentum going by buying a drink for two more gorgeous girls who were friends with the stripper.

Unfortunately, their grasp of the English language wasn't any better. They could say a few phrases and kind of knew what we were saying, I think, but nothing beyond that would build a rapport. Bob was worried that because I couldn't form a connection with any of these girls, that I wouldn't go through with taking one of them to bed. But by this point, having been cuddled up with a beautiful, half naked woman, coupled with the excessive alcohol consumption, was enough to get me to lose my inhibitions and prejudices against the world's oldest profession.

Bob took that as his invitation to move forward with the night. He bought out all three girls from their shifts at the bar so they could leave with us. By this time, James had squared away his beef with the security staff and rejoined the group. The six of us left the bar and made our way back to the hotel.

The breeze from the ocean was a welcomed cool down from the heat of the packed club as we waited on the hotel lobby's dock for our boat to arrive and taxi us back to our rooms. The girls changed into dresses at the club before we left. Although you could barely call them dresses, with what little cloth they actually contained. The hotel had dimmed their lights so that the moon and its reflection off the water was enough light for anyone to see. We continued to wait, laughing as each girl hung off our arms.

"So, who's going to share their room with us?" James points to himself and the girl dangling at his side. "Or are we all doing this thing in one bungalow? I'm cool with whatever's going down."

"Yeah, about that…" Bob slowly takes the girl James is holding onto and pulls her over to him, so now he has the two friends on both arms.

"Oh, fuck off, mate!" James blurts out. "Not okay."

"Are you picking up your girl's tab?" Bob's response shuts James down immediately.

The ferry to our villas pulls up next to us on the dock, as me and my escort slink away from the awkwardness and onto the boat. I'm expecting Bob and his girls to follow behind, but he's still standing there.

"James. We're going to go get another drink," Bob says this to James while looking at me, as I return a confused gaze. Bob directs the two girls into the boat with his hands on their lower backs. As the girls sit down next to me and cuddle up for warmth, Bob just smiles, looking back at his friend. The two of us unaware that this very well could be the last time we'll look at each other, the last time we'll share a smile, the last time we'll be happy together.

Bob takes James and turns him away as I sail off with my three companions on our way back to my room.

Two best friends drifting farther and farther apart as the boat streaks across the water.

*　　*　　*　　*

That night, for the first time since it was lost… For a brief moment… My happiness was back.

*   *   *   *

I should have fucking known, though.

I should have known that as soon as I start to let myself feel again, the universe would come back around with a cold kick to the dick. I woke up this morning in a luxury hotel's tropical oasis with three beautiful naked women in my bed, having been satisfied beyond compare. I didn't even care that they had been under my employ for that time. It was still worth every Baht. And to top it off, even though I had drunk a substantial amount of Thai rum, I wasn't the least bit hungover. Hell, I probably wouldn't even need a morning coffee I was so energized.

Then that fucking federal agent ruined it all. This motherfucker interrupted my euphoria by not only bringing me back to reality but shattering it at the same time.

The universe is a cruel bitch.

*   *   *   *

After…

Turns out they didn't give a shit that I had partaken in the local ladies. They were there because they had just detained Bob at LAX. This talking windbreaker with crumbs in his 'pervstache' sat on my hotel room couch and slid a file across the coffee table to me.

I didn't pick it up at first. I couldn't. Whatever was in that file was obviously a lie, so I let it stay unopened. I watched as my companions got dressed next to the bed, catching one last glimpse at their beautiful naked bodies before they covered their naughty bits and left to get on that ferry back to the hotel lobby.

"I'm giving this information as a courtesy," Agent Fuckhead tries telling me, even though I'm not paying him any attention. I'm focusing my gaze on the water outside my window.

470

The waves lapping against the posts that keep the room above it all.

Yet he keeps talking, "This will all go public in a few days' time.

Everything in that folder, our whole investigation, will be part of the

court filing and make it into the news cycle soon enough."

This isn't the first time some asshole has tried to come for

us.

As soon as the first few episodes hit the airwaves, we got a

full season order.

Shortly after that, we were renewed for a second and third

season.

We were a huge hit.

A cultural moment.

Everyone wanted a piece of us and if they couldn't get it,

they would try to take us down. Baseless claims of plagiarism,

character assassination attempts. Hell, we even got our first

protesters when we decided to speak out about homosexuality being

okay. And every time these fuck-nuts tried to swing at us, they would wind up hitting air. That's obviously what's going on here, just another attempt to smear a children's television icon.

I don't even want to keep thinking about this. I want to think about the night before. Go back to that sweet ecstasy, but this douche won't let me emotionally detach.

"Look, I know this must be quite the shock to you, and I know your first thoughts are denial. That's what most of us on this task force wanted to believe, that this was all just a series of misunderstandings. We were on your side because most of us are fans. We all have kids that either grew up with the show or are young enough to be watching it still. The last thing we wanted to do is destroy the childhood of our little ones." He puts his finger down on the manila folder, pointing at it with authority. "But the fact of the matter is, your partner is guilty. He is the monster no one knew about. The monster watching our children."

I finally turn to face this dipshit. I give him a 'get the fuck out of here' look and he's actually not too stupid to understand it. He lets himself out, leaving his file of lies behind. Good, because after all the crap he was saying about my friend, I was about two seconds away from being locked up for assaulting a federal officer.

But now that I'm alone, it starts to sink in.

I've gone numb. My mind, my body, everything is numb. It's like the sheer act of processing all of this has frozen my being.

I've been sitting on this couch for what feels like an hour now. It could very well have been five minutes since being left alone. I can't take this suspended time loop I've trapped myself in, so I do the unthinkable...

I pick up the folder and open it.

I'm not entirely sure what it is I'm reading at first, just a bunch of dates and statements. My adrenaline is also in overdrive so I can't fully concentrate, but finally it starts to come into focus...

For the past twenty years, ever since we first went on the air, possibly before, Bob has been sexually assaulting unsuspecting women. The evidence is so thorough and concise that it starts to overwhelm me. My denial is shrinking with the mountain of facts that I see before my eyes.

I can't breathe.

Luckily? This isn't my first panic attack, and I understand what is going on. The first time it happens, you are so scared that you might be dying that it just exacerbates the situation. Now I know I will live and just try to find my breath to calm down, though I'm not sure I want to survive. I drop the folder and rush to the bathroom mirror. To get my lungs and mind in check, I start to use a square breathing technique I learned from a child psychologist's book that I ended up using on the show.

I picture a box. Four sides.

I take a breath. Count to four, drawing a line in my mind. I let it out. Counting to four and drawing another line. I breathe in again. I count to four and continue the line. I let it out again. Counting to four, I draw a line that completes the box.

I do this again and again until I reset my brain and allow my emotions to calm.

I'm okay now.

I have always been okay.

The sins of my friend are not my sins.

I go back to the coffee table and can now read over the charges against Bob and try and find lies in the details.

Allegedly, he had used the touring show as his avenue for seducing single mothers and then would sexually assault them without their consent, and in a few cases, they weren't single. At first glance, I tried to rational that these were just women who regretted their slutty decisions and tried to blackmail a celebrity, but the pictures and reports painted a different picture. The women would invite Bob over or would wind up in his hotel room only to be drugged, tied up, and forcefully raped.

That's not even the worst of it.

That was his M.O. with the mothers. The next few reports are on the underage girls he had relations with. He drugged several girls as young as thirteen, keeping them in his suitcase as we would travel to different cities, nearly killing them from asphyxiation. He would then have his way with the girls, forcing them to perform lewd and sexual acts, since they had no choice. They were trapped in a strange city with no way of taking care of themselves. He promised to get them back home, but when he was done with them, he would drug them again and dump them in a random alley.

They were able to connect these reports to all of our travels across the country. There is also a file from Interpol alleging some international crimes. It says that in Amsterdam, he had raped a sex worker from the Red-Light District. In New Zealand, they say that he had exposed himself and groped a couple of teenage surfers. In Ireland, it's alleged that even though his accusers admit their sexual encounters started off consensual, he had ended up physically beating them so badly that most of them required hospitalization.

Many of the women reported these assaults immediately after they had occurred, but were met by unconvinced, condescending police officers. They didn't want to believe wholesome Mr. Bob was capable of such heinous acts, but still had to file the paperwork, even though most of the accusers later recanted their stories.

When asked why they recanted, a quote from one of the accusers. "Who was going to believe me? It's Mr. Bob. I don't want to believe me."

Some were even charged with filing a false police report. One woman who was charged, lost custody of her child due to being put on probation. The FBI finally got involved when enough women came forward and a strong enough case was possible.

Bullshit. It's gotta be bullshit.

Actually, they only really started to pay attention when he stopped just dumping the minors in random alleys and had decided to try and sell them to traffickers while in Brazil. The international trade aspect of it is what alerted the Feds.

There's more.

He kept up the psychological torture with women who "voluntarily" stayed at his mansion. I would come over to visit him and he would have these beautiful girls just lounging around all the time. I thought it was just typical Hollywood megastar stuff, but apparently, he had such a mental hold over these women that he literally branded his initials onto their bodies.

With every page, the picture of my friend gets more and more warped. Each act more depraved than the last. It was all too much for me and I again struggled to find my breath. I keep reading though, because somehow at the end of all of this, it has to be a mistake. Somehow, I have to discover this isn't Bob, because the more I read, the more it doesn't sound like him.

This is not my friend.

This is not my Bob.

This is not real life.

The Moment.

There's something about Los Angeles.

It's not the same kind electricity as New York, but it's a feeling in the air, possibility. It's like anything can happen. You never know what can lead to what. It's such a ton of the uber rich and famous and iconic that you get this sense that, somehow, you could be a part of that life. But in reality, no matter how close to it you get, you never really are.

I had just finished getting lunch with my sister, the adult film star who lived in the valley. It was one of those quick, casual kind of meet ups. I went in yoga pants and a hoodie, showing how much effort I was willing to put in. She was going through some typical drama with her piece of shit boyfriend. I really didn't feel like getting into it with her, since this was just supposed to be a quick visit, and I think she could tell I was kind of checked out. I mean, I only agreed to meet up with her because I was near her in Burbank.

I was in town because the boys were flying back in today to wrap up some reshoots for the latest season and we had to go over details for the tour. I was saying my goodbyes to my sister and hopping into my rental car when I got ambushed by Dan Lawson, the LA Times dickhead reporter I had a brief fling with. He was leaning against the restaurant's wall in the outside alley. He wasn't even trying to hide the fact that he was waiting for me. His long brown hair and equally big beard matched with the green denim jacket and jeans, giving off the hipster-hippie-beatnik vibe he meticulously arranged to make you think he didn't care.

"I heard you were back in town" he says to me through a stream of smoke he releases from his mouth before taking another drag from his cigarette like the chain-smoker he is.

"I'm not back. Just visiting." I reply without breaking stride towards my car. Dan kicks himself off the wall and chases after me.

"That actually makes me feel better." He flicks his smoke into the gutter as he matches my pace, *"Here I was thinking you had moved here, when you specifically told me you could never live in this hell hole, which lead to our breakup."*

"Yeah, that was the reason we broke up. It had nothing to do with you being an asshole." I roll my eyes as I unlock my rental. I'm about to jump in and burn rubber out of there, but Dan is now leaning against the rear door.

"That girl you were just eating with; where do I know her?" He asks.

"Dan what do you want? I've got a busy schedule while I'm here and don't have time for old boyfriends."

"Thought you might want to know about your show's star getting picked up by the Feds at LAX this morning."

"Fucking hell, what did Murphy do this time."

"Not him. Mr. Bob was taken away in handcuffs."

"Bob? What the fuck?"

"Apparently, good old Bob had some demons behind his funhouse door."

He then unloads the entire sordid details of Bob's double life. My legs start to go weak for a moment. Dan catches me even though I had already stabilized myself, any excuse for him to grab me, I guess. He proceeds to help me into the passenger seat, because I can't seem to catch my breath, and agrees to be my driver. I tell Dan I can't go to the studio now and he takes me back to Murphy's guesthouse in Malibu, where I'm staying. The whole time he keeps giving me more and more about what Bob is being accused of. I want to tell him to shut the fuck up, that he's lying, but I somehow know it's true.

We've dropped down the canyon and are only a few miles into the PCH when I tell him to pull over. He doesn't even get the car shifted into park before I fling open the door and roll out onto the beach. Dan gets out and tries to follow me, but I don't feel like hearing more of this bullshit and take off at a sprint. He kind of starts jogging, trying to keep up with me, bewildered the whole time, but eventually he gives up and lets me run along the shoreline. I run by smiling families, playful children, cuddling couples.

Happy people.

Eventually my lungs and legs give out and I collapse onto the sand. I position myself to sit and stare out at the ocean, bringing my hands to my mouth, resting my elbows on my knees. I want to keep running, but my mind has shut my body down.

How the fuck could this be real?

Bob was supposed to be the good one. It was always a running joke that if anyone was going to be canceled in our group it would be Murphy. Bob held us together. And just hearing all the disgusting things he had done just makes it worse. I used to listen to these True Crime podcasts or watch similar documentaries on Netflix and they would be so titillating. But when you know the man behind the crimes, it doesn't quite hit the tit.

I pull my headphones out of my purse and slip them on my ears. I need to focus on something else and hopefully the music can distract me. I play *Waves* by Mr. Probz as the only appropriate song in this moment. The original, slowed-down version, not the remix everyone knows. I listen all the way through and just before it ends, I hit the back button to start it over again. I do this a few times before just putting it on repeat to save myself the trouble.

Watching as the water hits land, it calls to me. I don't know how long I've been sitting here. The sun has gone down and I'm alone on this beach. I continue to hear the ocean as I stand up and take my pants off. I leave them with my bag, underwear, and shoes as I set out to dip my toes, the waves meeting me as it catches my ankles. My rational brain tells me it's supposed to be freezing cold, but I can't feel it as I trudge past my knees.

I can't feel anything right now.

I keep going.

My lower half is fully submerged, the water now beginning to soak my sweater, the only item of clothing I'm still wearing. Why I left it on, I don't know. I'm now neck deep in and having to use my arms to paddle forward.

My feet kick off the ground and I'm floating.

I let myself drift further out as only my head remains looking out at the dark sky. And I can't keep myself afloat anymore, both mentally and physically, so I let my body sink. I release my last breath and go under…

There's peace down here…

It's quiet…

I say goodbye….

To everyone…

And no one…

Except, it's not poetic like that.

Funny thing about the human body; it's buoyance doesn't allow it to sink. So, I kind of end up near the surface again, instead of down in the depths like I'd wanted. My headphones have cut off due to the water in its circuits, taking me out of my trance.

What the fuck was I thinking?

I've got too much shit to do to end it all. But as I try

swimming back, I struggle with the current and the cold water that's

actually numbed my extremities. Now that I'm trying to keep my

head above the water, it keeps overtaking me. I fight and I fight to

reach the surface, clinging to whatever amount of air I can collect

before I'm dropped under again and again. My vision starts to blur

thanks to the lack of oxygen my brain is receiving. My lungs burn as

they choke on the seawater. My arms and legs, already tired from

my impromptu jog on the beach, are on fire as the muscles strain to

keep me afloat.

My body is giving out now.

The final spasm of resistance has given way to succumbing

to the inevitable. But then a pair of powerful hands slip under my

arms and wrap around my chest. I'm pulled to the surface and take

in a giant, lifesaving breath. One arm remains around me, and I'm

dragged back to the shoreline, unable to see my rescuer behind me. I

collapse on the sand, coughing up seawater as my ass is out

mooning the moon.

I look over to see my savior, while pulling my sweater
down to cover my dignity, and expect to see a big strong, strapping
hero. Instead, my eyes are met by a scrawny black man, who
probably weighs less than me, in jogging shorts and a muscle tee.
The adrenaline alone must have been what channeled his strength,
because there's no way in a normal circumstance this man could
carry me. He's hacking up the ocean from his lungs just the same as
I am, leading me to believe his valiant exploit nearly killed the both
of us.

"Are you okay?" he says to me, "It's freezing in there! You
need a wet suit if you're going to surf…"

He trails off as his gaze finally takes me in. I can see the
realization move through his mind. He's discovering that I'm not
some late-night surfer without proper equipment, that my general
attire in this state screams, "I read Sylvia Plath."

But the look he returns to me is not of shock, or pity, it's
compassionate. My hero takes my hand, still buried in the sand, and
just holds it. He doesn't break eye contact with me.

"I'm glad you're here." I can see the tears start to streak down his face, like he's experienced what I'm going through, "Your story is not over."

I want to say something back to him. Tell him it was just a momentary lack of judgement, that I wasn't really going to end it all, but it wouldn't matter. He doesn't know me. He just recognizes a lost soul and felt the need to save it.

My tears now match his and he embraces me in a hug. We hold each other tight. I can feel the sun start to reach over the mountains and down to us. My rescuer releases our entanglement and after analyzing my face, genuinely believes that I am fit to go on my own and won't return to the ocean.

I let him know my car is nearby, at least I hope it is. I bet Dan left the key under the tire and got an Uber back to the Valley. He's the kind of guy that doesn't want to be bothered with 'female problems' and just walks away.

I tell my champion that I'll be fine, at least I hope I'll be. I truly don't know how to continue from here at the moment.

We don't exchange information; I don't even get his name.

He continues on with his life and leaves me to mine, while sitting on

the beach, shivering, with sand in my vagina.

And I gotta say, it's not the worst state a man has left me

in.

CHAPTER FIFTY-ONE

CLARK

After…

I often wondered about his sign off as Digg Dogg. He would use the ASL motion for "more" when most thought he should be pairing signs with his "Love Loudly" phrase. But Murphy said it was always a way of showing people, his fans, the children, that he will continue to love them more and more.

His love for them was ever growing.

Turns out the original idea for coming up with a sign off gesture came from Bob. He said they should have something with their hands so that they could hold them up in photos and no one would question where they were touching while with younger fans.

He actually inspired *The Wiggles* to use the same rationale with their

"Finger Guns" posing.

Even back then, he was a psychopath covering his tracks.

A pair of tits in a miniskirt who calls herself a journalist

sits in a chair across from Murphy. I've been working on being nicer

to other woman and to not treat them like competition as the

patriarchy wants me to do. But this famous-for-being-famous

woman wants to be considered a serious reporter all of a sudden, it's

something I just can't get behind. I know the only reason Murphy

suddenly decided to take this request from *this* news outlet is

because he wants to sleep with her. I'm watching this live feed from

the comfort of my hotel room couch as the camera cuts back and

forth between him and miniskirt. I haven't even made it back to my

condo in Brooklyn yet. I decided to stay at the hotel in Manhattan

with the rest of the cast to save me a commute.

It's an unusually warm fall day, so I have the nearby patio

doors opened up to let the New York breeze blow in from the

balcony. I decided to stick with the original boutique hotel we had

booked since we're at the end of the tour and fuck it the budget's already blown. Every inch of this room has unique features about it like the furniture was individually made instead of the mass-produced crap the rest of us peasants must sit upon. They've even got a vintage record player next to the love seat in the corner, stocked with contemporary vinyl. I put a Post Malone album on and the needle is currently humming out *Chemical*. I'm trying to zone out with the joint I've just rolled and lit up. My nerves from knowing Murphy's about to be on live TV addressing this controversy needs all the medicinal help it can get. After what felt like hours of lead-ins, they're finally ready to start.

"Welcome back. We're here with Murphy Harrison, star and co-creator of *Digg Dogg and Friends*. The show that brought joy to millions of children over the span of two decades. Having swept the Daytime Emmys for outstanding children's programming every year since its creation, this cultural touchstone has come under fire as of late. He's with us today, finally breaking his silence regarding the show's other star and co-creator, his creative partner, Bob Hale, and the scandal surrounding him. Earlier this year, Bob Hale was arrested and charged with thirty-seven counts of sexual assault. The accusations of drugging and raping women, some as young as fifteen years old, could have him locked away in prison for the rest of his life. Mr. Harrison, thank you for speaking with us today," she said all that in a tone that made it seem as if Murphy was the one accused.

"Thank you for having me," Murphy replies. His demeanor is attempting to be calm and collected, but he is visibly nervous.

"I want to start out by asking how you've been doing in all of this? How are you holding up?"

Hard-hitting questions right off the bat.

Really? That's how you start an interview? How are you feeling? How do you think he's feeling.

"Not good, actually." He lets out a sarcastic laugh. "No, um, yeah, it's been rough. I mean, it's nothing compared to what his victims have had to go through."

Smart, Murph. Smart. If he would have played the victim when there are actual hurt people out there, he would have been roasted alive online.

"Have you spoken to or reached out to the victims or any of their families at all?" the reporter asks.

"Aside from setting up a trust for them, no, I have not. I felt like I was the last person they'd want to hear from. I know monetary compensation won't erase the pain he's caused, but I felt I had to do something."

Fuck, Murphy, that's going to look like you're just throwing money at a problem.

"Plus, I was dealing with my own issues regarding Bob." he adds.

"Tell me more about that, the issues you were dealing with. How it was you dealt with them?" she asks.

You mean besides the whiskey, cocaine, and whores? He's been using a mix of denial and delusion to cope with his loss. You know, like any asshole would. I watch as Murphy just stares off for a moment before replying.

"I had to learn how to grieve a man that was not dead, somebody I loved very much that no one else loves anymore."

He brings his eye contact back to the reporter as she asks her follow up question, "Have you been in contact with Bob since the arrest?"

"I've talked to him once. Just recently. When I talked to him, I'm talking to the man I worked with and hung out with for over twenty years. I loved that man. I still love *that* man. I don't know the psychopath… the guy on trial… That's not the man I knew and cared about, built a partnership and friendship with."

He talked to him?

When the fuck did that happen?

How has he not told me he talked to Bob?

I should have been the first person to know right after he spoke to him. This is such bullshit. Just because we had an amazing night of passionate, angry sex and I completely rejected him afterwards, doesn't mean we can't still be friends.

Wait…

Yup, I'm wrong.

That's exactly what that means. I've messed it up by getting in his pants and that's why we haven't discussed his chat with Bob.

"Talk to me about the day this all came to light. How you found out?" Miniskirt asks.

"So, we had just finished shooting our latest episode—um, I mean our last episode... I was driving to my home in Malibu when my phone just kept going off. Like exploding. I had to pull over and check what was going on... The story broke, and it destroyed me... I didn't know how to react."

That's not entirely true.

That is how he found out the world knew the truth. I remember I had finally made it to set, worried I was going to have to be the one to break this news to him. Until I saw the look on Murphy's face when he took off the costume head.

He knew what I knew.

He had come back to LA in shock and just told the show's producers to finish the episode by cutting around Bob's coverage.

We sat down in his trailer's kitchen nook. Across from one another, he told me that Bob was accused of being a rapist. Murphy let me know he had been alerted by the FBI while in Thailand. I told him about the reporter friend who informed me, not adding the details of my relationship with said reporter for some reason. Murphy on the other hand shared graphic details of his encounter with a group of women in Thailand. I tried to focus him on the matter at hand, the whole Bob scandal. But he just kept wanting to tell me more and more about what he did to these escorts.

I wondered at the time why he fixated on talking about his sexual encounter instead of his friend being locked up. I'm slowly starting to understand how he was in denial. And that this was the first time since finding out a week earlier that Murphy had spoken about it. He told me and he instantly broke down crying. He was a ball of tears and snot. I had to have a production assistant help me load him into his car and I drove him back to his house.

But on the way, still crying, his phone went off.

Just as he told it.

The media jackals had gotten ahold of the story and the rest of the world had found out…

"After you recovered, what was your reaction?" Back on the hotel television, the reporter asks.

"Didn't believe it. This was my friend and partner that I had known for over two decades. How could he have done such terrible things." Murphy answers, having just dabbed the tears from the corners of his eyes.

"Did you have any inklings that he was prone to such acts?" she asks.

"None," Murphy replies. "You think if I knew he was capable of this I would have just stood by and let it happen?"

"I mean, you hear stories of people, celebrities and the wealthy, having things covered up for them in the past."

This bitch.

I almost throw my remote at the hotel television when I hear her, the accusation she tries to insinuate.

"I am not one of those people. I believe in my heart that if I knew something like this was happening, I would have shut it down."

"When this story first broke, you refused to speak on the matter. You were actually on tour with the traveling live show going across the country?"

"Yeah, not a lot of people know that I'm the one under the mask for the touring company. Bob had insisted we travel with the show since the beginning. He convinced me it was for authenticity to our product but turns out it was just a way for him to stay on the move when he committed his crimes," Murphy laments.

"Well, you're not behind the mask anymore. Is there anything else you would like to say?" She opens the floor up to Murphy.

"So, I've been avoiding making a personal statement about this until everything, all the facts come out, until after the trial… but the truth is… I was just afraid to confront it. I was afraid to confront my new life. If I spoke about it, that means my new reality is now in existence. And I wasn't ready for that new life… The fact of the matter is the show is done. Digg Dogg is done. Even if the network decides to bring us back for another season, even if we retool or reboot it, I just don't think it should continue. So, I wanted to officially announce that *Digg Dogg and Friends* will not be returning. We'll be closing out the current tour here in New York with our last set of shows and that will fulfill my commitment to the present production."

I'm up off the couch now. I already knocked over the record player in order to shut it up. I feel like I know what he is about to say but can't even fathom it could come out of his mouth. And, of course, this motherfucker takes a pause before finishing his thought. My face is practically pressed to the television screen, waiting for what Murphy delivers next.

"It will be the final time you see me as Digg Dogg."

Holy shit...

CHAPTER FIFTY-TWO

CLARK

After…

The sign on the marquee now has a sub-header alerting people that these are the final performances. The standard protest crowd has now dissipated, replaced with a crowd of fervent fans trying to secure themselves a ticket. The ushers at the front are being overwhelmed by the gathering audience, so I pull at the jacket of the theater's manager, yet another mouth-breather living in Manhattan off of daddy's money.

"Can you at least try to get more employees to the front? The crew there can't handle this crowd alone."

The champion of white male fragility escapes my grasp and runs off to find more staff to move to the main entrance. I can't fully blame him, though. I haven't had to deal with so many people in a while that I'm off my game too. I had been going through the motions with each city, but now that I'm in New York and we've become the hottest ticket in town, I actually have a job to do each night that requires more than just making sure my star isn't too blacked out to perform. Now I have to make sure the whole machine is running smoothly and there's nothing throwing off the gears.

Over at the merchandise stand, I see only a few stuffed Chesters dangling in the corners. I check in with the cashier and tell her where to find the emergency reserve of souvenirs boxed up inside a storage closet in the back. She holds up a long sheet of receipt paper that seems to go down to her knees. I can double check the numbers against inventory later. Right now I've got more important things to tend to.

The box office is packed with attendants dealing with rows and rows of people trying to secure access to the theater. I don't recognize half of the employees manning these booths. I'm guessing they had to hire temporary help for the new influx of customers. The only cashier I know is Katrina. She's worked at this theater for over four decades and has seen all sorts of hysterias for must-see programs being performed here. And every time she would remain calm, cool, and collected, handling everything thrown at her window. Which is why I was shocked to walk in and see her screaming at an adult holding their crying toddler in front of the glass, pleading for a seat inside.

"Hey, Katrina, how's it look so far?" I ask, knowing the obvious, but still checking in.

"How's it look to you? Sold the fuck out! We've had to open the balconies back up and those are already gone!" she barks back at me.

"Holy shit."

"If it wasn't a fire hazard, we'd put chairs in the aisles. That's how high the demand is right now for seats."

I need to get backstage.

This is madness.

It's the final performance tonight. Like, *final*, final. All the other shows this week have been sold out as well, but now everyone knows there's nothing after this and are clamoring to be a part of history. The tickets set aside for VIPs had to be opened up for the general public. Which means the celebrities tying to placate their nostalgia will be shit out of luck.

Before I can get backstage, I run across several cameras trying to document this unprecedented event. Aside from the local and national media outlets, we have a host of documentary crews trying to capture whatever footage they can for their unofficial retrospectives.

I cut across the stage to get over to the dressing room. I normally have to direct the crew and keep them from slacking off, but tonight everyone is moving with urgency. There's an electricity in the air that I haven't felt in a long time. Even before things went to nuclear shit the quality of the tour had gone downhill due to the trappings of longevity. But now, It's the knowing that this is the last time we will be in the presence of an icon that has rushed back all the nostalgia and washed away all the dirt from the last few months that Bob piled on us.

I give the sets a quick inspection while not losing step. The great big old doghouse has a fresh set of paint on it, making it look like it did twenty years ago when it was originally constructed to travel around this country. Remembering the first time I laid eyes on that thing brings a smile to my face, imagining the joy Murphy would bring to all the children when he would burst through that door. It wasn't long though that I was sticking plugs in my ears to block out the screeching that would accompany his arrival. I can't believe how quickly I became jaded to this wonderful job.

I pop my head into Ryan's dressing room, being greeted by the sounds of moaning and a faint smell of mint for some reason.

"Five minutes to positions, boys."

Inside the room, I can see Vinny and Ryan stretching their legs and arms, getting their bodies warmed up and limber while already in costume, aside from their helmet heads and leg bottoms. Vinny's calf is resting against Ryan's ear while Ryan's in a lunging position with a leg by Vinny's shoulder. If it weren't for the stuffing on the outfits, I'd swear they were having their regularly scheduled, pre-show rigorous sex.

"Soon as Kitty finishes my stretches," Vinny exhales.

"Loosen those quads, Ryan," I say to them as I leave them to their business, calling out behind me, "And get your frog legs on!"

Before I can make my way to the dressing room that's holding the star of the evening, I'm intercepted by Zoey in her mouse costume with the head under her arm. I don't break stride, but she follows right alongside me.

"Hey, Clark, just wanted to give you a quick logistics update, regarding moral. I miss the communal dressing rooms and the camaraderie it brought with it, but I understand why we didn't continue with that set-up."

"Because we're in a better theater?" I ask rhetorically.

"Because our lead is an artist and requires peace and tranquility before his farewell performance."

What the fuck kind of bullshit is that?

We've come to the door, and I need to leave her out here so I can have a moment alone with Murph. With all the chaos of our sudden popularity, we haven't really spoken much these last two weeks. I feel like now is the time for us to final say what we need to say to each other. And I can't really talk feelings with this mouse around.

Ah, what the hell? I'm all warm and fuzzy right now, knowing I'm about to be unemployed. I'll throw the little girl a bone.

"You know, I think *all* of the principal cast deserves peace and tranquility before and after their performances," I say, letting a sly smile creep across my face. "You should be able to change in Dressing Room Three."

"B-But that's Vinny's dressing room?" She's wondering if I'm playing a cruel trick on her.

"I'll talk to him if he gives you any grief. It should be fine."

Zoey's big blue eyes light up with joy as she puts on her mouse head and scurries off. I mean, she's already dressed and ready, so it's more of a symbolic gesture than anything. I'll give her a win tonight.

I've always, deep down, kind of seen her as my mirror. Or maybe more of a window, looking out at what I used to be. The enthusiasm I had, the love that this work gave me. That's probably why I hated her so much:

I hated me.

That realization hits me while my hand grips the cold dressing room door and I collapse to the ground. Not in the passed-out-and-dropped-to-the-floor kind of way, my knees just buckle, and I find myself sliding to earth to feel stable. Everyone is too busy getting ready that no one notices I've gone fetal. I've been so focused on the finish line that I never allowed myself to grieve my own loss. Murphy may have been able to fall apart, but I did not have the luxury or privilege to do such a thing. I compartmentalized my world and had goals that needed to be accomplished. Now that I can actually see the light at the end of the tunnel, the combination of the unknown and facing the reality of my relationship with Bob, it's all just too much to stand, literally.

But that's Future Clark's problem.

I'll let that asshole deal with her problems later. Right now, I've got to pull myself back up off the ground and get my shit together, using that cold handle as leverage to gain footing. The light at the end of the tunnel may be blinding, but I've still not yet reached it.

I take a deep breath before opening the door, stepping inside Murphy's dressing room. He's on the floor in his underwear and his whole costume is laid across the couch next to him, excluding the head hanging on the wall next to me.

His phone is playing music, but it's not his usual rotation. I walk over to see *Way Less Sad* by AJR finishing and then changing over to *Restless Radar* by StereoRiots. The header above the song states: Sisyphus Music.

A new playlist.

He's reading a book, *Greif Recovery for Teens.* I ask him

why he's reading that book, and he replies that it has some good

techniques for processing what he's going through. He's finally

letting go of Bob. He's treating him as if he's dead, like he should

have done from the start, and finding appropriate ways to

cope. Granted, the age range is slightly off from him, but I'm

guessing he can extrapolate the bullet points.

He sets the book down and I walk over to help him up off

the ground. I tell him he's got five minutes, and he starts to get

dressed. The costume slips on with ease as he's done a million times

over and over again. I just watch as we don't say anything, avoiding

eye contact with each other. I realize I'm going to have to be the one

to break through the silence. He may have matured when it comes to

his grief, but he's still a boy when it comes to adult relationships.

"Murph. About that night in Toledo…"

He finally meets my gaze. I can see the hurt this subject is

bringing him. I crushed his soul when I rejected him that next

morning. I didn't want to, but I had to. He's not ready to love

someone. He needs to get his own shit together first. Maybe

510

someday we can revisit this. He already seems to be trying to set a better path for himself. I express all of this to him, and he takes it better than my simple head shake had done in letting him down before.

And that's when I see it.

The spark in his hazel eyes when he smiles. That genuine smile that shows his happy sadness and makes his eyes disappear under his cheeks, letting only a little light shine out from the pupils. That sparkle would beam through Digg Dogg's mask and radiated on the screen and stage. That light is the reason I wanted to work with him in the first place, the reason I stuck around through all the bullshit he put me through.

I can't fucking stand it when he's sweet like this.

I smile back at him, and I know I'm going to end up going against my better judgment and fall for this man. This fucking train wreck of a human being is always going to be in my life because I always want him to be. I miss him when we're not on the road together and I know in my heart that he misses me, too. If he can just stop fucking up his life and getting in his own way, maybe, just maybe, this thing with us can happen.

"I don't know where we go from here, but I know we're going to go forward together, however that looks." I end with that. Murphy doesn't say anything in response. He just looks at a spot near the ground, but a million miles away.

"I once read a quote, 'it's dangerous to think of yourself as a hero and someone else as a villain. It gets in the way of empathy,'" is all Murphy can say to me, "I've decided to no longer let the memory of Bob hold my life in its hands."

"Where did that come from?" I ask.

"I don't know. Probably from a place of healing."

"Good."

The music cue to bring everyone to their seats and, of course, it's this fucking song. The earworm I've been listening to for over a decade. But now that I think about it, I'm going to miss it. I didn't realize how sweet the lyrics Murphy wrote were. Yes, they were simple, but it's the simplicity that made it so catchy.

I actually am going to miss this song.

My reciprocated smile seems to have re-energized him. He jumps up and down to psych himself up and prepare for his final curtain.

"One last time, Boss?"

He's back to calling me by my nickname.

Ever since we slept together, the only time we had to speak to each other he referred to me by my name. It was good to hear that moniker again. I grab the dog head off the wall and chuck it to him. He slips it on, and even though his face is covered, I can feel his eyes welling up under there. Probably because tears are coming down my face, too.

"I'm sorry, what was that?" I squeak out.

"One last time, Boss?"

I can't fight the tears back now, not that I want to.

I almost need to let it out, for me, for him.

This mad, merry, mess of a man of mine.

“One last time, Diggsy…”

Acknowledgments

This book would not have happened without the tireless efforts of all the children's entertainers and educators that helped in the development of young minds. If not for the creativity that these shows provided, I would not have pursed such an endeavor as being a writer.

But don't just take my word for it...

To the Lovers...

The Dreamers...

And me...

I also have to thank my mom for instilling in me a love of reading. The mountain of books she provided at my fingertips awakened an imagination that will never leave the clouds. My old man for demonstrating a youthful, playfulness while continuing to work harder than Superman. My brother for being my other half (apologies to my wife) I don't believe there is anyone on earth who I strive to impress more than my older brother. (Again, sorry, baby) My sisters, their children, all the significant others; there is no greater joy in my life than when we gather and create memories we'll talk about every time we get together again.

My Love. My Wife:

Words cannot describe how much you mean to me. ☺

Know there's nothing that I wouldn't do.

J, W, V:

You three are the reason I get out of bed in the morning. My only reason for being. Thank you, for being you.

It's *You* I like…